Bello:
hidden talent rediscovered!

Bello is a digital only imprint of Pan Macmillan,
established to breathe new life into previously published,
classic books.

At Bello we believe in the timeless power of the imagination,
of good story, narrative and entertainment and we want to use
digital technology to ensure that many more readers
can enjoy these books into the future.

We publish in ebook and Print on Demand formats
to bring these wonderful books to new audiences.

About Bello:

www.panmacmillan.com/imprints/bello

About the author:

www.panmacmillan.com/author/andrewgarve

Andrew Garve

Andrew Garve was the pen name of Paul Winterton (1908–2001). He was born in Leicester and educated at the Hulme Grammar School, Manchester and Purley County School, Surrey, after which he took a degree in Economics at London University. He was on the staff of *The Economist* for four years, and then worked for fourteen years for the *London News Chronicle* as reporter, leader writer and foreign correspondent. He was assigned to Moscow from 1942/5, where he was also the correspondent of the BBC's Overseas Service.

After the war he turned to full-time writing of detective and adventure novels and produced more than forty-five books. His work was serialized, televised, broadcast, filmed and translated into some twenty languages. He was noted for his varied and unusual backgrounds – including Russia, newspaper offices, the West Indies, ocean sailing, the Australian outback, politics, mountaineering and forestry – and for never repeating a plot.

Andrew Garve was a founding member and first joint secretary of the Crime Writers' Association.

Andrew Garve

NO MASK
FOR MURDER

BELL

First published in 1950 by Collins

This edition published 2012 by Bello
an imprint of Pan Macmillan, a division of Macmillan Publishers Limited
Pan Macmillan, 20 New Wharf Road, London N1 9RR
Basingstoke and Oxford
Associated companies throughout the world

www.panmacmillan.com/imprints/bello
www.curtisbrown.co.uk

ISBN 978-1-4472-1576-9 EPUB
ISBN 978-1-4472-1575-2 POD

Visit **www.panmacmillan.com** to read more about all our books
and to buy them. You will also find features, author interviews and
news of any author events, and you can sign up for e-newsletters
so that you're always first to hear about our new releases.

Author's Note

Fontego is a fictional place. It may appear to have certain resemblances, topographical or instituional, to any one of a number of British Colonies. Any attempt to identify it with an actual place, however, can only result in wrong conclusions.

Certain British Colonies have island leper settlements in their vicinity, but Tacri is fictional and is not intended to be a portrayal of any one of them or to reflect upon the management of any actual settlement. All the events described in connection with Tacri, including the contract for its rebuilding, and all the persons associated with it, are purely imaginary and have no foundation in fact.

In a story of this kind, it is unavoidable that certain characters should hold public office. There has, for instance, to be a Colonial Secretary, a Health Secretary, a Secretary of Education, a Superintendent of Police, and so forth. All the characters filling these and other posts are entirely fictional, and none is based on any actual person in any British Colony.

Chapter One

The launch from Fontego had been chugging through the forget-me-not blue sea for more than an hour before the last headland was rounded and the leper island came into view. The Negro boatman grunted and pointed ahead through the shimmering heat, and Martin West turned his binoculars on the jagged pile of salmon-pink rock which he would soon have to think of as "home."

In spite of all his misgivings, the appearance of the place excited him. At that distance it had an enchanted beauty of form and colour, like a wizard's grotto in a child's picture-book. A travel folder could have made it sound superlatively attractive—"bathed in tropical sunshine," "lapped by translucent water," "one of Nature's gems." As a tourist resort it might have earned badly needed dollars for the Colony. Or was it too parched? It certainly seemed to be almost bare of foliage. The dry pink rock shaded everywhere into dry grey cactus.

Martin swept the shore line with the glasses, and an expression of incredulity crossed his face. There seemed to be no flat ground at all. From the water the island rose steeply to two or three narrow terraces, on each of which was a scattering of wooden huts. Beaten earth tracks linked the terraces—there appeared to be no road. The long straggling building at the foot of the cliff must be the convent, and the wooden house at the far end of the bay would be his own residence. So there it was—that was the leprosarium. Somehow, five hundred leper patients and a staff contrived to live on this sloping shelf of barren ground a mile long.

A white-clad, sun-helmeted figure was waiting on the jetty: an elderly coloured man with greying hair, steel-rimmed spectacles and a sardonically drooping mouth. That must be Carnegie. As the launch sputtered to a stop he came slowly forward, smiling as though it hurt him.

"Welcome to Tacri, Dr. West." He shook hands. The irony in his tone and in his glance was unmistakable. "But where is your luggage?" he asked, peering into the empty launch. "Aren't you staying?"

"Not this trip," said Martin. "I've still things to do in Fontego. This is just a preliminary inspection. I thought I'd like to see the place before I talked to Dr. Garland. He's up country, I'm told, but he's expected back to-day."

"Oh." The old doctor's voice sounded disappointed. "I was hoping to hand over to you at once. When do you expect to take up residence?"

"In a couple of days, I suppose. Are you eager to get away?"

"Indeed I am," said Carnegie. "More than eager. I'm not a leprologist, you know. I'm not an administrator, either. I'm a surgeon. I've never understood why I was sent here, even as a stopgap. I suppose it was because everyone else refused to come." His tired eyes rested for a moment upon Martin, taking in the tall, loosely built figure, the shock of fair brown hair, the frank grey eyes framed in heavy horn-rimmed glasses. "You're younger than I expected," he said. "That's a good thing. There are too many weary old men in this Colony. I'm one of them."

"It's an exacting job, running a place like this," said Martin sympathetically, "particularly when you've no special interest in it. Have you been here long?"

"Six months, but it has seemed like sixty." They strolled slowly along the jetty. "Is there anything special you'd like to see? You can get a fair impression of the layout from here." Carnegie pointed with his sun helmet. "This shed here is the administrative office. If you're not careful you'll spend most of your time at a desk—there's far too much paper work. The two long buildings over there on the left are the male and female infirmaries. The smaller shacks scattered all over the place are the dwelling quarters. The hut with the new tin roof is alleged to be a hospital. Behind it there are a couple of storehouses, but as you'll see we have to store most things out of doors. Over on the right is the dining-room. How long have you got, by the way?"

"Two or three hours."

"Well, it's enough to get an impression. It takes quite a while to make a thorough round of the place because, as you see, there are no roads. To get about quickly you'd need to be a goat."

"How does one reach the house?" asked Martin.

"By launch, when it's not under repair. And we have also one small donkey."

"Is this really all there is of the place—just what we can see?" Martin indicated the narrow coastal strip.

"That's all. The rest of the island is just virgin rock, no good for anything."

Martin gazed at the leprosarium in growing dismay. It no longer seemed to have any beauty. At close quarters it looked what it was—a squalid slum, a concentration of untidy shacks with rusty corrugated iron roofs. The hard glare of the pink rock made him blink. "Do you ever get any rain?" he asked.

"Usually very little," said Carnegie. "The hills of the mainland take most of it. When there is a storm the place gets almost washed away, so I'm told, but it's a rare event. We're nearly always short of water."

"That's not very satisfactory, is it? Have they tried drilling?"

"They've tried everything, but there isn't any water. The idea now is to erect some very large rainwater tanks. There are going to be great changes here, as I expect you know."

Martin nodded. "I got a document this morning from the Assistant Health Secretary—what's his name?—Dubois. I've only glanced at the plans so far. They seem to be very ambitious."

"They are certainly far-reaching," said Carnegie, with a little warmth creeping into his voice. "It was a great personal triumph for Dr. Garland when the Legislative Council approved the proposals last week. It was a very close thing. Nobody could have pushed them through except him—he's been the life and soul of the scheme. He's the best Health Secretary we've had in my time. I'm sure you'll be impressed by him."

"I'm very much looking forward to meeting him," said Martin.

"Not everyone likes him, of course," Carnegie went on. "He doesn't suffer fools gladly, and he can be very ruthless. But he gets things done. As a matter of fact he's one of the very few men in the Colony who *can* get things done. He's almost stamped out malaria around Fontego City; he's got V.D. back under control in the towns, and he's just organising a big campaign against hookworm. He has immense energy, and when he's set on something he usually gets his way. It was he who persuaded me to come here." The old man quickened his steps. "Well, we'd better make a start. Do you want to see the Mother Superior?"

"Ought I to?"

Carnegie's eyes twinkled. "I think it will do next time. If you see her, you won't see much of the leprosarium. She's a very worthy woman, of course. In fact, all the sisters are very worthy women. It's a pity so many of them are inadequately trained."

Martin nodded. "I've come across that problem before."

"Ah well, then you probably know how to deal with it. The nuns have a lot of influence in the Colony, and it's best not to quarrel with them. Personally, I think their attitude to leprosy is sometimes old-fashioned and unscientific, but they're not bad housekeepers."

"I take it there *are* some trained nurses?" said Martin a shade anxiously.

"A few," answered Carnegie, "but not nearly enough. And many of them are quite the wrong type—we've had some unpleasant incidents. I believe things were better before the war, but everything was upset when the Military Base was built on the mainland. The rates of pay were so high during construction that most of the staff here left, and the leprosarium had to fill their places with anyone it could get." Carnegie's disapproving little cough spoke volumes. "We got the dregs, and for some reason they were allowed to become established civil servants, so now it's very difficult to sack them."

"I suppose trained nurses don't want to bury themselves in a place like this," said Martin.

"Of course they don't. And I for one don't blame them," said Carnegie with feeling.

They climbed a steep path and turned in among the shacks. The heat was fierce. The hillside afforded almost no natural cover, and knots of patients were grouped in the shade of every hut, sitting or sleeping on the dusty earth. All of them were coloured, and most of them were Negroes. On the whole, they showed few signs of their disease. Some of them smiled and called out to Martin as he passed, guessing he was the new Superintendent they had heard about. A lad of eighteen or twenty, with a bright face and sparkling teeth, cried, "Sah! Sah!" and leapt eagerly up the rocks. "Sah, ah wanna leave dis place. It ain't no place fo' me. Ah bin here two year—ah's tired—ah wanna go, sah."

Martin gave him a friendly smile, noting with practised eye the characteristic depressions in the back of the hand held out to him. "I'll talk to you about it in a few days," he said. "I'll be back. We shall have to see." The boy grinned broadly and rejoined the chattering group.

"He's a nice lad, Green," said Carnegie. "He takes it very hard being here. A lot of them do, I'm afraid." They climbed to one of the larger wooden huts. "This is the male infirmary," he said.

Martin surveyed the structure in silence. The walls were rotten from age and termites and had been patched in many places with sheets of cardboard and beaten-out tin cans. As Carnegie pushed open the door a wave of fetid air greeted them. Along each wall beds were packed so close together that it was barely possible to move between them. Old men and young boys lay side by side—a hutful of human wreckage, with quivering nerves and eroded faces and crumbling extremities swathed in bandages that looked far from clean. These were the patients who had been too far gone for effective treatment by the time they were discovered. This was what the disease could do, neglected and unchecked.

Sharp condemnation of the overcrowding, the bad ventilation and the dirt hovered on Martin's lips, but he restrained himself. His critical glance travelled to the roof.

"Hurricane lamps, eh?"

Carnegie nodded. "It's like Dante's Inferno after dark," he said. "You can imagine." He led the way through the ward. "Of course," he said over his shoulder, "under the new scheme we shall have electricity. A plant of our own."

"I wonder how long it'll take to install," said Martin. He looked curiously round the ward. "Shouldn't there be a nurse on duty here?"

"Why, yes, indeed there should be." Carnegie stopped by one of the beds, where a grizzled old man was holding a newspaper between his bandaged stumps. "Where is Edwards?" he asked.

"He jes' step out," said the old Negro.

Carnegie gave a gesture of helplessness. "That's what they do—'step out.' There's no discipline here." His tone of resignation seemed to disclaim any personal responsibility in the matter.

Martin walked on through the block and peered into the wash house and latrines. "Appalling!" he said, rejoining Carnegie. "My God, this is worse than anything I'd imagined."

The old doctor took off his spectacles and mopped his face. "I agree entirely, but what can one do? We have dry-pit latrines—everybody knows they're unsatisfactory. What with the habits, and the heat, and the shortage of staff, I'm surprised we haven't had serious trouble. It's the same old problem—lack of water. Now, under the new plan——" He saw the scepticism on Martin's face and broke off. "Do you want to see the women's infirmary?"

"Is it like this?"

"It's even worse, I'm afraid."

"Well, it's a damned disgrace," Martin said with heat. His thoughts travelled back to the little room in the Colonial Office where his appointment had first been discussed, and he could hear again the suave cultured voice of remote officialdom saying, "Conditions at Tacri are not perhaps ideal." Not perhaps ideal! He would have liked to have the fellow here now.

Carnegie said, "Are you surprised?"

"Frankly, yes," answered Martin. "I've seen some bad places, but this is unspeakable. Nothing in the reports I've read hinted at anything like this."

"The facts rarely get into the reports,"' said Carnegie. "Most civil servants in Fontego prefer to take the easy path and gloss over defects. Only Dr. Garland is outspoken. For years he has been condemning Tacri. You'll find him a kindred spirit. But improvements cost money, and the conscience of this Colony is not easily aroused if it means more expenditure."

"I'm astonished that there hasn't been a major scandal."

The look of resignation settled on Carnegie's face again. "People are not interested in this place. Out of sight, out of mind, you know. That, after all, was one of the chief reasons for putting the leprosarium on the island in the first place. There have been visitors, of course, but mostly medical men, who don't seem to have much political influence, unfortunately. A politician did come once, I believe. He shook hands with the less repulsive of the patients, to show how brave he was, and he said he thought the leprosarium was well run! At least, that's what your predecessor told me."

"You mean Stockford? Tell me, what did *he* think of it all?"

"Oh, I don't think Stockford had any illusions. He was a good man in many ways, but he made enemies, and so—he was persuaded to retire. I don't know the details. He was an idealist, I'm afraid, and Fontego is no place for idealists. The people who get on best here are the realists. You'll meet them. 'It is true,' they say, 'that conditions at Tacri are bad, but then they are also bad in the slums of Fontego City.' So they do nothing about either problem. The business men, Dr. West. They have the souls of pawnbrokers."

Martin made no comment. He knew the universal itch to find a scapegoat. "Let's have a look at the living quarters," he said.

Once again Carnegie led the way between the huts. "This is one of the standard dormitories," he explained. "Ten beds to a block, no sitting-rooms. The patients spend most of their time out of doors, of course."

Martin put his head inside. Three patients were lying on their beds, apparently sleeping. There was an almost complete absence of furniture or private effects, and a total lack of comfort.

"Is there no privacy at all, anywhere?" he asked.

"None," said Carnegie. "We just haven't the space. It is desirable,

I know, to have many sub-divisions of the patients, but we cannot even separate the young boys from the old men. It would be pleasant to have separate huts and a little normal home life, but that is quite impossible here."

"Are there no married quarters?"

Carnegie shook his head. "It's all in the plan. There's to be a great deal of new building."

"I can't think where," said Martin. "There's no space."

"They're going to use dynamite—blow up the rock and carve out new sites."

"They'd do far better to blow up the island," said Martin savagely.

"That," said Carnegie, "was your predecessor's view. That was why he made enemies." He led the way to the lower terrace, past a group of patients playing cards. He jerked his head towards them. "That is their chief pastime here—cards. Gambling. They play all day and every day. Almost their sole occupation."

"There must be *some* amenities for five hundred patients, surely? Some provision for communal activities?"

"Virtually none. There's been talk of a cinema, but there's no place to house it. We had a radio, but it broke down and there was difficulty about repairing it. There's no occupational therapy at all, because we haven't the staff. There's no level ground, so it's impossible to play games. There's no soil, so it's impossible to have gardens, which is a great pity because all our food has to be brought from the mainland at great expense. There's no education. There is, of course, fornication."

"So I should imagine," said Martin dryly. He gazed reflectively along the congested coastal strip. "At least there's the sea. I suppose the patients do some fishing?"

"Oh, no," said Carnegie. "There was trouble about that. They're not allowed to take boats out in case they abscond."

"Don't they abscond anyway?"

The old man gave his sour smile. "Of course they do. There is always some way of organising it. A small bribe—a *very* small bribe. We have two visiting days a week, and it can easily be arranged through relatives. Last year we had twenty absconders."

"Then what on earth's the point of stopping the fishing?"

"It was a political decision. Someone started a scare in the Legislative Council. If fishing were allowed, he said, the mainland would soon be overrun by escaping lepers. It was one of the planks in his election platform."

Martin's face hardened. He could see lots of trouble ahead. "What's this place?" he asked, peering into an almost windowless room built of loosely mortared rock.

Three or four sluttish-looking Negresses were tending a battery of black ovens along one wall. The place was thick with soot and stank abominably. From the open door came an eddy of scorching heat.

"That is one of the communal kitchens," said Carnegie.

"It's incredible."

"We are to have a wonderful new kitchen under the scheme, with electric stoves, stainless steel sinks, refrigerators and all the latest equipment." They strolled on a little way. "Here is the laundry."

Again Martin found himself gazing into a dark and dirty room. Women were standing at scrubbing boards and ancient coppers, their arms and faces glistening with sweat in the foul heat. "The place is forty years old," said Carnegie. "A nightmare. Nothing is ever washed clean. I need hardly go into details. Again, it's the old trouble—shortage of water. And no proper equipment. Now I'll show you the hospital."

Martin suddenly felt sorry for the grey old doctor whose job was surgery. "I'm not surprised you want to get away," he said.

"It would be different," said Carnegie wistfully, "if there were anything I could do. But where can I start? I'm single-handed, and it's much too big a job for me. There are too many patients—far too many. There's nothing for them to do—they eat their hearts out. There are not nearly enough nurses. There are no facilities for anything. All our stuff has to be brought from the mainland. Often our requests are ignored. There's no telephone—absolutely hopeless. I don't know how you'll ever make anything of it."

"I'm not so sure that I shall try," said Martin.

Chapter Two

The leisurely tempo of the Health Department in Fontego City quickened perceptibly as soon as it became known that the Secretary had returned. One of the office boys, who had been hawking sweepstake tickets in the street most of the morning, managed to slip back unobserved. The coloured girl typists, in their cool pinks and greens, stopped discussing the costumes they would wear at Fiesta and applied themselves with conscious diligence to their copying. The senior clerks opened more files and buried themselves in the contents. The Assistant Secretary, Ezekiel MacPhearson Dubois, mentally assembled the matters on which he would have to report and put on his jacket in readiness for the expected summons.

In the air-conditioned inner office Dr. Adrian Garland stood by the window, deep in thought. He was a striking rather than a handsome man, not particularly tall, but powerfully built, with a wide chest, big shoulders and strong hands. Though he was well over fifty his thick hair was still jet black except for a silver streak which grew in a freakish diagonal across his head. He looked what he was—a virile and energetic man, physically in his prime. His eyes were a brilliant blue, and of an unusual directness. They were eyes that could always command obedience, if not always affection.

At the moment the Secretary was not in the best of moods. His trip had borne some fruit, but as usual it had been exasperating. It was always the same at the start of a new campaign. Apathy—that was the main trouble. Apathy and obstruction. This rural health drive that he was planning would be expensive; he'd be in hot water again with the Financial Secretary for exceeding his estimates.

The Chamber of Commerce would probably accuse him of extravagance. The politicians would criticise him for concentrating all his efforts in one corner of the Colony—as though you could expect to win a battle with dispersed forces. The coloured doctors would bicker and scheme, as they always did. Was it worth it?

In his earlier years Garland had organised such campaigns with zest. He had been more ambitious in those days—professionally ambitious. He had enjoyed building a reputation as a first-class administrator, a man who got things done. He had enjoyed beating down opposition, particularly the opposition of the powerful. It had been very satisfying to inject a stream of energy and purpose into this lethargic Colony, to make plans like a general, to discipline and dispose his forces, and to get results. Very satisfying, ten years ago. But where had it got him? Where, for that matter, had it got the Colony? Disease was like the "bush"—it came creeping back as soon as the attack had weakened. These black fellows would never hold the line, once control of the Colony had passed to them. An idle, untrustworthy bunch, by and large—smart and slick sometimes, like Dubois, but without any guts. As for his personal position, he'd been marking time for years. Inadequate pay and no prospects. No financial prospects, anyway, not by honest toil. That aspect hadn't worried him until he'd married Celeste; indeed, he'd hardly thought about it. But it worried Celeste. The Colonial Service made no provision for expensive wives. Perhaps Celeste was right—perhaps he *had* been throwing himself away on an ungrateful Government. Anyhow, things would soon be different. If only she were less cold! It was odd how he missed her when he was away, considering how little she gave him. His marriage hadn't come up to his expectations, there was no use pretending it had; and Celeste was to blame. Some people might say she was a bit of a bitch—she probably was. But knowing it didn't cure him of his infatuation. He was even more in love with her now than when he'd married her a year ago.

He put Celeste out of his mind with an effort and rang for his secretary. "You might ask Dr. Dubois to come in now, Miss Chang."

Dubois arrived almost before the door had closed—swift, smiling, ingratiating. He was a coal-black Negro—slim, good-looking and obviously pleased with himself. His hair was carefully parted down the middle, his film-star moustache was meticulously trimmed, and his white teeth gleamed. His university tie was resplendent against a background of immaculate linen.

"Welcome back, Dr. Garland. I trust you had a very satisfactory trip."

"So-so," said Garland, regarding his deputy without pleasure and wishing for the hundredth time that he could get him switched to some other department. Everything about Dubois irritated him—the assiduously cultivated B.B.C. accent, the polite insolence, the perpetual hint of an *arrière pensée*. Dubois had too many ideas. Being educated in England had given him an odd twist. He could never stop talking about England—"the old country," he called it—and yet Garland knew that he disliked the British. A dangerous man, with too many friends and relatives among the local politicians, too much backstairs influence. An ambitious man, who'd almost certainly like Garland's own job. A trouble-maker.

"One or two rather trying matters have required attention in your absence," said Dubois, sitting down opposite Garland. "The typhoid outbreak at Preux is getting worse——"

"Of course it's getting worse," growled Garland. "If people will have latrines so near the river bank, what can they expect?"

"If there were alternative accommodation," said Dubois, "we could insist that the shacks were demolished. The Housing Committee has been very remiss."

"Yes," said Garland. He thought of adding that the most influential man on the Housing Committee was the owner of the shacks, but it hardly seemed worth while. "Anything else?"

"There has been an unfortunate incident at the Colonial Hospital. Dr. Crispin, who as you know has just come out from England, swore at a nurse in the operating theatre. It seems a case for disciplinary action." Dubois' eyes glistened with malicious satisfaction.

"Blast!" said Garland. "All right, I suppose you'd better let me see the report."

"And Dr. West has arrived."

"I know. He rang me this morning. He'll be along here in a few minutes. I'd like you to meet him after I've had a talk with him."

"Very good," said Dubois. "I sent him the memorandum on Tacri. He went out there yesterday."

"So he told me. I'm glad he's keen."

"He was sorry you were not in town," said Dubois.

Garland glared at his assistant. "I can't be everywhere at once. I've fixed up about the field crew. Mr. Spencer of Beauregard is taking his family to England for a holiday and he's kindly offered the Department the use of his house for as long as we need it. We ought to be able to clear up the area fairly quickly. I'll talk to you about it later. All right, Dubois."

The Negro retired. Almost at once Miss Chang entered. "Dr. West is here, sir."

"Good," said Garland. He went to the door and greeted Martin with a smile and a handshake. "Come along in," he said heartily. "Well, it's good to see a new face. I'm sorry I wasn't here to meet you."

"That's quite all right," said Martin. "Dubois told me you were away planning some drive."

Garland nodded. "It's a project I've been working on for some time—to isolate a small area and attack every disease at once. We may find some new patients for you. Cigarette? Well, tell me, how do you like the place?"

"Tacri?"

Garland laughed. "Good God, no, my dear fellow—nobody could like that. I mean Fontego."

"It's picturesque," said Martin, "but I think I'll reserve judgment."

"It's a very complex Colony," said Garland, "and a very difficult one. So you've been to Tacri already?"

"It seemed a useful way of filling in the time. I hope you didn't mind."

"Why should I mind? I like to see a little initiative—Heaven knows we need it. This place is moribund from the feet up. Well, what were your impressions?"

13

Martin found his chief's blue stare a little disconcerting, but he met it frankly. "To be honest," he said, "if I am to be a prison governor I think I'd sooner go the whole hog and have a place like Devil's Island."

Garland gave him a searching look. This young man wasn't going to be as simple to handle as old Stockford. He nodded slowly, sympathetically. "I know just how you feel. By the standards you're used to, Tacri must seem appalling. But that, after all, is why you've been appointed. I'm not up in your speciality, but I know you've got a big reputation and, according to the reports I've seen, you did a fine job building up that model settlement in India. If you can do half as well here, the Colony will be in your debt."

Martin said, "I'm a leprologist, not a magician. I couldn't make Tacri into a decent leper settlement in a million years."

"Oh, come," said Garland. "I don't expect to hear that sort of defeatist note already. Surely it's too early to judge. Besides, the place is going to be changed out of all recognition. Haven't you seen the plans?" The unwavering stare was almost an act of aggression.

"I've glanced at them. I haven't had an opportunity to study them in detail."

"Well," said Garland, "wouldn't it perhaps be better to avoid any dramatic judgments until you have? This scheme is no ordinary project. The whole place is to be rebuilt. There's to be ample accommodation for six hundred patients on the best modern lines. Small detached huts, mainly, with plenty of privacy and a quiet domestic atmosphere. The infirmaries are to be rebuilt. There's to be a new hospital and operating theatre, properly equipped; new administrative offices, a club, and a cinema; new kitchens and laundry, first-class accommodation for the staff, and a large additional recruitment of personnel, extra launches to carry the traffic—why, the place will be transformed!"

"But all that will cost the earth," exclaimed Martin.

Garland chuckled. "That was rather the view of the Finance Committee, but I managed to persuade them in the end that the job must be done. I told them that Tacri was a plague spot. I trod on a lot of toes, but I'm glad to say I got my way after a hard fight."

"I don't want to appear critical," said Martin, "when you've spent so much effort in getting reforms through, but——" He hesitated, then plunged. "Speaking as a leprologist, I can't feel that they're the right reforms. Where are you going to put all these new buildings? Carnegie said something about dynamiting the rock. Was he serious?"

"Quite serious. How else could we fit them in?"

"That's just the point," said Martin. "Why try to fit them in there? Tacri will never be a suitable spot. In my view it's pouring money down the drain."

"Wouldn't it be better to leave the financial arrangements in the capable hands of the Finance Committee?" suggested Garland dryly.

"Are they capable? I don't know. What I'm quite clear about, Dr. Garland, is that Tacri is hopelessly unsuited for the job it's been given. The whole conception of segregating lepers in a place like that is fifty years out of date. Whatever fine buildings you put up, that island will always be a prison—and a bad prison. There isn't room to move—there can't be. Most of the patients, I take it, got their living from the land before they were certified. How can they work the land on Tacri? There isn't an inch of soil on the island. And there isn't space to start alternative occupations. You'll never reconcile active young men and women to cramped idleness. They're bound to mope, and they're certain to try to escape."

"That's all true enough," agreed Garland. "I'm not a leprologist, but I know the case against Tacri. As a matter of fact I've written two long reports denouncing the place—if not three. The ideal, of course, would be an agricultural settlement here in Fontego, ten miles or so outside the city."

"Exactly," said Martin eagerly. "And in all probability it could be provided for a fraction of what these improvements on Tacri will cost. You'd avoid the sense of isolation, you'd have good land and stock and plenty of water, you'd recruit a better staff, and what's more, there'd be room to expand. I gather there may be well over five hundred additional leprosy cases still undetected in the Colony. How would you find room for those on Tacri?"

Garland smiled grimly. "They are, as you observe, still undetected. It'll take a long time to find them. In any case, that's beside the point. I admire your keenness, but you can't be a perfectionist in Fontego. We've got to face the facts, and the facts are that at the present stage it would be a political impossibility to move the leprosarium to the mainland. Just a moment—I'll get Dubois in." He rang the bell, and the Assistant Secretary was summoned.

"Oh, Dubois, I'd like you to meet Dr. West."

"It's a very great pleasure," said Dubois, shaking hands and beaming.

"Like the rest of us," Garland said, "Dr. West just hates the sight of Tacri. He doesn't think the improvements scheme can make the place a suitable leprosarium. He's all for a settlement on the mainland."

"But of course," said Dubois. "We're all in favour of that—in the Department. It would be in accordance with the best modern practice. But in Fontego——" He shook his head. "Quite impossible."

"Why?" asked Martin.

"There are powerful feelings against it in the Colony," said Dubois. "I am unusually conversant with the situation—my brother is a member of the Legislative Council; many members of my family have their ears to the ground. The people of the Colony are quite determined not to have the leprosarium on the mainland. If it were seriously proposed I believe there would be riots. It's regrettable, but it's true. Anyone who advocated such a plan would immediately lose his job. As Dr. Stockford did. These are democratic days in Fontego, and the people are beginning to feel their strength. If they don't like anyone they sweep him away."

Martin was unimpressed. "A quite spontaneous movement, I suppose? Was it the people who swept Dr. Stockford away?"

"Dr. Stockford made his position impossible by stubborn agitation," said Garland. The blue eyes drilled. "Resignation was the inevitable consequence."

Martin smiled. "If that's intended as a warning, I'm afraid it's wasted on me. At the moment, I'm much more scared of keeping my job at Tacri than losing it."

"It wasn't intended as a warning, of course," said Garland, more amiably. "There's plenty of room for differing opinions as long as we have a little discretion. But Dubois is right. I don't know about the people, but the politicians here are very powerful and—with all respect to your relatives, Dubois—they're usually against everything that makes sense. God knows I hold no brief for them, but they can't be ignored. They think that a leprosarium on the mainland means risk of contagion, and they've got the ear of the masses."

"But we all know it means nothing of the sort," said Martin.

"*We* know," said Dubois, "but we can't hope to persuade the people of that."

"Have you tried?"

"It's been constantly emphasised in reports," said Dubois, "that leprosy is not a particularly contagious disease."

"In reports! Who reads reports? Have you tried getting down to the people? Couldn't you enlist the support of the schools and the churches, use the radio and the newspapers and posters and so on? Present the facts in the simplest possible way? I should have thought that would have done the trick."

Garland shook his head. "I'm afraid you've got a lot to learn about Fontego. You don't appreciate how deep the prejudices are."

"I can imagine," said Martin. "It's hardly a new thing where leprosy is concerned. I've found it wherever I've been. You simply have to break down the prejudices—if necessary, override them. This isn't a matter where you can afford to defer to popular superstition. Once there's an accomplished fact, the people will soon find out they were wrong."

"You can't force things on the people these days," said Dubois.

"Why not? I take it the Governor still has some authority?"

Dubois looked pained. "We are well on the way to responsible government," he said.

"I see no sign of it," said Martin shortly.

Garland intervened. "I don't think this discussion is going to lead anywhere," he said. "I respect your views, West; I think you're ninety per cent right about Tacri. But Dubois is certainly right about the political aspect—it's extremely tricky. There are plenty of ugly feelings about already in the Colony, and we don't want to make the situation worse. I'm not a politician, thank God, but I can sense the mood." He contemplated Martin's indignant face with a slightly sardonic smile. "If you feel that you'd care to raise the matter personally with the Colonial Secretary you're welcome to do so, but I don't think you'll get much change out of him."

Martin gave a non-committal nod of acknowledgment. "I appreciate your permission, anyway."

"The fact is," said Garland, "that, politics apart, we've gone too far now with this Tacri project to reopen the subject. The contractors, a very enterprising firm, are ready to start work. Tacri has been a blot on the Colony for years, and as I told you, it's been the very devil of a fight to get the plans through. Dubois will bear me out. At last the money's been voted—three-quarters of a million pounds. If you start advocating an alternative scheme at this stage the whole thing may be thrown into the melting pot again and those poor devils on Tacri will go on stewing for another decade. As it is, in three or four years we should be able to make the place fairly comfortable."

"I'm entirely unconvinced," said Martin, "but I see your point. Anyhow, I'll study the plans carefully."

"In the meantime," said Garland, "what about some cocktails? My wife is looking forward to meeting you, I know. You'll stay to dinner, won't you? She's expecting you."

"It's very kind of you both," said Martin.

Chapter Three

Celeste Garland stood back to admire a great bowl of exotic flowers she had just arranged, and held the pose as she heard her husband and Martin enter the drawing-room. Behind her head a panel of tropical wood, gleaming with a dark brilliance, made the perfect background for her upswept blonde hair. She was wearing a low-cut dinner dress of white piqué. A stiffened sheath of the same material encircled her shoulders, curving down into the bodice with a line of exquisite simplicity, reminding Martin in a vague way of arum lilies. Against the whiteness of the dress her skin had a warm bronze flush—not the acquired tan of the Hollywood beauty but the deep rich glow that spoke of southern blood. Her eyes were brown with golden lights. She was quite arrestingly lovely, Martin realised, and her dress was a work of art. He wondered for a quick moment if the Secretary of Health had a large private income. It looked as though his wife might be an expensive item in his budget.

Garland kissed the cheek of Celeste prettily offered to him and presented Martin. Her eyes flickered over his face and she gave a welcoming smile. He heard her voice, rich and low, murmuring some polite phrase.

"Shall we sit in the garden?" she suggested. "It's just beginning to get cool. The others will be here soon. Dr. West, what would you like to drink? Have you got used to our *reki* yet, or would you prefer a civilised cocktail?"

"Could you manage a gin and something?"

"Of course. Salacity makes a wonderful Martini."

Her visitor looked startled. "I beg your pardon!"

Celeste laughed—an attractive chuckle. "That's the maid's name, believe it or not. Salacity Brown! I suppose her mother heard some hot gospeller use the word and liked the sound of it. The Governor's wife thinks I ought to call her Sally, but I wouldn't dream of it." She smiled at her husband's faint air of disapproval. "So you're going to live on that horrid island, Dr. West. I don't know how you can bear the thought. Won't you be dreadfully lonely?" The warm brown eyes rested on him with a speculative look.

"I expect I shall be much too busy to feel lonely."

"Oh dear," said Celeste, "are you another of these active conscientious people? Adrian's like that—he's always rushing around like a Boy Scout."

"Not always doing good deeds, I'm afraid," said Garland lightly. He was watching his wife, watching the way she looked at Martin. The old jealousy smote him. She was always the same with anyone new, if he were at all presentable. It was just her manner, of course—it didn't amount to anything serious. It couldn't, in the small white circle of Fontego—not without gossip. All the same, he felt glad that young West was going to Tacri. Young men were a damned nuisance. Garland couldn't ever forget that he was twenty-five years older than his wife.

The tropical night was just beginning to fall as Celeste led the way on to the terrace, where deck chairs and little tables were set out in the light of carefully arranged lamps. The air was cooler now and deliciously scented. From the bottom of the garden came the gleam of water.

"It's a pity it's too dark to show you the grounds," said Celeste. "You must come along in the daytime—the garden is quite lovely. The hibiscus is a picture, and we have two enormous mango trees and some wonderful shrubs that I haven't seen anywhere else."

"Is that the sea at the bottom?"

"It's a sort of lagoon," said Garland, "very shallow, but it gives us a pleasant bathing beach of our own. That's one thing we can always do here—swim."

"I think you're fortunate to live in such a delightful spot," said Martin. He lay back in his chair and felt at peace. The familiar evening orchestra of frogs and cicadas was well into its overture, and fireflies were dancing among the bushes. This was easily the pleasantest time of day in the tropics—better even than the crack of dawn.

"I like the place myself," Garland was saying. "The only thing I miss in these parts is a smooth green lawn. I suppose we all do. I've experimented with a dozen different sorts of grasses, but they all come up coarse. Ah, here are the drinks." A black and smiling Salacity placed a tray on one of the tables and Garland handed round the glasses.

"A garden like this must need a tremendous amount of attention," said Martin.

"It needs more than it gets," said Celeste. She was lounging gracefully in the corner of a long rustic seat, one bare brown arm stretched invitingly along the back. She glanced at her husband. "Johnson Johnson's quite useless. He's much more interested in his banjo than he is in the garden, and I find him asleep in the oddest places."

A tolerant smile crossed Garland's face. "He's not too bad. We were lucky to get him. You know what the servant problem is." He turned to Martin. "These chaps were all spoilt during the war. They were paid fantastic wages for doing practically nothing, and now they just won't work. Johnson Johnson is a poor relation of Dubois—that's how I got hold of him."

"A deplored relation, I should say," remarked Celeste. "But Dr. Dubois takes his family responsibilities very seriously. He sounds exactly like an old patriarch, always talking about 'my people.' Why doesn't he get married, Adrian?"

Garland shrugged. "He will, I dare say, when it suits his plans. He's a cautious chap. By the way, I remember now he's going to bury one of his relatives tomorrow morning. You ought to see a funeral here, West. It's quite a sight."

"I suppose that means that Johnson will want the morning off too," said Celeste. "And he'll spend all the rest of the day sleeping off the effects."

"You're prejudiced about him," said Garland. "He has his points—he's one of the luckiest men with a rod I've ever come across. Do you do any fishing, West?"

"I haven't done a lot. I've always been too far from water."

"We must take a trip sometime. You'll need to get away from Tacri occasionally. I've a little ketch over in Darwin Bay, on the other side of the Base. It's a fine spot for mackerel and snapper. I don't get over very often, but I enjoy it when I do. The essential thing in the tropics, as you know, is to take plenty of exercise."

"I told you he was a Boy Scout," said Celeste. "It makes me hot just to watch him. You should see him playing tennis. I've never known such energy."

Garland laughed, but Martin had the impression that he wasn't too well pleased by his wife's teasing.

There was the sound of cars pulling up in the drive. "Now you're going to meet the social life of Fontego," said Celeste to Martin. She gave him an amused intimate smile, as though they already shared a secret, and rose to greet the newcomers. Martin was presented to a plump woman of about fifty; this was Mrs. Sylvester, wife of the Office of Works Secretary. Sylvester himself was a slim grey-haired man with an air of calm self-assurance. There was a much younger man named Carew, who was the Secretary of Education; his wife, a small pretty girl with auburn hair and a Scottish accent; and another man named Forter, who was a member of the Executive Council.

Salacity came pattering on to the terrace with more drinks, and for a moment there was a general buzz of conversation. Then Mrs. Sylvester's resonant voice rang out as she called to Celeste. "Darling, did you hear about Susan's smash? I always knew that girl was asking for trouble, driving the way she does."

"No, what happened?" asked Celeste with languid interest. "Is she hurt?"

"Nothing to speak of. Her right hand is cut rather badly, but that's all. She was extremely lucky. She was driving along the Cobra Lane—at not more than forty, *she* said, but you know what she is—and one of those awful taximen came hurtling round the bend on the wrong side, as usual. The next thing Susan knew was that she was buried in sugar cane, and there was blood and broken glass everywhere." Mrs. Sylvester's voice ended on an almost exultant note.

Garland said: "You haven't met Susan Anstruther yet, have you, West? She's the Colonial Secretary's daughter—a charming girl, but a bit reckless with cars. These taxi fellows are a menace, of course, even when they're sober."

"They're a race apart," said Celeste. "They all have a sneering look, and they all wear little black moustaches and dirty straw hats. I believe they're all one family—a race of demons, with one big black taximan as their father, who makes them give him all their takings."

"Anyone who drives in this Colony takes his life in his hands," said Forter. He was short and bald, with little twinkling eyes. "The roads aren't exactly built for speed."

"Come off it," said Sylvester, helping himself to salted almonds. It was Sylvester's department that built the roads.

"What always puzzles me," Forter went on banteringly, "is why you never finish off the edges of the roads. They're always left anyhow, and they crumble away until there's barely room for two cars to pass."

"It's a simple matter of cash," said Sylvester, quite unperturbed. "If you chaps in office will vote the money for us, we'll make decent roads."

"Seriously," said Forter, "there's one thing you ought to attend to, Sylvester—that bridge over the Silver River on the Main Trunk Road. It's just not good enough with all the airport traffic. It gave a distinct wobble when I drove over it yesterday. The Trunk is the only fast road we've got in the place, and I think it ought to get priority."

"That's only a temporary bridge," said Sylvester.

Everybody laughed. "One of the things you'll discover here, West," said Garland, "is that almost everything is temporary. The Colony has a genius for starting things and not finishing them—particularly the Office of Works, eh, Sylvester?"

"What can you expect," Sylvester broke in, "when you collar a cool three-quarters of a million for a new leprosarium?"

"Now there, Sylvester, I agree with you," put in Forter, who ran one of the Colony's big factories when he wasn't serving on the

Council, and like the rest of the business community was always in favour of reducing public expenditure. "With due sympathy for Dr. West, of course, who's got to live there ... Anyway, it's an absurd place for a leprosarium, as I said in Council. Do you know how much it costs to run the visitors' launch service? Literally thousands! Personally, I'd sooner see the place rebuilt over here—it would pay in the long run."

"Me too," said Sylvester. "Building costs three times as much on Tacri as it does on the mainland."

"But we don't want that ghastly place here," cried Celeste. "All those horrible people rubbing shoulders with us! Ugh!" She gave an exaggerated shudder, and her own beautiful shoulders shrank back as though already warding off contamination.

"They wouldn't actually do that, you know," said Martin mildly.

Garland caught his eye and smiled grimly. "It looks as though your propaganda will have to start in my home, West."

"I'm sure Dr. West wouldn't start anything so dull," said Celeste with a provocative glance at him. "And anyway, why do we always discuss such dreary topics?"

"You shouldn't have married a department, my dear," said Mrs. Sylvester. "That's the mistake I made. I get so tired of hearing about improving this and improving that. It isn't as though it does any good. You'll never make anything out of these black people. They're a good-for-nothing lot. All they can do is breed like rabbits." She turned accusingly to Dr. Garland. "Now if you spent that three-quarters of a million on birth control clinics instead of a leprosarium, you might get somewhere."

"You know perfectly well they'd never use them, Marion," said Celeste with a laugh. "Remember what happened to Lavinia."

Martin, who was making a whole series of mental notes, said:

"What happened to Lavinia?"

Mrs. Sylvester explained. "Lavinia is a Miss Hollis, a most respectable maiden lady with a passion for good works. She keeps house for her brother, who works here, but she interests herself in the social welfare of the natives. Well, she was visiting a hospital and in the maternity ward she got talking to a black woman who'd just had her fourteenth child. Lavinia tactfully suggested that the woman ought to do something to prevent her family growing any bigger. It wasn't easy to get the idea across, and Lavinia had to go into quite a bit of detail. The black woman looked terribly shocked and said, 'Dat may be o' right fo' de likes o' yo', ma'am, but I'se in Holy Wedlock.'"

There was a general laugh. Celeste said, "Considering the way you feel about them, Marion, you manage to imitate them awfully well. You know, Dr. West, there's a common belief that English is spoken here, but it's quite a mistaken one." She glanced mischievously at the Education man, Carew, who was sitting quietly listening. "What *is* the language you teach them, David?"

Carew smiled. "We do the best we can with the raw material we've got," he said.

"I suppose there's the usual shortage of good teachers," remarked Martin sympathetically.

"There is indeed," said Carew. "There's a shortage of everything, of course, but particularly of teachers. And half of those we have are quite unqualified—little more than uneducated kids themselves. If the teacher doesn't speak properly, obviously you can't expect the children to."

"Tell Dr. West about the Inspector and the cat," put in little Mrs. Carew in her musical voice.

Carew smiled reminiscently. "It was last week," he said. "One of our Inspectors was sitting in at a lesson and the subject was the domestic cat. When the lesson was over he thought he'd test the children on it, so he asked. 'How many feet has a cat?' The children just gaped at him and didn't say a word. He repeated the question and still no one answered. The Negro teacher was getting quite restive, and suddenly he called out sharply, 'Chillun, how much foots puss have?' Immediately a forest of hands shot up."

Carew himself joined in the laughter that followed, but he added ruefully, "The trouble with most of us expatriate English is that we expect too much. These people are making progress in a lot of ways. I've seen enormous changes since I came here, and that's not so long ago. The general standard of education may seem very poor—it *is* poor, it can't be anything else—but we do manage to turn out some quite good scholars, and in time they may leaven the lump. They're more likely to do it themselves than we are to do it for them."

"Oh, nonsense," cried Mrs. Sylvester in her emphatic way. "There are exceptions, of course, but most of the black people I see have no more intelligence than animals. And they certainly behave like animals. I heard of a man who boasted of having children by twenty-three different women. I think it's disgusting."

Garland again caught Martin's eye, and his lips twitched. "They're not usually quite as promiscuous as that," he said. "A good many of them are content with more or less faithful concubinage, and the parents quite often get married as soon as the eldest daughter is old enough to be a bridesmaid."

"*I* think they must have rather a good time," said Celeste in her lazy drawl.

"Darling!" said Mrs. Sylvester reproachfully. Martin felt that if she had had a fan in her hand she would have rapped Celeste's knuckles with it.

"If you ask me," said Forter, "the worst fault of the people here is that they're bone idle. They'll never make anything of the place until they've learned to do an honest day's work." He turned to Martin. "Do you know, West, we actually have to put up notices saying, 'Any employee found asleep at his work will be instantly dismissed.' They're quite shameless about it—they drop off at the first opportunity. You know that, Garland."

Garland was no lover of the black population, but his professional sense was aroused. "I admit I've found them a pretty useless lot," he said, "but the trouble isn't just idleness. They're riddled with disease, you know. If we could take a small area, as we want to, and treat the entire population there for all its complaints—hookworm, V.D., yaws, malaria, and so on—on the spot, you'd be amazed at the change in them. I know I shall never persuade you, Forter, but honestly it's a most shortsighted policy to grudge the Health Department additional funds. It would be an investment to let us spend the money."

Celeste laughed. "I do hope Dr. West isn't believing all this. The only thing that happens as a result of medical science here is that fewer people die, the population increases, and there's less to eat for everybody. *I* don't think it's a kindness to cure them of things. And anyway, who'd trust a Government department? They nearly all fritter their money away in graft."

"That's a gross exaggeration," said Garland. He looked at his wife almost angrily.

"Is it?" said Celeste coolly. Her eyes rested on Garland with something like contempt. "Anyhow, Dr. West, you'll soon find out for yourself. Mind you," she added cynically, "*I* don't blame people for making a bit on the side if they can—it's a tradition here—but I don't see any point in pretending they don't."

"To say nearly *all* Government departments," said Sylvester, "is going a bit far, in my opinion. In any case, I think you should make it clear to Dr. West that it's only the coloured population that's involved. You don't find the whites doing it—at least, not those from England."

"You don't find them, no," said Celeste, "but I wonder how many of us would bear investigation."

"Oh, I don't agree with you there at all," said Carew. "It is a fact that the Colony's public standards are pretty shocking, but all the same, the white administration's not corrupt."

"It's everything else," said Celeste, adroitly changing her ground. "It's tired, bored, afraid——"

Martin intervened in what seemed like a family squabble. "From what I've heard this evening," he said, "I would have thought it fairly vigorous."

"Oh, this is just an act we're putting on for your benefit," said Celeste, her eyes dancing. "We like to sound intelligent when there are strangers about. You don't imagine we always discuss these portentous subjects, do you? We talk about the shortcomings of our friends, and the best way of mixing drinks, and why we played the four of clubs instead of the three of diamonds last Wednesday week. Nobody cares a hoot about the Colony, and why should they? It's a hopeless place."

There was a chorus of protest, but Celeste ignored it. She was enjoying herself. "The men here," she went on, "are overworked, underpaid, and disillusioned. They know there's no future for them here. They know they'll have to hand over to the blacks pretty soon and that then everything will go to pot, so they're just waiting patiently for their pensions to fall due. The women are so bored with inactivity that they can hardly bother to yawn. Week after week we do the same things—play bridge and tennis, give cocktail parties, go to cocktail parties, dine and dance at the Country Club, gossip about each other—and always with the same people. It's so tedious. We'd all like to break out, only we're too scared."

"I'm sure *I* don't want to break out," said plump Mrs. Sylvester, who looked as though she was about to do so.

Garland's annoyance seemed to have passed. He was looking at Celeste with the expression of an indulgent parent watching a precocious child. "You must take everything my wife says with a grain of salt," he told Martin.

"Well, look at you," Celeste persisted. "Aren't *you* disillusioned? You've given your life to this place, and what thanks do you get? Everybody criticises and no one's any the better off. I know *we're* not." The implication of domestic penury was belied by her appearance, but Celeste seemed unconscious of the fact.

"Personally," she continued, "I'd be happy to take a plane to Honolulu to-morrow and never come back." She nodded to Salacity, who stood beaming at the french windows. "Anyhow, dinner is ready. Shall we ban politics? I'm sure Dr. West is tired of all our grumbling."

"On the contrary," said Martin, "I'm extremely interested. After all, I'm in it too."

Chapter Four

Dinner was over. The party, now appreciably mellower, had gathered again on the terrace.

"You'll have to make sure they let you off that island for Fiesta," Mrs. Sylvester was saying to Martin. "You've arrived just in time for it."

"Is it fun?" asked Martin. "What happens?"

"What *doesn't* happen?" said Celeste. She was sitting close beside him and he was pleasantly aware of a subtle perfume.

"Think of a Musical evening at Government House," said Sylvester with a grin, "and then think of the opposite. That's Fiesta." He caught his wife's reproving glance. "Sorry, my dear."

"It's an orgy," stated Celeste.

Martin laughed. "It doesn't sound quite in my line. Do you want to get me struck off?"

"I only meant you should watch it, of course," said Mrs. Sylvester. "I don't approve of white people taking part."

"They used not to," said Forter. "At least, only in the most decorous way. A few years ago their contribution was simply to drive around in fancy costumes and throw confetti and paper streamers at their friends."

"They go a good deal farther than that now," said Mrs. Sylvester. "It's shocking how some of the women behave. People who are most respectable all the rest of the year. They seem to lose all control. I suppose they get carried away by the things they see."

"It's being able to wear masks," said Celeste. "They feel they can discard all their inhibitions quite safely. It must be a wonderful sensation."

"I'm still not quite clear what goes on," said Martin. "I take it Fiesta's a sort of national holiday?"

"That's the idea," said Carew, who had made rather a study of it. "It's always held during the first week in May—actually on the anniversary of the ending of slavery in the Colony. It's quite indescribable—a free-for-all, with no holds barred. You'll have to see it for yourself. They start at six o'clock on Wednesday morning and go on till midnight on the Thursday. Everybody parades in the streets, with costumes and masks according to taste, and they dance and sing and shout and generally make whoopee until they're exhausted."

"*Reki*, rhythm, and rowdyism," said Forter. "It's very colourful, but it's a darned nuisance all the same. The jails are always full when it's over. Personally I don't like it."

"I'm with you there," said Garland. "I always try to get as far away from it as possible. In my view, Fiesta's the best time for a fishing trip. I think it's high time a stop was put to it."

"At least at Fiesta we're not watched by servants," said Mrs. Carew. "Normally one can't get away from them, but at Fiesta they simply disappear. I can't see that it does any harm. It's probably a safety valve."

"I don't like to see white people being undignified before the blacks," said Mrs. Sylvester grandly. "No wonder they've lost every scrap of respect for us."

"Oh, I wouldn't go as far as that," said Forter.

"I would," said Celeste, "but I don't see what can be done about it. After all, there's no clear-cut division. Who is white, and who isn't, if it comes to that? I think that's one of the horrible things about this Colony—the way everyone's mixed up."

"A lot of people would say it was one of the good things," observed Carew. "It does mean there's practically no colour bar."

"There may not be a colour bar," said Celeste, "but there's a frightful colour problem, as you'll have to admit. Almost everyone's got a complex about colour, and the black people are the worst of all. They all envy a light skin. Isn't it true that most black men want to marry someone lighter than themselves?"

"Yes, I think that is so," admitted Carew. "I had an example of it at one of the schools only the other day. I was watching a young Negress teaching her class. She was very competent, and I thought extremely attractive. I said to the head teacher—a Negro himself—'You won't be keeping her long; she'll be getting married.' He shook his head and said, 'She not get married—she too black.'"

"I don't understand," said Martin. "Surely in a country of black people——"

"What he meant," explained Carew, "was that the sort of Negro she'd be willing to marry—an educated man with some culture—would be on the look-out for a brown girl, or even a white one. After all, some of these Negroes do quite well as doctors and lawyers—they certainly make a lot of money—and there are plenty of white girls without any prospects who don't mind marrying them for what they can get out of it."

"And the result of it all is," said Celeste, "that a snobbery of colour has developed. What matters here is not so much social status or wealth, but how much of the tarbrush there is. Anyway, that's what matters with a lot of people. Why, it's a popular sport at the Country Club to watch the girls dancing and pick out the white ones with a touch of colour. I think it's all horrible."

"But if they're white," said Martin, "how can you tell?"

"Oh, you can usually tell by the way they 'traipse'."

"'Traipse'?"

"That's what we call the shuffling dance that's so popular here. The coloured people do it with a sort of sinuous wriggle that the whites find very difficult to imitate. It's done to the calypso tunes—you know about calypso, surely?"

"Not very much," said Martin.

"Oh, calypso is all tied up with Fiesta. They're just beginning to practise the new ones now."

"Calypsoes are just rather primitive topical songs," said Forter, "set to an African rhythm. They're not indigenous to this Colony—actually they were first brought here from the West Indies, weren't they, Carew? I've never seen much in them myself, but it's devilish difficult to keep still when they're being played and some people rave about them."

"They can be quite amusing," said Carew. "They began as a pretty low-class sort of entertainment, but they have a certain amount of wit. I like them best when you get two calypso singers improvising as they go along and making cracks about each other. Some of the chaps are very smart—they develop an eye for significant and humorous incidents, preferably a bit scandalous. It can be rather dangerous, of course, if there's anything you want to hush up. They have a knack of picking up spicy gossip, and when they do it goes through the calypso huts like wildfire."

"I'm surprised West hasn't been approached by any of them," said Sylvester. "There's a kind of racket some of them work. When a newcomer arrives one of these chaps writes a calypso about him, very fulsome and flattering, and offers to sing it in public—for a consideration, of course. If he gets a few shillings, that's the end of the matter, but if he doesn't he's quite capable of writing a different sort of calypso *and* singing it. There's definitely an element of blackmail. Of course, we don't know what these people are singing about us half of the time—or saying, for that matter."

Garland's voice came from the shadows. "If you'd like to hear a calypso, West, I'll get Johnson Johnson along for you. He's a great enthusiast."

"Must we?" said Celeste. "I hate the things." Seeing Martin's look of disappointment she added, "Besides, he's probably gone home."

"Not he," said Garland. "He's more likely to be asleep somewhere. You know he always hangs around with his banjo when we have people to dinner. Salacity will find him."

Celeste called, "Salacity!" with a mischievous look at Martin, and the maid came running down to the terrace.

"Find Johnson," said Celeste. "We want him for a calypso."

Salacity went off, and they heard her voice calling, "Hey, Johnson, man, where am yo?"

"Listen," said Garland to Martin. "You'll like this."

Another voice was heard near the house, oddly coming from somewhere between earth and heaven. "What 'appenin'?" it said.

"What part yo is, man?"

"I'se up here, 'omans," came the suspended voice, now located in the branches of a mango beside the house.

"Yo one bad foolish mans droppin' asleep up dar," Salacity chided him. "Yo fall off an' break yo neck."

Johnson seemed annoyed. "Wha mek yo mout ah run laka ribber so?" he said sleepily. "Leh yo tongue rest."

"Yo stop throwin' words at me," cried Salacity indignantly, "Cumna man down, massa want yo fo' play calypso."

The word acted on Johnson like magic. In a moment he had scrambled down from the tree and was blinking sheepishly in the circle of light. He was a slim youth in an old garish blazer and a battered felt hat. He stood grinning with his head a little on one side and his long arms hanging loosely. Round his neck was his cherished banjo.

"Johnson," said Garland, "you sing calypso for Dr. West?"

Johnson's grin broadened. "Yes, sah." He tentatively plucked the strings of his banjo. "Wha you like, sah?"

"Can you do a calypso about Dr. West? He's come to look after the lepers at Tacri."

"Yes, sah, ah knows. Ah heard 'bout um."

"Smart boy. All right, see what you can do."

"And keep it clean," said Celeste. "They often don't," she explained to Martin. "They think we don't understand, which is usually true. I've a vivid recollection of the Governor's wife enthusiastically applauding the most awful obscenities in a calypso hut. I think she thought it was a sort of native hymn!"

Martin laughed. "I hope I understand him better than I did when he was in the tree."

"Oh, you'll manage. He makes a special effort for calypsoes. Professional pride, you know."

Johnson's eyes had taken on a trance-like look, and he began to strum. As he played, his whole body started to jig in time with the rhythm—his feet tapping on the ground, his shoulders jerking, his hips waggling, and his head nodding. The tune was simple. Suddenly he began to sing in a pleasant tenor voice:

> "Doctor Wes', believe we very 'appy
> Dat you wid us now so willingly
> To do big tas' which will certainly
> Make fo' better livin' in dis Colony."

Martin was so fascinated, he was hardly aware that Celeste was holding his hand. For several verses Johnson continued in a similar vein, making the most of the little information he possessed, leaning heavily on words ending in "y" for his rhymes, and not bothering about scansion. But whatever odd collection of words came tumbling from his lips, the beat of the music never faltered, and somehow the words managed to catch up with the tune before each verse finished. By the fourth verse the young Negro had worked himself up into unrestrained admiration of his subject.

> "In you we put our trus' mos' willingly
> We glad dat we bin blessed wid such a personality
> A man of yo greatness of heart an' strength an' brain capacity
> An' we honoured to 'ave yo 'mong us in our company."

"Bravo!" cried Martin, and led the applause.

"There you are, West," said Garland, "that's the calypso at its most generous."

Johnson was still twitching and tapping as though he had St. Vitus's dance in all his limbs.

"Let's have just one more," said Carew. "You don't mind, Celeste, do you? I like the one about the 'santapee'."

"I'm the country cousin," said Martin. "What on earth's a santapee?"

"A centipede, but it would be all the same if it was a hippopotamus. It's the idea that counts."

"You'd think Carew was a woman-hater," said Celeste. "Listen!" Johnson was singing again:

"Man santapee bad too bad
But woman santapee mo' dan bad."

"The female of the species," whispered Celeste in Martin's ear, "is more dangerous than the male." She had had, he suspected, just one drink too many.

Chapter Five

It was nearly midnight, and the guests had departed. Celeste, wearing a diaphanous *négligé*, was brushing her hair at the dressing table. Garland, sitting heavily on the edge of one of the twin beds, was watching the rhythmical sweep of her bare arm.

"Shall I do that for you?" he asked presently.

"Oh, would you, darling? Thank you so much. You know how I love having things done to my hair." Celeste gave a voluptuous wriggle and settled herself comfortably. Her mouth curved into an ironical smile as she studied Garland's reflection in the mirror, his face serious and intent as a small boy's as he brushed the hair with long even strokes.

"That was a rather attractive young man you brought along to-night," she said, just to see the alarm leap into his eyes. "It's so nice to see a new face. And, above all, a young one."

Jealousy surged through Garland again. He knew he ought to make some light-hearted remark, but he couldn't for the life of him. Celeste was the one person in the world, he told himself bitterly, who could undermine his self-confidence.

"I'm sorry you find life so dreary here," he said coldly.

Celeste laughed. "Oh, I get by," she said, holding her head farther back for the caress of the brush. It amused her to observe how vulnerable this man was, even after twelve months of her sort of marriage. It was such a pity he wasn't wealthy as well as respected. Then he'd have made the ideal husband. Perhaps, in her anxiety for status, she had been precipitate. But it wasn't so easy to find money *and* the rest, and so far, while there had been plenty of the rest in her life, there certainly hadn't been much money nor even, until now, the solid professional standing and authority which Garland represented.

"I like this thing you're wearing," he said, touching gossamer frills. "It's new, isn't it?"

"Yes," said Celeste. "Julia Gore brought it back from San Francisco for me. It *is* rather lush, isn't it?" She preened herself.

"You always look lovely," said Garland. The shadowy line of a breast stirred him. "I missed you while I was away."

"Did you, darling? Naughty thoughts?"

"It wouldn't be surprising, would it?" he said, resentment breaking through. "That's about all I do have."

"Well, darling, really, this heat! And if you *will* expect me to play the charming hostess so often . . . What are you going to do during Fiesta?"

His face brightened. "I thought we might spend a few days together in the hills. It would be a change for you."

"Not the sort of change I want," said Celeste. "The same people in a different place! I think I'll stay here and have a nice quiet rest. You'd better go fishing."

"I don't mind staying here."

Celeste stood up. "That will do for my hair to-night, thank you . . . No, Adrian, it's sweet of you, but you know you don't like sitting about doing nothing. I shall be quite all right. It'll be a relief not to be cluttered up with servants."

"As you wish," he said. He recognised the note of finality in her voice. "Perhaps I'll take West along with me."

"Now that *is* a good idea."

Garland felt an absurd sense of relief. He'd been a fool to worry. Just because she sometimes seemed rather aloof to him, it didn't necessarily mean that she was hankering after anyone else. He said rather breathlessly, "When this new campaign is over let's take a plane to Honolulu and have a holiday."

Celeste swung round in surprise. "Adrian! What's come over you? Have you been saving up and not telling me?"

"I've had a small legacy—from an aunt. Nothing much—a few hundreds. I thought perhaps you'd like to help me spend it."

Celeste put her arms round his neck. "Darling, what fun! I didn't know you had an aunt. She must have been frightfully ancient. How soon can we go?"

"In a few weeks."

"How marvellous of you to think of it! I'll be able to get some clothes. It's awfully unsatisfactory having things sent." She leaned her head against his shoulder. "You're rather sweet to me, aren't you?"

Garland looked down at her bright eyes. "I'd do anything for you," he said huskily. "You know that, don't you?"

Celeste was thinking how like a lovesick boy he was. No one seeing him now would believe that he had a reputation for ruthlessness among men. Even his eyes had lost the steely glint they showed to the world, and were hot and greedy. He didn't look his age, in spite of that white lock, but he wasn't her idea of romance. He must be nearly fifty-five. Still, *faute de mieux*—and the evening *had* been rather stimulating. . . .

With an enigmatical smile she loosened the *négligé* as he took her in his arms.

Chapter Six

Johnson Johnson lived among a collection of shacks known, without intentional irony, as Paradise Heights. The denizens of Paradise had probably received more headlines in the newspapers and been the subject of more speech-making by indignant members of the Legislature than any other body of citizens in the Colony, for the place was a notorious slum. A clearance scheme had long existed on paper, and there, for the lack of funds, it was likely to remain.

From a distance of about one hundred yards, the settlement looked as though it might recently have been hit by a large bomb. It had a dusty, littered, and partially disintegrated appearance. Its site was an almost bare hillside of breakneck steepness, the surface of which was without steps or paths. Deep ruts had been scoured by the heavy rains of the wet season. On this slope had been erected dozens of wooden huts on stilts, many of them now leaning precariously as a result of eroded foundations. The best of them might have been mistaken in a more favoured country for rather neglected henhouses, but the worst gave to the site an appearance of almost unbelievable squalor, being crudely patched with wads of newspaper, bits of cardboard, old rags, rusty corrugated iron, and flattened tins. Most were single rooms, airless, windowless, and dark. In some, no more than ten feet square, two parents and as many as a dozen children might sleep at night. The incidence of tuberculosis was increasing. A Commission of Inquiry, sent out to inquire into the causes of local unrest, had boldly referred to these homes as "unsatisfactory."

Scattered among the huts, in the interests of hygiene, were numbers of communal wooden privies. Some of these had leaking or overflowing cesspits, so that dark and noxious rivulets trickled down the slope to form stinking pools under the homes of the more luckless.

The Paradise dwellers were class-conscious, but in a way peculiarly their own. Those who lived at the top of the slope, where the rents were higher, were inclined to despise those who lived at the bottom. This was understandable, for in the rainy season it was those at the foot of the hillside who were liable to be swept away by torrents of filthy water and the swirl of accumulated refuse.

In one of the huts at the top of the hill Johnson Johnson stirred and sleepily rubbed his eyes as a ray of morning sunshine sneaked through a crack. For a moment or two after waking he stared around him a little uncertainly. His head ached—Salacity had been generous with the *reki* after his calypsoes. His slow gaze took in the rickety wooden table, the old rocking chair, the chest of drawers, the ten-year-old insurance calendar on the wall, the magazine picture of a pretty white child that the barber had given him, the banjo hanging on its nail. A contented smile stole over his face. Perhaps it wasn't much of a shack for twelve shillings a month, but it was better than the one he'd had down the hill before Eke had badgered him into taking the job with Dr. Garland. And at least he wasn't crowded. He was a smart boy—he'd been careful not to burden himself with a permanent woman.

He was aware of a core of happiness. Those white people had liked his calypsoes. He had been a popular figure—they had applauded him. He had shown them what he could do. They'd been different from Eke, who looked down on him and thought he was only fit to do odd jobs for Dr. Garland. One day he would show Eke too. Perhaps very soon now, if he continued to study the technique of the "Howler" and "Orpheus" and "Genghiz Khan" and other masters, he'd be making up his own "le'gos"—his own smash-hits. In time, he might even have his own band, and then he'd get big money from the people who ran the calypso huts. After that, perhaps Eke would stop being so superior. Who was Eke, anyway? Just because he'd been lucky and had an education!

Suddenly Johnson remembered what day it was. Of course, this was the day they were going to bury Ephraim. Johnson sat on his plank bed, in his grimy shirt and shorts, hugging his knees and dwelling pleasurably on the prospect. It wouldn't be a slap-up funeral, of course, not the way it would have been if Ephraim had been a big shot like Eke. A ten-pound one, maybe. Still, there'd be singing and the procession behind the hearse and no doubt a bit of a celebration afterwards.

Johnson wished he could look smarter for the occasion. What a good thing it was that Salacity had managed to beg a pair of old black trousers for him! They'd look all right with the clean white shirt he'd been saving up. And that wasn't all. He got up carefully, stepped over the grass-filled sack which served him as a pillow, made a little detour round the rotten floorboard, and opened the top drawer of the chest. Lovingly he fingered the black tie that he'd bought for one-and-sixpence. That would show respect. That would show Eke that he knew what was what.

He stripped off his shirt, took up a piece of soap and a bucket, and stepped out of doors in his underpants. The sun was already hot—he reckoned it must be seven o'clock. Paradise was fully awake. O'Connor, the barber, was lounging beside his chair, watching without impatience for early morning customers. A little way down the hill Miss Jones, the dressmaker, was spreading out her washing on boxes, while the three black babies she had inadvertently acquired in the course of a passionate spinsterhood scrabbled happily in the dirt beside the door. Between the huts scores of other children, some naked, most of them bare-foot, a few pot-bellied, were beginning the long day's play.

Johnson responded amiably to the shouted greeting of his neighbour's "mistress," who was routinely engaged in picking lice from her eldest daughter's woolly head. Most people greeted him in a friendly way in Paradise; he had something of a position there, as a calypsonian. Full recognition had still to come, but at least he was beginning to be appreciated.

He sauntered to the nearest standpipe, idly kicking stones and humming to himself. A comely young Negress named Delta, who had not so far responded to his rather half-hearted advances, was washing her hair at the tap. She pretended not to see him. He seated himself on the ground and waited. He was in no hurry. Presently his fingers began to beat a tattoo upon the hard earth and his bare toes to wriggle in time with the tune which had come into his head. He wished he had brought his banjo.

> "A young gel washin' of her hair
> Can't do nuffin' 'bout it ef folks stop an' stare."

Maybe he could turn that into a "le'go." He frowned. Popular taste was very uncertain. He watched a lizard peep from under a stone and then skid down the hill with one flick of its tail. He loved watching things; he found everything full of interest. He might lack Eke's prepossessing exterior, but he had the soul of an artist.

The girl squeezed the water out of her hair and departed unconcernedly. Johnson sighed, filled his bucket at the stand-pipe, poured the water over his head, and began to soap himself. He didn't take his underpants off; he just soaped over them. The decencies were usually observed in Paradise, and everyone soaped over their underclothes. The sun soon dried them.

Having washed himself, Johnson hummed his way back to the hut. While his shorts dried he went into the lean to kitchen and lit the paraffin stove. He was rather proud of his kitchen; he had built it himself out of old wooden crates, one of which still bore the words "Made in U.S.A." When the water boiled he made himself some cocoa, emptying the last of his condensed milk into it. With the cocoa, Johnson ate some bread. Then he put on his black trousers, his white shirt, and his precious tie and set off for the church at a loitering pace, for the sun was hot. It was very pleasant to have the morning off. On the way he stopped and had a shoeshine. He decided that when he succeeded in composing a "le'go" he would style himself "Prince Banjo."

As he had feared, it was only a ten-pound funeral. The church was an obscure building with a rusty iron roof, and forty people inside it made it seem full. Johnson wasn't a near relative of the deceased, so he contented himself with a modest seat at the back. He saw Eke a couple of pews away, but failed to catch his eye. He felt annoyed at first, but as soon as the service started he forgot about everything else.

When the mourners fell in beside the purple-draped hearse, Johnson established himself at Eke's side. The great man condescended to nod gravely. A tall Negro in a top hat seated in the back of the hearse behind the coffin wound up an old horn gramophone, and with the first strains of the "Dead March" the cortège started off. This was the part that Johnson liked—the long slow shuffle behind the corpse. It was slow rhythm, but it was rhythm. His step was sedate but springy. People stood on the curb, respectfully watching the solemn black and white men, the fluttering heliotrope women. It was almost as good as being in a pageant. He glanced at Eke, who was sweating profusely. It must be fine to be dressed up like that, thought Johnson—a complete black suit, without a speck of dust on it, and white gloves. Eke had certainly got on in the world. Johnson could remember him, long long ago, also sitting in the dirt of Paradise, also strumming a banjo. Eke wouldn't like to be reminded of that now.

The ceremony at the graveside was brief but satisfying. After Ephraim had been interred the mourners gathered in a hired room in the town. Johnson continued to stand close to Eke, who at last deigned to address him.

"Well, Johnson," he said loftily in his fine accent that was so hard to understand, "how are you getting on?"

"Ah'se all right, Eke, man," said Johnson.

Dubois frowned. He very much disliked being called Eke. Perhaps it was too much to hope that his old intimates would drop the name, but the trouble was that it had spread into circles where he expected to be called MacPhearson Dubois—or at least Dubois. The familiarity jarred on him.

"A dignified farewell to poor old Ephraim," he observed.

Johnson nodded, his mouth full of sandwich. "Ah bin like fo' to see de way dey open dey mout whan dey bin sing de song 'Fight de Good Fight'."

"Very stirring," said Dubois. "Well, is Dr. Garland satisfied with you? You've not been wasting your time, I hope."

"De wuk's mo 'ard dan clark's job," said Johnson sadly. "Ah cuts de grass an' grows de wegetables an' cleans de auto an' sometimes ah goes fishin' wid Dr. Garlan'. Aw Gawd, yo shud see dem fishes wha we ketch."

Dubois regarded him coldly. "It's a pity you can't learn to talk the King's English," he said.

Johnson looked crestfallen. "Yo tink ah's foolish an' hignorant?"

"I think you're lazy. I'm told you spend most of your time sleeping."

"Wha yo tark ain't true," said Johnson indignantly. "Who bin tel yo dat? Ah ony sleeps whan ah's tired." His expression became sullen, but only for a moment. "Las' night ah sings calypso fo' Doctor Garlan's frien's."

Dubois shook his head in disapproval. "That strumming will never get you anywhere. There are too many good-for-nothings in this Colony who think they can make a living by calypso. You must learn to work hard, and then you'll get on."

"Dey say dey wan calypso an' mek me fo' to sing," Johnson protested. "Anyways, yo aw wrong 'bout calypso. Ah's goin' fo' to be big calypsonian. Ah ain't so chupit as you tink. Yo tink ah sleeps al de day an' al de night but dat ain't so tal. Ah sits up in de mango tree an' ah listens. Ah 'ears wha plenty mens say. P'raps ah sing calypso 'bout um."

"Eavesdroppers always come to a bad end," said Dubois sententiously. "And what do you hear, pray? Nothing of any significance, I'm quite sure."

Johnson felt flattered by this faint stirring of interest, and searched his mind for scandal.

"Ah 'ears 'bout de feller Salacity bin cosy wid de dark out night."

Dubois smiled. "You surprise me."

Johnson was further encouraged. It was pleasant to surprise Eke. He dug deeper into his memory, "An' ah 'ears all 'bout dat deh leper place an' wha dem peoples going fo' to do deh."

"You could have read all about that much more safely in the newspapers. One day you'll fall out of that tree."

"Ah knows tings yo nah know 'bout deh leper place," said Johnson, provoked. "Doctor Garlan' 'e tark wid dat man wha come from Australy 'bout deh leper folk. Deh tark 'bout all de new 'ouse an' tings dey goin' fo' to mek dey at Tacri an' de Australy mans 'e say 'e give fifty tousan' pound."

"That's a likely story," said Dubois. "You mean Rawlins, the contractor? He wouldn't give a penny. He's a very smart business man, not a philanthropist."

"An nah childs, ah grows up," said Johnson. "De fifty tousand pound nah fo' lepers, et fo' Doctor Garlan'."

Dubois face suddenly lost its bantering look. He dropped his voice and said in a sharp tone, "You'd better be careful what you're saying, Johnson. You ought to be ashamed of yourself after the way Dr. Garland's helped you. If you talk like that, you'll soon find yourself in jail."

Johnson looked hurt. "Nah don't go fo' to put yo fut 'pon me. Ah won't lan' in jail, please Gawd. Doctor Garlan' 'e very good mans. Wan de Australy mans say 'e give fifty tousand pound, Doctor Garlan' 'e shek is 'ead."

"I tell you, Johnson, you mustn't talk like this. The whole thing would be against the law. Rawlins would never have said a thing like that."

"Ah trus' de vice ob me own airs," said Johnson obstinately. At least there was no doubt now that he'd gained Eke's full attention. "Ah was in de mango jes by de hopen winder an 'ah sees Doctor Garlan' an' dis Australy mans an' dey bot drinkin' whisky an' ah 'ears wha dey say 'bout de leper place, an' de Australy mans say it am big portant job an' 'e wan fo' to do um bad an' den' 'e say 'e pay fifty tousand pound fo Doctor Garlan'."

Dubois looked incredulous. "What did Doctor Garland say?"

"Doctor Garlan' 'e say dat sort ob ting all right fo' de blacks peeple but de Australy mans 'e say jus lil present. At las' Doctor Garlan' 'e say 'e tink 'bout um an' Australy mans say p'raps 'e pass back. Aw Gawd, man, it's de truf ah's tellin' yo."

"Listen," said Dubois earnestly, "you're not to talk about this to anyone else, do you understand? If you do you'll get into serious trouble. I'm glad you told me—you were quite right to do so—but it must be a secret between us. Is that clear?"

" 'Course ah's nah goin' fo' tark 'bout et," said Johnson, pleased to share a secret which he had not realised had so much significance. "Doctor Garlan' 'e nice mans, good good mans." Eke, he thought, was making a surprising fuss about nothing.

Chapter Seven

The Colonial Secretary, Jocelyn Anstruther, sat with his daughter
Susan on the terrace of Martin's house at Tacri, drinking
lime-squash and relaxing after a gruelling two-hour inspection
of the leprosarium. Martin was playing the assiduous host and
feeling moderately pleased with himself. It had been a useful visit
from his point of view. The Colonial Secretary had tramped
doggedly from block to block, more and more appalled, his face
wearing the abstracted look of a man compelled suddenly to
adjust preconceived views in the light of new facts. Susan had
taken the horrors in her stride and had asked a great many
questions.

"You know, West," Anstruther was saying, "this place has always
had a bad reputation but I'd no idea it was quite so shocking. I
really think I'll have to persuade H.E. to come out." He lay back
in the deck chair and tied his long legs into what was presumably
a comfortable knot. He was a tall, slender man in his late fifties,
with a manner suggesting the scholar rather than the administrator.
Some illness had left one arm and shoulder slightly paralysed, so
that his head was held always a little to one side, giving him the
appearance of an extremely sympathetic listener. Martin had been
needing a sympathetic listener, and as he now contemplated the
expression on the Colonial Secretary's face, he felt that he had not
wasted his opportunity.

"As a matter of fact," said Anstruther, as though troubled by a
sense of neglected duty, "I would have come before if the place
hadn't been so inaccessible." He caught Martin's eye and smiled.
"Yes, that's a point for you. I should need to give the problem

more thought before conceding your case as a whole, but I admit that the difficulty of getting here is a major defect."

"Personally, I think Dr. West's case will be extremely hard to answer," said Susan. "He's quite convinced *me*, for what that's worth."

Martin smiled his thanks. He was impressed with Susan. She seemed to be clear-headed and practical, but she was none the less attractive for that. She looked fresh and pretty in pale green linen, her chestnut hair cut short and clustering in thick soft waves round her head. Intelligence and good looks—a fairly rare combination. She would be a useful ally.

The same thought appeared to strike her father. "I won't have *you* taking sides in this controversy," he told her, with mock severity. "If there's one thing I can't bear, it's propoganda at the breakfast table. Anyway," he added, "I thought you seemed remarkably unmoved by Tacri."

Susan raised an eyebrow. "What did you expect me to do—faint? It's revolting, but I've seen living conditions almost as bad on the mainland."

"Oh, surely not," Anstruther protested.

"I have, though. You ought to see the exercise yard at the Mental Hospital—it's grim. Or the workhouse—you could hardly have anything more squalid than that. And think of the huts on the estates—think of Paradise—think of the sleepers-out."

"What sleepers-out?" asked Martin.

"Oh, they're one of the sights. The pavements of Fontego are littered with them every night—mostly old people with nowhere to go. Scores and scores of them. The only time they see a bed is when they're lucky enough to be rounded up by the police and spend a few hours in the Colonial Jail. There's no social security here, you know. You can't lift a stone in this place without finding something horrible underneath."

"And yet you lift the stones?"

"Of course. I like to know what's going on."

"I wish I had your opportunities," said Martin. "I'm afraid I may find myself chained to this rock."

"Oh, you can't possibly stay here all the time," said Susan. "Surely there's someone you can leave in charge."

"Not since Dr. Carnegie went, but I've asked for an assistant."

"They'll give you one, of course."

Martin smiled. "I very much hope so. I expect they will in time. The point is, you see, that the problem of leprosy can't be tackled from here. It isn't enough just to look after the leper patients that we know about. The disease will never be stamped out, as it could and should be, until we can make a thorough survey of the whole Colony. That means a network of out-patient clinics on the mainland, the training of personnel, and a great deal of organisation. It's only field work that will give us results. That's why I want to be able to travel around—to set up the machinery."

Susan was listening with interest. "You don't want a chauffeuse, do you?"

Martin's eyes dropped to her bandaged right hand. "That depends," he said with a grin.

Susan made a face. "How people chatter! *I* couldn't help it if an idiotic taxi-driver drove straight at me."

"One of the big mistakes of my life," Anstruther confided, "was to buy Susan that car. All the same, West, if you happen to have nerves of steel you could do worse than take her up on that offer. Susan knows the Colony a good deal better than most people."

"I'll be delighted to have a guide," said Martin. "So far, I haven't received a very favourable impression of the place. I was at the Garlands' a week or two ago, and most of the people there couldn't find a good word to say either for the Colony or for its inhabitants."

"Could they find a good word to say for anything?" said Susan. "You mustn't pay too much attention to Celeste—she always makes a point of disparaging things. And most of the whites are more or less fed up. The Colony *is* in a mess in many ways, but it's a fascinating place all the same. You'll find the people most likeable and amusing once you can understand what they say, and provided you don't expect too much. It's hopeless to judge them by our standards, of course, but then why should we? You'll have a good opportunity to study them *en masse* soon—at Fiesta."

"Yes," said Martin. "I've heard about that. I gather from Mrs. Sylvester that it's rather a lurid festival—definitely not quite nice."

"Neither is your leprosarium, but that's no reason for not seeing it. Whatever you do, you mustn't miss Fiesta. Why not come to dinner with us on Tuesday and stay over? Daddy, you must see that Dr. West gets his assistant this week."

"If you think I'm going to poke my finger into departmental pies just to provide you with an escort for Fiesta, you're very much mistaken," said the Colonial Secretary.

"Oh, don't be so stuffy, darling. That's settled, then. And please, Dr. West, don't believe everything you hear about the Colony until you have had an opportunity to judge for yourself. It's by no means all bad, and a lot of the whites are very superficial. They're so busy running the place that they never have time to get to know it."

"I'm told it may be under entirely new management soon," said Martin. "At least that's the impression I got from Dr. Dubois. Do you know him?"

"Know Eke? I should say I do. He's rather priceless, isn't he? We both spent some time at the London School of Economics—different years, of course—and he regards it as a bond between us. Almost every time I see him he manages to drag in some reference to the 'London School of Ec.' Affectionate diminutive! He's intelligent, in spite of his complexes. He'll probably play quite a part when the Colony gets self-government."

"I suppose there's no doubt that it will get it?"

"None at all, I should say. The politicians at home have given the people here all sorts of promises, and they can't back out now. Isn't that right, Daddy?"

Martin turned to Anstruther, who lay smoking peacefully. "And will the people be better off or worse? What do you think, sir?"

"That's a big question," said Anstruther slowly. "I'm inclined to think they'll be worse off to begin with, but in the long run it may not make very much difference. It depends a good deal on what sort of leaders they throw up. Anyhow, there's not much we can do about it. The transition is well under way. The local people run most of the services already, and we're being more and more pushed aside. British rule is getting very nominal. I think we've just about shot our bolt."

"Eke would say it's a pity we didn't clear out a long time ago," said Susan.

"Well, he's wrong there, of course," said Anstruther firmly. "We may not have taught them as much as we ought to have done, but we have given people like Dubois himself some sort of education and training, and we have given them a pattern of government and set them on the road to wherever it is that we are going ourselves."

"The trouble is," said Susan in her forthright way, "that we've given them the framework but we haven't provided them with enough money to finish the building. In fact, we've taken away what there was. If they had now what we removed in the old days, when cocoa was doing well and sugar was profitable, they could really do something about their slums and hospitals and schools. It seems to me that we've milked the cow, and now that it's running dry we're handing it back to its owner and expecting him to say 'thank you'."

Her father demurred. "As things are at present, Susan, money from outside wouldn't be a permanent solution. Look what the Americans have lavished on Puerto Rico—and it still hasn't given the place a stable economy. Look what happened here over the Base—it brought Fontego a considerable amount of temporary wealth, but most of it's been squandered. I think some help will be necessary, of course, but the most important thing for these people is to shake down by themselves, to find their own natural level of production and population."

"Do you think they'll manage to make ends meet?" asked Martin. "From what I've seen and heard, I should say there's a very small margin between what they've got now and starvation."

"That's true enough," said Susan, "and it's partly their own fault. Everybody knows that Fontego can only survive as an agricultural country, but the people have got used to the bright lights of the towns, and they don't want to go back to the land. I think we've been a bad influence in that respect. We've dazzled them with a sort of life they can't ever hope to have. Most of the young people to-day think there's something degrading about manual work. Directly they get a little education they want to be doctors or lawyers or civil servants or shop assistants or taxi-drivers—in just about that order. Nobody ever wants to grow anything."

"Perhaps they'll feel more like getting down to it when we've gone," suggested Martin. "More incentive, do you think, knowing the place belongs to them?"

"I wonder," said Susan thoughtfully. "It's a demoralising place, you know. Quite the pleasantest way of passing the time here is to lie in the shade and sleep. The people can scrape along on a minimum of food. Why should they bother? Perhaps they'll forget the bright lights and revert quite happily to subsistence level."

Anstruther untwined his legs. "Could you bear to postpone this discussion of the Colony's future? I'd like to stroll to the end of the jetty with you, West. You'll excuse us, won't you, Susan? We shan't be very long."

"Poor old civil servants," said Susan, with a twinkle at Martin. "I shall lie in the hammock and snooze." She watched the two men stroll away.

"I hope you didn't mind my mixing business with pleasure in this way," Anstruther said. "My bringing Susan, I mean. There were several things I wanted to talk to you about, but I thought it would be much better to discuss them informally than across an office desk."

"Of course," said Martin.

Anstruther marshalled his points. "Well, now—first of all, this feeling of yours that the leprosarium should be moved from Tacri. It's an old problem, it's been discussed over and over again. There seems to be no doubt at all that your general argument is sound. In fact, Garland is strongly in agreement with you, in principle. At the same time, there *is* the political aspect to consider, and in any case I think he's right that having got so far it's really too late to reopen the subject."

"I suppose so," said Martin. "I gather that the contract for the rebuilding programme has just been signed. That seems to settle the matter, doesn't it? I won't pretend that I'm reconciled to the project, because I'm not. I'm one hundred per cent against it and I always shall be. But I can imagine that it's too late to do anything effective about it, and quite frankly I've too much on my hands now to worry about what can't be helped. I'll carry on as best I can, and we'll see what happens."

Anstruther looked relieved. "I'm very glad to hear you say that—very glad indeed."

"I only hope that Dr. Garland won't be misled by his easy victory," Martin added.

Anstruther laughed. "Not he. He'll think you're a sensible fellow. Tell me, what do you think of the reconstruction plans themselves, now that you've gone into them?"

"I find them quite incredible," said Martin. "Didn't Dr. Garland tell you my opinion? The more I look at them, the more they amaze me."

Anstruther raised his eyebrows. "Oh? Why?"

"They're so lavish. They go from one extreme to the other. The intention seems to be to turn Tacri into a sort of Shangri-La."

"Surely the idea is to make it comfortable and up-to-date?" said Anstruther.

"The plans go far beyond that. For instance, there is to be an elaborate reception station near the jetty, with enormous reinforced concrete pillars sunk about five feet into the rock. It's going to cost ten thousand pounds. That money might just as well be dropped into the sea."

"H'm. I remember there was some debate about that. It was Garland who persuaded us. He pressed the view very strongly that if we were going to make Tacri a permanent home for the lepers, everything must be done to give them a good first impression."

"With all respect to Dr. Garland," said Martin impatiently, "a good second impression is what matters. They're not going to *live* in the reception room. But that's only one little item that happened to catch my eye. The whole scheme is on the same exaggerated scale. The new administrative offices will be far more luxuriously equipped than is necessary in a place like this, and far too big. The new kitchen accommodation would be appropriate for the feeding of the five thousand—but we shall only have five hundred. The capacity of the new laundry is so great that it'll be idle half the time. As for the hospital——"

"What's wrong with the hospital?"

"There's nothing wrong with it—it's going to be marvellous. The operating theatre would delight Carnegie's heart. But what a crime to put it on Tacri when hospitals are so badly needed on the mainland. All we want here is a modest building with modest facilities, costing about a quarter of what's proposed. Major operations will have to be done on the mainland anyway. As for the cost of clearing the new housing sites—well, I guessed it would be high, but the actual figure shatters me."

"I think it's possible that the scheme does err a little on the side of extravagance," the Colonial Secretary admitted. "The point *was* made, several times. But Dr. Garland was most insistent that this was a case where no expense should be spared. His attitude was that if the Colony was determined not to have the leprosarium on the mainland, then it must be prepared to pay for its prejudices. I must say he presented his arguments very skilfully, and with much force. He's a great fighter, you know, and I've never seen him more determined than he was when he attended the Finance Committee."

"I still can't understand it," said Martin. "It's a shocking waste of money when there are so many other things that need doing. Dr. Garland himself must see that."

"Well, there it is," said Anstruther. "The plans are passed and the contract is signed."

Martin gazed across the water at the tiers of shacks. "It'll certainly be a showplace when it's finished. Fontego's Folly! Everyone will be happy except the patients. Still, I've given my view and I'll say no more about it." He glanced at the Colonial Secretary's worried countenance. "Is there anything else, sir?"

"There *are* one or two minor matters," Anstruther told him. "At least," he amended, "they're minor at the moment. You've been making some changes here, haven't you?"

"Quite a lot. And I plan to make a lot more."

Anstruther nodded. "That's quite natural. After seeing the place this morning I'm all in favour. You must expect, though, to encounter criticism."

"I do," said Martin. "Has it begun?"

"It has, as a matter of fact. I had a talk with Garland yesterday and he's a bit concerned. He's not against anything you are doing, not in principle, but he doesn't want trouble at this stage. He's absolutely set on getting the new leprosarium built as quickly as possible, and he doesn't want any sort of complications which might hold it up."

"I don't see any likelihood of that," said Martin.

"Well, he thinks that if people get the impression that conditions at Tacri are too free and easy, they'll begin to ask themselves what they are paying for."

"You mean they're buying complete segregation, and they want their money's worth?"

"To put it bluntly, yes."

"I see. I suppose the charges are that I'm letting some of the patients use the boats for fishing again, and that I allowed young Green to visit the mainland."

"They're the main criticisms."

Martin nodded. "Well, let's take the case of Green to begin with. He's a young active chap who's been shut up here for two years. He hates the place. He came to me last Friday morning, looking very anxious, and showed me a letter saying that his brother in Fontego City had had a bad accident. Green asked me if he could go over to the mainland for the day to see him, and I let him go. I can think of no valid objection."

"I suppose it does rather undermine the principle of segregation," suggested Anstruther.

"If the leprosarium is going to remain on Tacri," said Martin, "it'll be impossible to enforce segregation rigidly. It's inhuman. Think of some of those youths we talked to this morning—vigorous young fellows who feel quite fit and have the ordinary human feelings and interests and urges. You've seen for yourself that many of them show virtually no outward sign of the disease, and in the early stages they don't feel any, either. The way things are, unless some new cure is found, they may be here for twenty years. They can't be treated as criminals with a life sentence—they've got to be given some latitude."

"I quite agree with you," said Anstruther. "But there's the community to think of as well. What about the danger to others?"

"From occasional contacts like that of Green, there's no danger. After all, we let relatives visit them here—why shouldn't they visit their relatives? Leprosy isn't a thing like chicken-pox, or a cold in the head that you catch from a sneeze. It's transmitted only as a result of prolonged and intimate contact. Why, even in the closest relationship of all, marriage, it's passed on to a healthy partner in only about four per cent of cases. But apart from that, we've simply got to be realistic. Take the case of the boats. People are saying, no doubt, that some of the patients will take the opportunity to abscond. Suppose they do? They'll merely be the same chaps who would have absconded anyway—it's quite easy. My aim is to take away the feeling of close confinement that so many of the patients have, and then perhaps they won't want to abscond. There oughtn't to be *any* absconders from a well-run leprosarium. There ought to be a waiting list of voluntary patients, eager for treatment. There's no better safeguard for the community than to make people want to stay here. I think a judicious amount of freedom will help to do that. Look at young Green, for instance. If I'd said no, he'd probably have taken the first opportunity to slip away, and he might have stayed away. As it is, he's come back, and he's much more contented. Now he thinks it may be possible to leave the place occasionally he doesn't particularly want to go. He'll be an excellent influence."

"I see your point," said Anstruther, impressed.

"There's another aspect," said Martin. "Would you come into the house for a moment? I want to show you something." He led the way to his study with eager steps and stopped in front of a large wall map of the Colony.

"This," he said, "will show you what a lot of nonsense segregation is when it's carried to extremes—in our conditions, anyway. Here's a map showing the place of origin of all the leprosy cases that have been traced. All this was done by my predecessors, of course. Each red dot is one case. As you see, there are quite a lot of dots in and around the capital, and scattered about the towns and villages nearby. But look at this vast undotted space." He swept a hand over the greater part of the map. "The absence of dots doesn't mean that there aren't any lepers there. It means we haven't looked for them. In fact, there are certainly five hundred and possibly a thousand undetected cases in that area—people who are free to go into town, sit in restaurants, ride in buses, and go to bed with anyone they want. Honestly, in those circumstances does it make any sense to forbid the unlucky five hundred on Tacri to leave the island for a single day? Our most important task is to track down the hundreds of undetected cases and make sure they can't spread the disease. Then it'll die out. But at present we are hopelessly handicapped because people who've got leprosy realise that if the fact becomes known they'll be sent to Tacri, which they regard as no better than a penal institution. If there were a decent settlement on the mainland they'd soon be coming in of their own free will. Well, that's ruled out now, but at least we can try to make Tacri as bearable as possible and reduce people's fear of it. Then perhaps they'll give us some co-operation."

Anstruther looked at Martin with respect. "You're an enthusiast, Dr. West."

"I'm angry," said Martin. "This Colony has had the opportunity to solve its leprosy problem in a generation, to wipe it out in a decent humane way, and it's thrown away the chance. I've been given a set of blunt tools by stupid selfish people and I know I can't do much with them. But that doesn't mean that I won't do what I can. I'll have things on Tacri the way I want them, or the Colony will find itself with a repetition of the Stockford case."

"That would certainly be a pity. What else do you propose to do?"

"Win the patients' confidence, if I'm given the chance. Tell them about the improvements that are coming along. Treat them as individuals with rights. Get them interested in all sorts of occupations. If only I had a few acres of good soil!"

"One thing is very clear to me," said Anstruther. "We now have another fighter in the Colony. I do hope that you and Garland will get along."

"It certainly won't be my fault if we don't," said Martin. He looked questioningly at Anstruther. "Have we exhausted the charge sheet?"

"Not quite," replied the Colonial Secretary with a faint smile. "There's been a complaint—from a religious body, as a matter of fact—that you are paying insufficient attention to the moral welfare of the patients. I thought I'd better pass it on to you. It's just as well you should know what you're up against. The specific accusation is that you're indifferent to the fact that leper patients with husbands or wives on the mainland are openly cohabiting with other patients on the island."

Martin looked grim. "I share with Dr. Carnegie," he said, "a profound distaste for the interference of ignorant laymen with religious prejudices. It's outrageous that because a man has the misfortune to contract leprosy he should be regarded as fair game for moral busybodies. The whole thing's an impertinence. The patients aren't here to be disciplined—they haven't done anything wrong. They're entitled to all the rights of free men and women, provided they don't endanger the community. If they want to sleep with each other, that's their affair—they haven't many other pleasures. Anyway, most of them can never hope to rejoin their husbands or wives on the mainland. In effect, their marriages are already at an end. I'd much sooner have them making homes together here if they want to than sneaking off to Fontego City. After all, they can't infect each other."

"But what about the children?"

"Children of lepers are always born healthy, and don't contract the disease if they're removed straight away. It may seem tough on the children to start life that way but it's a situation that's bound to arise and it must be dealt with in a practical manner."

Anstruther nodded thoughtfully. "You know, West, I'm appalled to find how little I knew of all this. It's been a revelation coming here to-day, and I've really Susan to thank for it. It was she who wanted to see the place. Well, I think we've covered everything. I'll see Garland, and I'll have a talk with H.E. as well. Of course, we must be prepared to answer the critics."

"Nothing would give me greater pleasure," said Martin. "As soon as they come out into the open we'll give them a broadside."

Anstruther gave him a friendly look. "I wish you'd arrived three months ago," he said, "before this programme was settled. We've a lot of excellent fellows, conscientious hardworking chaps, but it's hard to persuade tiptop men to come to these large backward Colonies. Garland's one of the few men here of really first-class calibre—no doubt that's why he's had such an impact on the place."

They walked slowly back to the terrace.

"Hello," called Susan from the hammock. "Have you settled all the problems of Tacri?"

"We've had an extremely interesting discussion," said her father, smiling at her disappointed face. "It's a pity you weren't there—you'd have enjoyed it!"

Chapter Eight

It was getting on toward noon on the Tuesday before Fiesta, and the employees of the Health Department were preparing to leave the office. Shouts and laughter echoed through the staid corridors. Everyone was in the highest spirits at the approach of the holiday.

Almost everyone. The noise irritated Ezekiel MacPhearson Dubois, who was sitting nervously in his room waiting to see Dr. Garland. For him this was a day of crisis. He wished that the summons would come, that the matter were already put to the test. He felt dreadfully hot and sticky. If he were kept much longer he would sweat his confidence away.

Ever since his talk with Johnson Johnson he had been trying to make up his mind what was the best thing to do about Dr. Garland. His emotions had been very mixed. For a long time he had had doubts about Johnson's story. The man could hardly be considered a reliable witness. Honest enough perhaps, but simple. He could easily have misheard or misunderstood that conversation. After all, was it credible that Dr. Garland—the great Dr. Garland who was so vain about his own reputation and so stern in his judgments of others—would risk everything for a sum of money, however large?

That had been Dubois' first reaction. But as the days passed his doubts had weakened. *Was* it so unlikely? Dubois himself had advocated the Tacri scheme because for a man with his political ambitions it had seemed more profitable to bow to a popular prejudice than to fight against it. But he had always felt that the scheme was unnecessarily ambitious. It was Garland who had driven it through. Dubois had been surprised at the time by the vehemence of his support for such dubious expenditure. A bribe would explain it, and nothing else would.

It was said that every man had his price. Dubois knew very well that most of his countrymen had a pretty low price. In Fontego you could buy a vote or a verdict or even a life for a pound or two. But a white man? His white chief? That took some believing. In spite of his outward assumption of colour equality. Dubois had inwardly a streak of romanticism about white people. It went against the grain for him to believe it. And yet, he argued, why not, if the price were high enough? Fifty thousand pounds sterling was a tempting bait for anyone. A staggering sum. Garland had always *seemed* a man of integrity, but who could be sure? He was a man of strong passions, Dubois knew that. The sort, perhaps, to give way to strong temptations. There had been a change in him lately; he had become more irritable, more cynical. At times he had given the impression of being fed up with everything. Still, Dubois didn't want to believe it.

Later on, Dubois the man had receded and Dubois the politician advanced. This just showed how hollow white superiority really was. Just a façade. People like Dr. Garland were ready enough to denounce Fontegan corruption when all the time they were no better themselves. What a scandal it would make if it came out—what a wonderful weapon for those who were demanding the departure of the whites! Indignation swelled in Dubois' breast. He imagined himself, the honest tribune of a fleeced and misruled people, flaying this rotten administration in powerful speeches, being elected to the Legislative Council on the issue, leading the Colony to self-government and freedom.

The righteous mood, the public-spirited mood, passed. Narrower considerations prevailed. If Garland had done this, and it could be brought home to him, his job would fall vacant. Dubois himself would get it—a key position, carrying prestige and authority and a good salary.

But how to bring it home? Many times Dubois had envisaged the interview which at last was about to take place; many times he had rehearsed his lines. But always he had felt afraid. He feared Garland. He hated to have those steely blue eyes boring into him; he mentally recoiled when those powerful shoulders moved. He knew, without admitting it, that Garland was twice the man he was. He tried to imagine himself going into Garland's room and saying bluntly, "You have taken bribes!" and inwardly he trembled. Garland's anger would be like a tornado; he might become violent. Dubois had seen him very near to violence once or twice when the provocation was nothing more than the crass incompetence of an underling out in the "bush" where everything was primitive. What would he be like when his dignity and vanity were injured?

Thus Dubois pondered, and waited. He had considered the possibility of some less direct approach—the spread of rumour, a whispering campaign, using his friends on the Legislative Council to help. But he realised that whatever means he adopted, the report would be traced to him. Ultimately, the showdown with Dr. Garland would still be unavoidable. Night after night he had lain awake, going through conversation after conversation with Garland, until finally he had evolved a course of action which he believed would be at once safe and sufficient.

A knock at his door made him jump. Miss Chang came in, handbag in hand. "I'm off, Dr. Dubois. A pleasant holiday! Oh, Dr. Garland is ready to see you now."

"Thank you, Miss Chang," said Dubois. He got up, a little unsteady, his stomach a pit of emptiness. He was dreadfully frightened. Perhaps after all he would say nothing. He went in. Garland was sitting at his desk.

"What are you hanging about for, Dubois?" The Secretary's tone sounded friendly enough. "We've cleared everything up, haven't we?"

"Yes," said Dubois. He stood in front of the desk like an erring schoolboy, fingering his striped tie.

"What is it, then?" asked Garland. "Sit down, man, and for Heaven's sake stop fidgeting."

Dubois sat down. He tried to look Garland in the eye, but his gaze faltered. It was like matching glances with a basilisk. "I wanted to speak to you privately, Dr. Garland, about a rather serious matter that has come to my attention."

"All right," said Garland, "there's no need to be so pompous about it. You are speaking to me privately. What's troubling you?"

"I know you will agree," said Dubois, taking courage from the sound of his own voice, "that it is of the first importance that all the activities of this department should be carried out in such a way that they are above public criticism."

"They never have been," said Garland ironically.

"What I mean is," said Dubois, "that nothing should be done to cause a suspicion in the public mind that anything at all underhand had been done."

Garland became suddenly wary. The hand outstretched across the desk stopped its patient tapping. "What exactly are you talking about?"

"It concerns the leprosarium," said Dubois in a dry cracked voice, and the blood pounded in his head.

Garland sat motionless. "What about the leprosarium?"

"You will agree," said Dubois, "that the project at Tacri is going to be very costly. I am told——" He was caught in the blue stare as though in a searchlight, and he couldn't finish. "Are we not perhaps spending too much money?" he ended lamely.

"For Heaven's sake!" exclaimed Garland. "Why raise that again? You know the whole thing's been decided."

"I know, Dr. Garland, but I have been thinking about it. It seems to me that perhaps we have been unnecessarily extravagant. On reflection, I am inclined to believe that we might have had the necessary work carried out more cheaply. We could have allowed more time for tenders. Do you not think that perhaps we were a little hasty? There is a very large profit to be made by the firm of contractors. If we had been less impatient, others might have undertaken the work on a smaller margin—and perhaps to less luxurious specifications."

"Well, upon my soul!" ejaculated Garland. "You must need a holiday, Dubois. Why bring this up now? We discussed it all very thoroughly at the time. You helped to draw up the plans and you were strongly in favour of them. I think you were quite right—they're very good plans. Anyhow, the contract's signed—we can't change things now."

"I agree that I had a hand in drawing up the scheme," said Dubois. "I believe now, however, that I allowed myself to be led away by my strong desire that the leprosarium should not be moved from Tacri. I feel that I may have been guilty of a dereliction of duty, and it is on my conscience."

"If that's all that's on your conscience, Dubois, you're a lucky man. You'll feel better after a couple of days off."

"I think not, sir. I feel I should have probed more carefully into the scheme before giving my approval."

"May I remind you," said Garland with cold formality, "that the responsibility is mine. With all respect, Dubois, it would have gone through with or without your approval. You can give your conscience into my keeping. The scheme is sound, and I'll stand up for it anywhere."

"I think, Dr. Garland, you would perhaps adopt a different attitude if you knew all that I know. I'm sorry to have to say this, but I'm afraid that your enthusiasm for the scheme—which infected us all—has been made use of by unscrupulous people."

Garland suddenly hammered on the desk. "For the last time, Dubois, will you tell me what's on your mind instead of beating about the bush like this?"

Dubois took a deep breath. "I understand that the firm of contractors paid a consideration in money in order that it should get this contract."

"To whom?"

Dubois wriggled evasively. "That I don't know, Dr. Garland."

Garland looked at the Negro with cold hatred. The smarmy little swine! Of course he knew. So that was what all these smooth circumlocutions were leading up to—an accusation. How on earth could he have found out? Garland's hands clenched in anger and the veins in his muscular forearms stood out. Desperately he struggled to control himself. The only hope was to bluff it out.

"It sounds to me a most unlikely story, Dubois. Unless you've got cast-iron evidence I'd advise you to be extremely careful what you say. There could hardly be a more serious charge."

"That is precisely my own feeling," said Dubois. The crisis seemed to be passing, and he felt more assured.

"Anyhow, you'd better tell me who your informant is."

"I regret that I am unable to do that at the moment," said Dubois. "For the time being, I am under an obligation to regard my informant's name as confidential."

Garland shrugged. "You can't expect me to attach much weight to an anonymous witness. Frankly, I don't believe a word of it. The firm would have got the contract without resorting to bribery—in fact, I don't see whom they could have bribed. After all, I myself pushed the scheme through. I take it you're not suggesting that I was bribed?"

Dubois looked deeply shocked. "Of course not, Dr. Garland. Indeed, no. It is true, as you say, that you were the inspiration of the scheme, the chief mainspring and the motivating force, but it was the Finance Committee which accepted your advice. Unfortunately, as I say, my informant was unable to state what person or persons received the bribe, but there seems to be no doubt that it was paid."

"There's plenty of doubt in my mind. It seems to me almost inconceivable. A reputable firm——"

"There have been similar cases in the history of the Colony," said Dubois.

"Yes, but at least nothing of the sort has touched my department before. I'm sure it'll prove quite untrue, but I'm glad you told me. I hope in any case that it will be possible to avoid a public scandal. The reputation of the department is at stake."

"Only if an employee of the department is concerned," said Dubois smoothly. "I realise, of course, that it may put you personally in a somewhat embarrassing position until the matter is fully explained—that is a thing that I deeply regret." He added as an afterthought, "But I must also take my share of the blame."

"You know, Dubois, I can't possibly begin looking into this until I know who your informant was. What have I to go on?"

"It seemed to me," said Dubois, "that as the bribe was probably given to someone outside the department, very likely to a member or members of the Finance Committee, the proper course would be to pass on all information to His Excellency, who would no doubt institute the necessary inquiries. I should be prepared to give the name of my informant to His Excellency."

"That would mean a major scandal," said Garland, "if your story is true."

"The offence is very serious," said Dubois. "One of the things I came to admire most during my valued years in England was the tradition of integrity which is the pride of the Civil Service. I should like to see the same tradition take root here. It is in the public interest that cases of corruption should be brought to light, and duty seems to require us to give all possible assistance to that end." He fingered his tie complacently.

"You'll have to let me be the judge as to our proper course of action," said Garland sharply. "I expect you to keep your own counsel until I have reached a decision."

"It has always been my privilege," said Dubois with growing confidence, "to carry out your wishes in all matters relating to the department, but in this case I feel very strongly that my first duty is to my own people, whose confidence I think I possess, and must deserve."

"You're a civil servant, not a politician. As long as you're in this department you'll kindly do as you're told, and keep that hustings stuff for your private conversations."

"I have a duty," Dubois repeated. "With all respect, if you feel unable to take this matter to His Excellency I shall consider myself obliged, with the very greatest regret, to do so myself."

"I see." Garland got up and went to the window, fighting down his panic. For the moment, he couldn't think of any way out. He must play for time.

"Don't think, Dubois," he said, turning, "that I don't agree with you on the main issue. Of course the thing must be investigated to the last detail, and perhaps you're right about the means. Perhaps it *will* be advisable to pass the whole thing over to H.E. and let him deal with it. As you say, it's only indirectly a departmental matter. Let me have the weekend to think it over, and we'll discuss it again immediately after the holiday. If I come to any decision during the weekend, perhaps I'll let you know."

"Very good," said Dubois. "I should naturally prefer to leave it in your hands." He was suddenly aware that he and Garland were alone in the building, and was seized with an urgent desire to leave.

"I take it that I can rely upon you," said Garland, "not to mention the matter to anyone until we've had another talk? The utmost discretion is necessary."

"That is quite clear," said Dubois. "Good day, Dr. Garland. May I wish you a pleasant holiday?"

"You may," said Garland.

Chapter Nine

Garland sat on at his desk after Dubois had left him, deep in thought. With appalling clarity he saw that his life was in ruins.

His moment of fear had passed, and given way to a colder emotion—something like despair. No good telling himself that he had done what he had done deliberately and with a full knowledge of its nature and its possible consequences. That didn't make the situation any better. The fact was that he had miscalculated the risk, and now he didn't want to meet the bill.

He could remember vividly that evening at his home—months ago, now—when he and Rawlins had discussed the problem of the leprosarium over a glass or two of whisky. It had been such an academic discussion at first. Rawlins had been visiting Fontego to negotiate a contract for a housing estate, and to begin with he had shown only mild interest in the leprosarium and its problems. Garland had steered the conversation, had begun to talk about Tacri, had indicated that big changes were in the air. Finally, Rawlins had scented large profits from a development of Tacri.

For an hour their conversation had been free from any impropriety. Garland had made it clear that he personally favoured a leprosarium on the mainland. He had stressed the huge expenditure that would be involved if Tacri remained the site. He had intimated that the Fontegans might, in certain circumstances, be prepared to pay that price. The contractor's appetite had been whetted. Finally, Rawlins had said with a deprecatory smirk, "Of course, if this were like some places I know we should have a contract for rebuilding Tacri in no time." A rascal, Rawlins, in spite of his benevolent appearance.

The matter could so easily have ended there. But Garland had taken him up, very cautiously, feeling his way. "If this were like some places you know," he had said, "what sort of consideration would you offer?"

Rawlins had given a little shrug. Something of the order of fifty thousand pounds, perhaps. For a rich contract, with plenty of expensive frills—the sort of contract Garland had in mind.

It had been so much more than Garland had expected. The key to a golden path through life. A stake big enough even for him. He remembered how circumspectly the conversation had developed, how wary each of them had been as they had probed each other's minds. Garland had talked about the conservatism of the Finance Committee, the penury of Fontego, the jealous scrutiny of local politicians when they were not lining their own pockets. Rawlins had become glib on the general subject of bribery. He hadn't called it bribery. He had found euphemisms—"commissions," "recognition of services," "legitimate rewards for expediting necessary work." Not a good practice, of course, in ordinary circumstances, and unthinkable in an efficient well-run country like England. But one had to adjust oneself to the accepted standards of the place one was in. "When in Rome, you know——"

Garland had listened with a sardonic smile. He had felt contempt for Rawlins—not because the man was moving crab-wise to an infamous arrangement, but because he seemed to imagine that Garland could be made to believe that black was grey. Still, what Rawlins thought hadn't mattered. Step by step, each had committed himself equally until at last the common intention was plain and all that remained to be fixed were the details.

Garland had known precisely what he was doing, and why. His life had run into a dead end. Exasperation and frustration had made him reckless. Since he had married Celeste his values had been steadily eroded. He was tired of labouring on projects that never bore satisfying fruit, of endless ineffective drudgery with tiresome dolts and half-men. Dissatisfaction had eaten into his soul. At fifty-four, if he continued on his present course, he could see nothing to look forward to. Another five or ten wasted years, and then a pension that Celeste would think derisory. He might even lose Celeste. Whereas the alternative . . .

Fifty thousand pounds! A round attractive sum.

He had weighed the risk, and thought it reasonable. On his second meeting with the contractor the bargain had been struck. A substantial sum of money down, in cash, as a token of Rawlins' good faith and an earnest of what was to come; the rest to be deposited by Rawlins himself in a safe place in Singapore, for Garland's use, directly the contract was signed. He would take with him a specimen signature which Garland would provide—in an assumed name. Rawlins, it seemed, had made similar arrangements before; he knew the ropes, and anyway, no one was fussy in Singapore.

Garland had pondered the arrangement, aware of his own inexperience in all business matters. Rawlins had persuaded him. The deal would be a personal one, and would be executed with the utmost discretion. Neither man would ever dare to talk, for both were too deeply involved. And no one would ever suspect. Garland would be the last man in the world to come under suspicion of such behaviour—the stern unbending Garland! That, at least, was how it had seemed.

And yet someone had found out, and had told Dubois. It was inconceivable that Rawlins would have mentioned it to anybody. The second conversation had taken place in the open air, out of earshot. Someone must have overheard that first conversation. There was no other possible explanation. Celeste had been at the Country Club, dancing. Garland himself had made sure, at the appropriate moment, that no one was in the garden. Salacity and the other maids had been in their own part of the house. Johnson Johnson . . .

Of course! The mango tree! And who else would have thought of going to Dubois with the story?

Sudden fury possessed Garland. These black men! Apes! How he loathed them! It was an unbearable humiliation that he should be in their power. A cringing, half-educated underling and a pinhead of a banjo player! God!

The spasm passed. Anger wouldn't dispose of them. Dubois held all the cards. Nothing would give the man greater pleasure than to go to the Governor. The informant would name Garland. Investigation would follow—investigation which might bring the financial transaction to light and which in any case would lay bare his recently increased personal expenditure. Garland could not doubt that investigation would mean ruin.

He could imagine the headlines in the newspapers, the smug gloating editorials, the merciless contempt of the white population, the disgust and incredulity of his friends. The shame of it all! The arrogant administrator humiliated, the sea-green incorruptible dragged down from his pinnacle!

And disgrace wouldn't be the worst of it. There would be other things immeasurably harder to bear. Degradation. Garland felt rivulets of perspiration trickling down his spine. The day had gone by when an erring colonial servant could be discreetly spirited away to England and punished there. In these enlightened days, when every black politician was watching for a chance to complain of race favouritism and every white administration was straining itself to enforce equality before the law, there could be no question of slipping away. He would become the plaything of people whom he despised. He would be arrested by a black policeman and imprisoned with black men in the Colonial Jail. He would be sent for trial by a black magistrate and pronounced upon by a black jury—how they would love it! He would have to listen to the homily of a black judge, in the presence of his former friends. And he would have to serve his term with black men, eating with them, sleeping with them, working with them, in the sordid equality of convicted crime. He knew just what it would be like. He had once seen a white man in that jail.

No, that at least couldn't be allowed to happen. If the worst came to the worst, he had a revolver at home. A bullet would be infinitely preferable.

All the same, suicide was the last resort. Perhaps it wouldn't come to that. Systematically he considered the alternatives.

There was flight—but that would be ignominious and probably

fruitless. And it would mean leaving Celeste—she would never stick by him. The thought flashed through his mind that he must buy off Dubois—if not with money, then with the offer of his own immediate retirement. He rejected it out of hand. The mere idea made him squirm. Not for anything in the world would he put himself in the position of crawling to Dubois. Not even for life itself. In any case, it wasn't likely that Dubois would agree. He would like nothing better than to drag Garland down. It would please him personally, and would do him good politically. And there would still be the problem of that chattering half-wit, Johnson.

Garland rose heavily from the desk. All the savour had gone out of life—even what little there had been. He would have to talk to Celeste as though nothing had happened, and she read him so easily. He must get away as soon as possible, get to the boat and think it all out. On his own. Perhaps by the time Fiesta was over he would have thought of some solution.

And in case not, he would take his revolver with him.

Chapter Ten

At first light on the Wednesday morning, well ahead of the time laid down by law for the start of the holiday, the warm clear air of Fontego began to pulsate with a tantalising rhythmic beat. Fiesta had begun.

For a time, the notes and tones of separate instruments could be distinguished and located. Very soon, however, all identity was lost as innumerable streams of sound swelled and floated together into a mighty sea of noise. Life in Fontego had become a communal din and hubbub, a drumming syncopation which would end only with the final spasm of Bacchanalian revelry in forty hours' time.

From now on, movement was everything—movement in time with the sensuous African beat. The whole town was as restless as a tray of jumping beans. It was as though a sudden spell had been cast on all, compelling continuous movement of every joint and muscle. People no longer stood or walked. If they were standing they jigged, and if they were walking they fell into a languorous shuffle. Black abdomens writhed sinuously, loins gave suggestive jerks, shoulders twitched, hips swayed, and buttocks shook. The women swung their breasts provocatively. Fingers fidgeted and toes tapped and heads nodded in tempo.

Already, at this early hour, the streets were filling up. There had been a time when only the poorest class, the backstreet dwellers, had taken part in these morning promenades on the first day, but now almost everyone was eager to get out of doors, and crack of dawn was like a starting gun. Along the main thoroughfare a confused and shapeless procession was beginning to move in the wake of a percussion band whose members, mostly in drab old clothes and some in rags and tatters, were beating out the time. One or two carried old oil drums, skilfully divided into segments like an orange, so that each segment gave out a different note when struck. Some were banging rusty motor-car brake drums, disused garbage pails, and empty tins picked up on the city dump. Some were hammering on dustbin lids and old saucepans, or extracting metallic notes from half-filled bottles beaten with spoons.

Mixed up with the band were the bearers of banners and flags, some with strange inscriptions like "Saviours of the East" and "Charlemagne's Avengers." It was flamboyance that mattered, not significance. Many of the revellers were in fantastic garb. There was a fat man dressed as a bride; there was a painted clown in a torn football jersey; there was a man who had somehow contrived to make a headpiece of an alligator's jaws. There was a woman in a policeman's jacket and a schoolboy's cap, and a pseudo-priest in a white nightshirt with a black cross, and two men in flowing robes of scarlet and ochre with tawny artificial hair streaming down their backs. A group of shuffling men were pushing steel rods ahead of them along the road as though engaged in a demining operation. One individualist kept up a piercing whistle as he walked, pretending that the sound came from a long cane. Another man was juggling with two enormous dice, and yet a third, with no great precision, kept throwing a pole into the air and catching it.

Cars and buses mingled with the shuffling dancing mob in inextricable and satisfying confusion. What did it matter, since nobody wanted to go anywhere? And one could dance just as well inside a bus as outside. Loads of tight-packed Negresses in gaudy cotton frocks stood and jigged in the buses like pistons in a cylinder block, their bosoms bouncing and their smiles wide.

On the pavements there were still a few who took no part as yet. There were young men prospecting for a good "pick-up," and young girls showing off their big hats and their new backless shoes from which pink heels protruded in startling contrast to their shiny black legs. There were small boys racing up and down, apparently impervious to the heat, anxious to miss nothing. Already the street vendors were doing a fine trade, selling wedges of crushed ice dipped in syrup, and the delicious water of fresh green coconuts whose tops they so dexterously sliced off with murderous-looking cutlasses.

By midday all the streets were so jammed with sweating ecstatic humanity that movement was hardly possible any more, except vertically. The respectable roads in the better-class suburbs were hardly less crowded. Earlier generations of middle-class revellers would have concealed their identity with masks even at this stage, but now caution was thrown away. On a day when nothing was barred and *reki* was flowing, immodesty could quickly become competitive and every advance in flirtatious impropriety win new applause.

Normal eating hours meant nothing to anyone. The programme was continuous. As the sun rose higher the crowds were joined by fresh holiday-makers with a greater variety of costumes, so that soon the open spaces were brilliant with fancy dress. Popular uniforms were parodied. There were policemen with huge whistles and tailors with shears and top-hatted doctors with long thermometers. There were cowboys, and men in white steel helmets with U.S. insignia painted on them, and Chinamen in pigtails riding lions with rope manes; and clowns and devils and dragons with long tails, and minstrels with banjos and flour-whitened faces; and all of them were in continuous movement. Parties of young men and girls were beginning to go round from house to house on the outskirts, dancing and singing, each with its own noisy band and its collection of ludicrous costumes.

Indoors, in the calypso huts, great crowds were tapping out the monotonous savage rhythm to which all were tuned, while professionals who had been practising for weeks in readiness for this occasion tried out their new songs and scored points off each other in sarcastic duels of calypso war.

In the afternoon the better-off and more inhibited section of society contributed its quota of colour and gaiety. Limousines, driven by black chauffeurs who jigged in their seats, and gaudy trucks on which topical tableaux had been arranged led a parade round the outskirts of the city. Beautiful women, brown and white and olive, displayed the gorgeous clothes they had ordered for the occasion from Paris and New York, proudly escorted by wealthy men. The jigging *hoi polloi* looked on, mildly derisive, enjoying the polite restrained spectacle but knowing that downtown that night the masks would be on and that many of the respectable wealthy would be joining avidly in an orgy of *reki*, women, and calypso.

When the swift night fell and electric lights blazed out on the swaying, yelling, and exultant black mass, the pulse of the rhythm seemed to beat more strongly, and excitement rose. The day was for colour, and the night for *reki* and debauch. Policemen became alert for trouble-makers and night robbers, though the noise and confusion and *reki*-fired emotionalism were the perfect cloak for crime, and the dark hours would take their toll of property and life. There was little the police could do except keep their batons at the ready. It was understood that, as far as possible, they should stay out of things and let licence have its head. All night long the dancing would go on and the drinking and the heated copulation on the warm grass, and the drumming of the steel, and the blaring orchestras and radios. By morning the first wave would have spent itself and there would be a brief respite. But not for long. Dawn would bring the second wave into the littered streets, with still brighter costumes, still greater energy and zest, until the long carousal ended with the midnight stroke and the orgy was over.

Chapter Eleven

As the first Fiesta crowds began to flock into the streets on that Wednesday morning, Garland set out for Darwin Bay. He was driving a rather dilapidated station wagon, for Celeste always liked to have the car when she was left alone. His rods and tackle were stowed in the back, though it seemed unlikely that he would use them. He wasn't in the mood for fishing. He felt such a depression as he had never known before.

If he could have drawn a little warmth and comfort from Celeste, that might have helped. Last night he had wanted to tell her everything; probably he would have told her if she had shown the slightest interest in him. But she had been as detached as she always was. He didn't believe that she could ever have been in love with him, even when she had appeared so during their early meetings. She certainly wasn't now. Nobody could have been more coolly indifferent about a husband's departure than she had been last night. He found himself speculating how she would spend the holiday—what she would find to do. He always wondered that when he was away from her, but when he asked her afterwards she was always off-hand and vague.

He felt that he had really very little to live for. In all the circumstances, logic pointed remorselessly to self-destruction. It would, of course, be easy to find excuses for weakness, to defer action, to cling desperately and at all costs to life, because simply to breathe was something—particularly easy in the soft enervating climate of Fontego, where mere existence was a sensual pleasure. If Celeste had been fond of him, and this hideous danger had not been hanging over him, his morning's drive could have been a heavenly thing. The sky was blue and the sweet air was alive with the song of tropical birds. The Bay would be a delight; the sea would be perfect for swimming and sailing. What an enchanting holiday he and Celeste could have had together—if everything had been different! If he had had a carefree mind, and Celeste had wanted him to love her. Instead, here he was driving alone with thoughts as bitter as aloes, his only comfort the pressure of a revolver butt against his thigh.

He drove slowly and mechanically. The traffic on the road was increasing. Whole families were crowding in for the sight-seeing, on foot and on the backs of donkeys and jammed into crawling bullock carts. In the villages that he passed through, local merry-making had begun, so that the streets were becoming congested with dancing groups. The foolish animal ecstasy on the faces of these grinning Negroes somehow increased his sense of loneliness. He despised them too much to envy them, but at least they were glad to be alive, and would still be alive to-morrow.

Presently he drew up at the sentry box which guarded the entrance to the Base, for the road to Darwin ran through the middle of the leased territory. There were no restrictions on through traffic by day or night, though the number of each car was noted as it entered and left the area, to make sure no unauthorised person remained there. Garland took his pass from the sentry and drove slowly on through the beautifully-kept grounds. Driving through the Base always made him feel more dissatisfied with the rest of Fontego—it was so clean and orderly, with fine living quarters and superb road surfaces and well-kept tennis courts and swimming pools and clubs. It threw into vivid relief the unkempt squalor of the Colony.

He gave up his pass at the exit, and almost at once caught the gleam of the Bay behind a copse of flaming immortelles. Down on the beach all was deserted. There were three yachts at anchor, including his own, but of life there was no sign. Even the fisherman who was supposed to keep an eye on his own yacht, the *Papeete*, had gone into town with all his brood. No scene could have been more peaceful or more lovely. A faint wind blew from the sea—just enough to stir the graceful fronds of the coconut palms which ringed the semicircle of golden sand. Garland parked the station wagon under a tree and walked to the hut where the dinghy was kept, trying as best he could to ward off the venomous sand flies with flailing movements of his arms. The sooner he got on the water the better. Even though he might be going to put a bullet in his brain, sand flies were irritating.

He unlocked the shed and heaved the ancient dinghy down the beach. The last time he had been here, he had had Johnson Johnson with him to do the chores. He ploughed heavily back through the sand and collected the hamper that Salacity had packed for him. By the time he was ready to push off, his shirt was soaked with sweat, but on the water the air was pleasantly cool. The *Papeete* was only fifty yards from the shore. Behind her the horns of the Bay curved and almost met, forming a perfect anchorage. Outside the surf was beating.

Aboard ship, Garland methodically stowed his things. Then he stripped, and slipped over the side into the milk-warm sea. The gently heaving water caressed his naked body like a lover. He lay for a while on his back, floating and basking. Then he swam round the ship with powerful strokes, enjoying his strength.

Presently he climbed back into the yacht and let the sun dry him. He poured himself an iced lime-squash from the vacuum flask. It was delicious. Everything external to him was delicious this morning. His problems had already begun to take on an air of unreality. They couldn't be as serious as he had supposed. The revolver on the bunk looked melodramatic and absurd. He had been idiotic to bring it. He had got things out of proportion. After all, he was strong and vigorous—yes, and wealthy, if he could keep his freedom. Life still had a great deal to offer him. He wasn't afraid of death, though it did occur to him that it would be ghastly to bungle the job in a lonely place like this. But for a man like him, suicide was cowardly and silly—the resort of the weakling. There must be another way out.

He lay on the bunk and tried to forget the magic of the tranquil sea and the scented air. Deliberately, he tried to get back into the mood of those moments after Dubois had left him. It was easier than he had expected. Logic reasserted itself. If Dubois told what he knew, disgrace was inescapable. And he would tell.

Garland's eye dwelt upon the revolver. Unless, of course . . .

Murder! That was an alternative. The path of logic forked. Suicide or murder.

Put that way, was there any real choice? Murder wasn't a thing to contemplate lightly, but then most people weren't forced by events into such desperate decisions. Garland wondered how he would feel afterwards, if he killed Dubois. He decided that he would feel very little—except, perhaps, satisfaction. And how that one simple act would change the whole prospect! His self-respect would be preserved, his career would be saved, and with money to burn he might even find Celeste less cold. How could he hesitate?

There was, of course, Johnson Johnson to think of. The little banjo player would have to be silenced too. Two murders! Garland dwelt darkly on the double enterprise. Anyhow, Dubois came first. He was infinitely the more dangerous, with his stored up resentments and his scheming mind. And the danger was immediate. Directly after the holiday he would want to act. If he was to be killed, it was vital that the deed should be done before the end of Fiesta.

Garland's depression lifted. The prospect of action always stimulated him. If he were careful, it should be fairly safe to kill Dubois. The apparent absence of motive would be a great safeguard. Garland would be the last person to be suspected of such a murder, provided he made no blunders. The chief problem would be to get away from the scene of the murder unobserved. A white man could not easily pass in a crowd in Fontega. Whatever movements he made might well be noticed. Not so much, of course, during Fiesta—people would be much too busy with their pleasures.

Garland wondered what Dubois would be doing with himself during Fiesta. Not dancing in the streets, that was certain. Probably sitting at home with a departmental report, feeling superior! He lived, Garland knew, in a small detached house in one of the middle-class suburbs, with a man to look after him. The man would almost certainly be out celebrating.

Garland considered the advisability of calling on Dubois at his home and killing him there. It was the most direct way, but the risk of being seen and identified was great. That suburb wasn't one that men like Garland frequented. It was mainly a Negro district. If a white man were seen entering the house the circle of suspects would be dangerously narrowed. In a building, too, traces might be left.

The ideal thing would be to get Dubois out of the house and mixing with the crowds. Say to-morrow evening, at the climax of Fiesta, when bedlam would break loose and the town would be so full of noise and drunkenness that the killing of a man in the dark would pass unnoticed. Would it be possible to get Dubois out? Garland thought it would. He could telephone—he could say he had come to a decision about Dubois' disclosure, and stress the urgency of a meeting, and name a rendezvous. Dubois would respond automatically. He might think it was odd, but he would certainly come.

No, that wouldn't do. The killing might pass unnoticed, but someone might see them together before the killing, and that would be fatal. Garland was too well known. If only he could wear some disguise.

A disguise! Why, of course—what could be simpler? The thing to do was to dress up in some outlandish costume and wear a mask, as thousands of other people would be doing. Dubois would be astounded, of course, knowing Garland, but he would be dead before he could draw any conclusions.

Garland's blood stirred with excitement. This was going to be far better than putting a bullet in his own head. He would drive in to-morrow at dusk, ring up Dubois, and make the appointment, dispatch him and return to the boat as though nothing had happened. What about a weapon? Clearly not a revolver. Poison would be simpler to administer if they were having a drink somewhere—but poison was too difficult for the ordinary man to get hold of. It would be safer, perhaps, to use a knife and make the murder seem like the result of some native brawl. Garland knew he would have no difficulty in driving a knife with precision to a man's heart, if the man was unsuspecting. He had the very thing in the tool chest—a short double-edged knife in a leather scabbard that he used for various jobs around the ship and occasionally for hacking out the pulp of coconuts. He could sharpen that until it would go into flesh as easily as into a coconut. And he could wear the scabbard at his belt, under his clothes. He went to the chest and took out the knife. It was a little rusty but would soon polish up. He would have to hold the handle in a handkerchief or something, if he was going to leave it in the body. Afterwards, on his way back to the Bay, he would throw the scabbard into one of the muddy rivers.

The disguise was a problem. It must be something that he could fix up here on the boat with the materials available to him. It wouldn't matter how fantastic it was as long as there was nothing about it to suggest a masquerading white man. He would have to do something about darkening his hands and face and neck.

He looked thoughtfully round the boat. There was very little that he could dress up in. A few old clothes, but it wouldn't be safe to use them. He really needed something long and enveloping, like a robe. His eye fell on a thin coarse blanket, off-white—a covering that was sometimes necessary in the cool hour before the dawn. He should be able to make something of that. He tried wrapping it round himself like a toga. It was the right size, and would admirably conceal the knife. Somewhere he had a leather belt. He searched in the lockers and found it. When he had strapped it round his waist and examined the effect, he decided that he looked rather like a Moslem priest. Perhaps he could develop that motif. A towel was the obvious thing for a headdress. He set to work to make a turban. It was some time before he could get the knack of tucking the ends under so that the turban remained tight. But finally he was satisfied. His appearance was bizarre enough, but the disguise was excellent, and at Fiesta anything would pass.

The mask presented greater difficulties. If only he had thought of all this before, he could have made some preparations. Still, there was safety in spontaneity. The only thing he could see that would be at all suitable for a mask was an old piece of sailcloth. He made a rough pencil sketch on the canvas and cut out the mask. The slits of the eye-holes must be just wide enough to see through comfortably, but no wider. A small hole would be needed for his nose; otherwise the mask wouldn't lie against his face. For some time he experimented and adjusted. Finally, he attached four lengths of string and tried the effect. The mask looked amateurish, but wasn't improvisation the keynote of Fiesta? There was no doubt that it completely concealed his identity, and that was all that mattered. He took the scissors, cut the remainder of the sailcloth into a dozen pieces, and stuffed them back into the locker.

Once more he went over the plan in his mind. There would be an element of luck—all depended on his finding Dubois at home when he telephoned. But if that hurdle were passed, the rest should be straightforward. A suitable rendezvous—some night spot with large crowds; a carefully chosen moment; a swift blow—and all would be done. He would mingle with the throng, pick up the car, and be out of town within the hour. There would be risks, of course, but not undue risks, considering the stake. Garland felt eager to put the plan to the test. Even if he failed he would be no worse off than now. He could still use the revolver on himself. He had nothing to lose.

Chapter Twelve

It was seven o'clock on the second evening of Fiesta, and dusk had fallen. Ezekiel MacPhearson Dubois was sitting out on his balcony overlooking the brightly lit street. With conscious superiority he was refraining from taking an active part in the celebrations, though it was quite impossible not to participate passively. Through every open door and window loudspeakers which had been left switched on blared their calypsoes, while every few minutes a group of rowdy revellers would come dancing and singing their way past the house. Dubois was thus able to sniff the bouquet of the heady drink which he felt a man in his position ought not to touch. He must set an example. Nevertheless, the rhythm beat in his blood, and his neatly shod feet tapped upon the concrete.

Dubois was hoping for a telephone call. His mind had not been at peace since he had left Dr. Garland at the office, and he would be thankful when the whole matter was cleared up. He felt that temporarily he had lost the initiative. Dr. Garland was a bold and intelligent man, capable of swift action. He might be devising some countermove. Not that Dubois could imagine anything effective, but he nevertheless felt unhappy about the situation.

His chief worry, as he realised upon reflection, was that the evidence against Garland so far in his possession wasn't really very strong. If it had been, the wise course would have been to take it without further delay to the Colonial Secretary or the Governor. But, whatever might turn up later, at the moment there was nothing to go on but the unsupported word of that feckless fellow, Johnson Johnson. In the circumstances, Dubois decided, his correct and cautious approach to Dr. Garland had undoubtedly been sensible. The question now was, what would Dr. Garland do?

If by any chance Dr. Garland *hadn't* taken the bribe, he'd certainly be all for an investigation. In that case, Dubois would keep as far in the background as possible and Johnson Johnson could take the rap. But if Dr. Garland had done it, he simply couldn't afford to face investigation—unless of course he thought he could bluff it out. He had always had unlimited confidence in himself. It was more likely, though, that he'd try to get away from the Colony, knowing the game was up. Dubois didn't much mind whether he got away or not. Whether he ran or whether he stayed, the humiliation would be complete—though Dubois rather liked the idea of the great Dr. Garland taking to his heels. He couldn't quite see it happening, but it was a pleasantly ignominious thought. Of course, a man in Dr. Garland's position and of Dr. Garland's character might well commit suicide. That was what often happened in such cases. That would be quite satisfactory.

As he sipped his *reki*, Dubois' imagination explored several attractive paths. With Dr. Garland humbled and out of the way, he would get the department. There was no doubt about that. No other claimant existed, and the Government was always anxious these days to appoint a coloured man whenever possible, "even though it may involve some decline in efficiency," as the policy decision had impudently put it. With the department in his hands, Dubois would make many changes. There were one or two white doctors who could usefully be dispensed with. They only caused bad blood in the services, simply by being there. They could be encouraged to ask for transfers and their places could be filled with reliable local men, friends of Dubois. He could begin to organise the department as his instrument. He could use it for his political purposes. He would take steps, for instance, to see that suitable statements reached the press. The Colony's health was appalling, and the administration could be blamed—not directly, perhaps, but by implication.

He would begin his campaign by exploiting Dr. Garland's lapse. One of the greatest blunders, his argument would run, had been to entrust such an important charge as Public Health to a corrupt expatriate white instead of to a trustworthy local man who had the interests of his own people at heart. That particular situation had been dealt with, he would let it be known, as a result of the vigilance and public spirit of Ezekiel MacPhearson Dubois. But there was still much to be done. The department was starved of money, and the poor were neglected, because the white business men who were taking so much out of the Colony didn't want to pay higher taxes. (It was true that some of the wealthiest business men were coloured, but the fact could be slurred over for the time being.) Simple people were suffering and dying because of the whites—that was the line. A scandalous state of affairs. It would be necessary to see to it that the press had every opportunity to publicise the facts about the neglected health services. It should have greater access to the hospitals, particularly some of the very bad provincial ones. Pressmen should be shown round the maternity wards, where over-crowding was so bad that more than a hundred mothers were delivered every year in each bed, and some of the children's wards, where it was common to find two or three in a bed at the same time, and the observation block, which was a fire-trap. Yes, the observation block would provide some valuable headlines. In a short time, so much trouble could be stirred up that the Finance Committee would have no alternative but to vote more money. He, Dubois, would lead the agitation.

It wasn't perhaps the traditional role of the responsible civil servant, but at this stage no one would dare to attempt to discipline him. Only Dr. Garland would have done that. Dubois would be too strongly supported by his friends in the Legislative Council. Sooner or later, in any case, he'd have to abandon administration for politics, and get himself elected to the Council. The people needed an educated leader. They had plenty of ignoramuses who were ready enough to set themselves up as leaders—men who couldn't speak English or write a grammatical pamphlet; dangerous agitators whose one idea of political struggle was to set fire to sugar cane; fanatical evangelists who had "got" religion in one of its thirty-odd local manifestations and thought that it was an adequate substitute for a practical knowledge of affairs. Dubois would soon oust them. Education always won in the end. He was young—not much over thirty—good-looking and eloquent. He might well become Prime Minister when the Colony was granted responsible government. Dubois took another abstemious sip of *reki*. Yes, the future looked extremely bright.

Suddenly, above the racket of the street, the telephone rang. He got up quickly, automatically adjusting his tie as he walked to the receiver. Despite his forthcoming elevation to Prime Ministership a choking feeling came into his throat when he heard Garland's voice. Ridiculous to feel so nervous of a man who would soon be in disgrace! He steadied himself and said with dignity, "How are you, Dr. Garland? I trust you are having an enjoyable holiday."

"Not so bad," came Garland's voice, terse and brittle. "Listen, Dubois, I've been thinking over that matter we talked about and I'd like to have a word with you right away. I'm in town—what about meeting this evening?"

"You know I am always very ready to fall in with your wishes," said Dubois. "Where would you like me to meet you?" He felt suddenly apprehensive about what Garland might do, and he had no desire to be alone with him, out of the public gaze.

"I'd ask you along to my place," said Garland, "but my wife is entertaining, and it wouldn't be very convenient. I suggest we meet for a drink somewhere. Somewhere in keeping with the spirit of the holiday, eh? What about the Blue Pool? It won't be very quiet, but then it's not quiet anywhere tonight."

Dubois hesitated. The Blue Pool! Not exactly the place he would himself have suggested going to. It had—well, a reputation. He had always rather wanted to go, of course; it was supposed to have a rather *risqué* floor show. And after all, it was Fiesta, and being there with such a respected figure as Dr. Garland would surely make everything all right.

"If you think that's a suitable place, Dr. Garland," he said, putting the responsibility squarely on his superior, "I shall of course be very happy to join you there. Would you like me to come immediately?"

"If you don't mind," said Garland. "I'll be inside—you shouldn't have any difficulty in finding me. I'll expect you in about half an hour."

"Very good," said Dubois. He smiled as he replaced the receiver. It would be rather pleasant, doing his duty and yet enjoying himself at the same time. Listening to Garland trying to talk himself out of the mess he was in, having a drink or two, watching the girls, and at the same time feeling quite secure.

He brushed his crinkly black hair, ran a delicate finger over his moustache, put on his white linen jacket, and descended to the street. It would be hopeless to look for a taxi—no car would get through the crowds. He would stroll along by the sea front, where there was the best chance of a breeze. He wanted to feel cool when he arrived—one was always at a disadvantage at an interview when one was perspiring and the other man was not. As he walked, he prepared a few suitable phrases with which to meet the various situations that might arise. "A great tragedy for the Colony as well as a personal tragedy for you, sir. . . ." That would be appropriate if Garland broke down and admitted his guilt. Dignified, statesmanlike. Or, "I fear your decision leaves me no alternative but to go at once to the Governor. . . ." That would counter any attempt to hush things up. Or, "Of course, Dr. Garland, I fully share your belief that the inquiry will dispose of the whole thing as an empty rumour. . . ." That would do if Garland seemed inclined to face an inquiry. Dubois wished he knew what Garland was going to say. Obviously he had a proposition of some sort to make or he wouldn't have suggested the meeting.

Dubois realised with a shock of embarrassment that he had automatically fallen into a sinuous shuffle. He tried hard to correct it, but the rhythm beat at him from all sides, and the example of the crowds was contagious. He threw back his shoulders and strode ahead; avoiding the worst of the crush. Twice he looked at his watch. He didn't want to be too early—that would show servility. But he didn't want to be late—Dr. Garland hated unpunctuality. Precisely thirty minutes after Garland's call he turned into the grounds of the Blue Pool.

The place was built on the lines of a modern roadhouse, with a large white two-decker restaurant and dance floor brilliantly lighted, several bars, and an orchestra on the balcony. On the ground below the balcony was a large circle of polished wood where the floor shows were staged under a spotlight and where, at other times, customers could dance. Round the floor were scores of tables, some of them set in the open and some discreetly concealed among flowering bushes and coconut palms in the grounds. Beyond the building was the private lagoon and beach which gave the place its name. Altogether, it was a popular, vulgar, and stimulating spot.

To-night, of course, the Blue Pool was packed and very rowdy. By no means all the customers had been able to find tables. Crowds were milling around the bars, and more crowds packed the sandy beach and the lagoon itself, from which shrieks of female laughter rose above the general din. Everywhere there were groups of people drinking and shouting and jigging under the coloured lights festooned among the trees. The central floor was alive with men and girls "traipsing" in a continuous snaky circle to the tune of the old "le'go," "Who Dead Canaan?" Almost everyone was in costume of some sort, and about half the people were masked. There were, Dubois saw, quite a lot of whites or near-whites. Liquor was flowing freely everywhere, and so was money. The Blue Pool was no place to go for a cheap evening. It was a good thing that Garland would be paying.

Feeling very sober and somewhat conspicuous, Dubois elbowed his way rather diffidently through the vast throng, keeping his eyes open for his chief. A dusky girl accosted him and took his arm, but he shook her off impatiently. It really oughtn't to be hard, he thought, to pick out a man like Dr. Garland, even in a crowd like this, though it might take time because it was so difficult to pass between the tables. After a fruitless search in the neighbourhood of the dance floor he turned in among the coconuts. Perhaps Dr. Garland had chosen one of the quieter spots—if such a word could be used of such a place on such a night. Perhaps he'd been unable to get one of the tables near the floor. That was a pity; obviously you had to be near to get the full advantage of the floor show.

Just inside the belt of palms, beside a gorgeous hibiscus, a masked white woman at a table turned her head and seemed to regard Dubois with more than casual interest before devoting herself again to her male companion, who was also masked. A few yards farther on, a coloured man wearing a turban and a long white robe sat alone. Not much fun, Dubois thought, coming alone to a place like this. Or perhaps he was waiting for someone. Dubois stepped aside to let a party of chalk-faced minstrels pass and was about to resume his search when a familiar voice said quietly, "Ah, there you are, Dubois. Have a seat."

Dubois whipped round, his face frozen in astonishment. He stared for a moment at the turbaned figure and the bright steady eyes and then flopped into a chair. "Good gracious me!" he said, breaking into the sweat he had tried so hard to avoid.

"Quite an effective costume, don't you think?" said Garland.

Dubois, who had not yet recovered his poise, gazed at the brown hands, the brown skin around the turban and under the chin, the rough cloth mask tied with bits of string. "I'm very surprised," he said, "very surprised indeed!"

"I thought you would be," said Garland. "My wife made me do it—she said it would amuse the guests. Personally, I find it damned hot. It all comes of changing my mind and not going fishing."

"I should never have recognised you," said Dubois. He felt that he ought to sound disapproving. Actually, he was puzzled and a little worried. If Garland had been in the mood for dressing up and family merry-making, it didn't look as though he could have very much on his conscience or be greatly troubled about the future. That numskull Johnson had probably got everything mixed up after all. Dubois wished Garland would take off the mask—it looked hideous, and talking to a masked face was very unsatisfactory. In a conversation such as they were about to have, expression was everything. Perhaps that was why Garland had put on the mask. Perhaps, after all, his conscience wasn't so clear. Anyway, he'd hardly take it off now. He wouldn't want anyone to recognise him in that fantastic get-up.

"You'd better have a drink," said Garland as a waiter came

weaving through the crowd. "What shall it be—*reki?* Cheer up, Dubois. You look as nervous as though you'd just walked into a brothel for the first time."

Dubois, whose fascinated eyes had switched to the table under the hibiscus, said, "I'm not quite sure that I haven't." The two white people seemed to be pretty drunk. The woman, her hair completely covered by a white silk scarf and her body less completely covered by a gay beach wrap, was making what appeared to be half-hearted attempts to ward off the exploratory hands of her male escort. Garland also turned to look, with a spasm of irritation. He wouldn't have taken this table if he'd known that white people had reserved the adjoining one, but by the time they'd arrived it had been too late to change. He wondered who the woman was. It was quite likely that he knew her, but she had obviously gone to great pains to make recognition impossible—just as he had. A good thing too, considering her behaviour. A frustrated exhibitionist, no doubt. Apart from the wrap she seemed to have very little on.

With a conscious effort Dubois averted his gaze. "Disgusting!" he exclaimed. "I'm afraid some of your people don't set us a very good example, Dr. Garland."

"No," said Garland indifferently. The sooner he got this over, the better. He'd nothing to say to Dubois. The mere sight of him, sitting there so neat and smooth and complacent, made his gorge rise. All that was necessary now was to choose the right moment, and strike hard and true. People kept passing the tables, but they were interested only in themselves. With care, the crowd should be a safeguard. He must watch for his opportunity, and deliver the blow unobserved, and go.

The waiter, jostled by an unsteady passer-by, slopped the drinks on his tray and nearly dropped it. "Sorry, sah," he said. "Too much peoples, sah!" He put down the two glasses, and slipped away through the trees.

Dubois took up his glass. Surely Garland wasn't going to attempt to drink in a mask! He felt that this whole business of the costume was very inconsiderate and ill-mannered. Here he was himself, in his ordinary clothes and easily recognisable, in a place of dubious repute that he wouldn't normally have come to, and the shield of respectability on which he had relied turned out to be no shield at all. From the slots of the mask, Garland's eyes stared. Dubois' nervousness increased. He ought not to have come. He wished Dr. Garland would start talking. He raised his glass and said, "Your very good health," glad to moisten his dry lips. Garland said, "Long life!" and carefully applied the glass to the mouth slot in the mask.

At the next table the man and woman were in close embrace and oblivious of everything but themselves. An extra loud crash came from the distant orchestra, and a white spotlight was turned on to the dance floor. It looked as though the show was about to start. This seemed to be the moment for action. Garland leaned forward. "By the way, Dubois," he said quietly, "the reason I asked you to see me was that I think I've cleared up the whole business. It was just a misunderstanding, I'm glad to say. This document explains everything."

He got up, went round to the other side of the table, and thrust a sheet of paper before Dubois' disappointed eyes. As he leaned over, his right hand fumbled for the knife handle. Dubois, his eyes screwed up in concentration, read a few lines of the typescript but could make nothing of it. He looked up at the masked face in puzzled inquiry, just in time to catch the glitter of the descending knife. His mouth opened to yell, but before he could utter a sound, agony tore his body. The knife, directed with precision, pierced his heart. He slumped face downwards upon the table, knocking his glass to the ground.

The woman in the beach wrap looked up at the sharp sound of breaking glass. Garland had already turned to go when a group of carousing men and girls came rollicking into view and converged unsteadily upon him. In his haste to get away Garland collided with a big Negro. The man, tipsy and showing off to his girl, replied with an unceremonious push. Garland stumbled and almost lost his balance, and as with an effort he prevented himself from falling, his turban dropped to the ground.

He snatched at it and thrust it back on his head, but not before the woman at the next table had given a gasp that spelt recognition.

Her glass was poised in mid-air, halted in the act of drinking, and the eyes behind her red mask were fixed on him. He was seized with desperate fear, but there was nothing he could do about her. At any moment the newcomers would discover the knife in Dubois' back. Garland gathered up the hem of his long robe and rushed away into the crowd. He had not gone more than a dozen steps when there was a shriek behind him. The murder was out!

Chapter Thirteen

Once again Garland was leaving town in the station wagon, but this time he was driving fast. He was in no immediate danger, for he had reached the car without being pursued, but his foot on the accelerator instinctively obeyed the impulse of flight. He had stopped only long enough to divest himself of the mask, robe, and turban, which were now tucked well down in the back of the wagon.

His mood was grim. He had done the job but he had made a mess of it. Up to the last moment the plan had worked perfectly, and then luck had turned against him and that clumsy oaf of a nigger had ruined everything.

Garland had no doubt at all that he had been recognised. That sudden astonished immobility had been unmistakable proof. By now the police would be on the spot, and the woman in the beach wrap would be disclosing the identity of the man in the turban. That silver lock of hair would have been enough; it was unique. At various times the wives of most of his acquaintances had commented on it. The briefest glimpse was all that anyone would need to recognise him.

All his plans had been made on the assumption that no suspicion would fall upon him. Now there would be worse than suspicion—there would be accusation. By to-morrow morning at the latest he would be wanted for questioning, even if there wasn't actually a warrant out for his arrest on a charge of murder. Now he would *have* to use that revolver—and quickly, before the means of killing himself were taken from him. Otherwise, he would find himself not merely being tried and sentenced by black men, but taken from his cell at eight o'clock one morning and hanged by one.

Somehow, the thought of suicide was even more repugnant now than it had been on the previous day. Since then, he had become buoyed up with hope. With action, the will to live had flooded back more strongly than ever. He had let his imagination dwell on splendid plans. It was unthinkable that the security which he had bought by such desperate and bloody measures should now escape him; that after all his planning and bold unflinching execution of the plan, he should still have to die by his own hand.

Perhaps, he reflected, he should at least wait until tomorrow morning, wait to see what happened. There was still the one-in-a-million chance that the woman hadn't recognised him. No point in advancing to meet disaster. He would drive cautiously back into town first thing in the morning, and learn the news. No, he could do better than that—he would tune in to Radio Fontego on the yacht's receiver. Dubois' murder would cause a tremendous sensation in the Colony, and the radio would probably tell him all he wanted to know.

Meanwhile, he must act on the assumption that the identity of the man in the turban would *not* be known, and must cover his tracks as he had planned. At a bridge over one of the little streams which ran under the road, he stopped and disposed of the knife holster. It was a plain holster, of common design, with nothing about it to identify it as his, but he felt it was better not to have an empty holster aboard the yacht.

The distant gleam of Darwin Bay brought a feeling of relief. It had been an exciting, exhausting evening—he would be glad to get aboard. He found the Bay as deserted as ever. As soon as he reached the yacht he unwound the towel which had served as a turban and hung it in the wash-room. The leather belt went back into its locker. He carefully examined the blanket for bloodstains, and having found none he folded it and placed it at the foot of the berth where he slept. The mask was more of a problem. After a little reflection he put it into an old paint tin, poured petrol over it and burned it to ashes, which he scattered overboard. Finally he set to work to remove the telltale brown stains from his hands and wrists and around his face. It was a long job, requiring much scrubbing, but at last he felt satisfied with the result. He had disposed of all the evidence. Dead tired, he turned in and slept till daybreak.

He awoke completely refreshed, and swam before breakfast in the tepid sea. This might be his last swim, but there was no reason why he shouldn't enjoy it. He shaved carefully and drank some iced orange juice. Just before eight, he tuned in the radio for the morning news. He tried to tell himself that he was resigned to the worst, that the first few words of the news bulletin would seal his fate, but the suspense was unbearable.

Here it came! "Radio Fontego regrets to announce——"

He listened with grim concentration. The news item was more succinct than usual. Ezekiel MacPhearson Dubois, Assistant Secretary of Health and prominent public figure in the Colony, had been stabbed to death at the Blue Pool by an unknown assailant . . .

Garland's breath came sharply. An unknown assailant!

Up to the moment of his murder, the announcer went on, he had been in the company of a coloured man wearing a greyish-white mask and a crude Moslem costume. A fairly accurate description of Garland's disguise followed. The local C.I.D., under the active leadership of Superintendent Jarvis himself, had been working all night in an effort to trace this man, so far without success. The murderer had been seen by a number of people just before he made good his escape, but the police were particularly anxious to interview a white lady and gentleman who had been sitting at a neighbouring table and might possibly have seen something of the incident. The announcer then read a flattering obituary notice of Dubois before passing on to list the other crimes which had been committed in the Colony during the forty hours of Fiesta.

Garland snapped off the radio and relaxed. How sweet and fresh was the morning air! How right he'd been not to be hasty with the revolver! Unless the police were deliberately keeping something back, they had no idea who the man in the turban was. It looked as though the man and woman at the nearby table had cleared off when the trouble started. The question was, would they respond to the police appeal?

As Garland reflected, he began to realise that they might not be at all anxious to show themselves—particularly the woman. It depended a good deal, of course, on who she was. She might easily be the wife or daughter of some eminent person in the Colony, out on an uninhibited spree with some equally well-known man. If that were the case, it wasn't surprising that she had slipped away when the murder had been discovered, and left the Negro party to deal with the police. If that were the case, she'd be likely to go on putting her reputation before her civic duty. The very last thing she would want to have known was that she had been disporting herself in public, half drunk and half naked, at the Blue Pool. At this moment she was probably feeling as apprehensive as he was. But at least she was safe as long as she kept quiet. She knew Garland's identity, but he didn't know hers.

He tried with all his powers of concentration to recall the visual picture he had had of her in those few seconds before his flight. There was a remarkably clear impression in his mind. He could see, almost photographically, the white silk handkerchief, the red mask, the white beach wrap with its purple arabesques, the smooth olive-skinned hand holding the poised glass, motionless as a statue. Yes, the picture was vivid enough, but it wouldn't help him to identify her. Hundreds of people must have worn white silk handkerchiefs. The mask was of a kind which was sold in every stationer's at Fiesta time. Of course, if he ever saw that unusual and rather gaudy wrap again, he would recognise it, but the woman wasn't in the least likely to wear it any more. He tried to remember something about the man who had been her companion, with less success. Brown hair; tall, Garland thought, like the woman; a similar red mask; a well-cut tropical cream suit. He could have been anybody. It was an odd situation. In Garland's acquaintance there were several dozen white women—wives of Government officials and business men and planters—any one of whom might have been the woman behind the mask. A most unsatisfactory situation! It was true that, provided the woman didn't come forward, he was safe enough, but he would have precious little peace of mind. From now on he would be looking into every woman's eyes, sizing her up, mentally equipping her with a red mask and a purple and white beach wrap, and wondering whether it was she—or someone else—who had the power to hang him if she felt like it.

He threw off his anxiety. There was still hope—that was the main thing. The fact that the man and the woman had cleared off was an excellent sign. Obviously the thing for Garland to do now was to return to town as he would have done in the normal course of events after the holiday, and play the part of a man to whom the unexpected news of Dubois' death came as a great shock.

It would, he knew, be a difficult part for him to play. As he drove back over the familiar road he made an effort to empty his mind of everything that had happened during the past two days and start afresh. He had been fishing, that was all; fishing and swimming and lazing. He was going back with mind and body refreshed after a perfect two days' holiday. He would call at his home for a quick bath and a change of clothes, intending to go on to the office and there take up with Dubois the many threads of the department's affairs. The one fatal thing would be to know too much—particularly with Celeste, who was damnably intuitive. It was a pity he had to see her first, but that was his normal routine. She would be expecting him, and on this day of all days it wouldn't do to break with precedent.

He found her lying in a swing chair in the shade of the mango. She looked very attractive, with shining hair drawn smoothly behind her ears and a dreaming look in the brown eyes, but for once Garland didn't stop to think of her charms. He kissed her cheek and wondered furiously what the newspaper reports contained.

"Well, darling," said Celeste in her usual lazy manner, "did you have a good trip?"

"Very good, thank you," he answered mechanically. "How did you enjoy yourself?"

"It's been a heavenly rest," she said, stretching and almost purring. "Susan came along with Martin West yesterday afternoon and we had a swim. Otherwise I haven't done a thing. Just lazed and kept cool. You've heard about Dubois, of course?"

Garland tried not to overdo the look of surprise he gave her. "No," he said. "What about him?"

Celeste gave a wry smile. "I'm afraid you'll have to look for a new assistant."

"What do you mean? What's happened to him? Nothing serious, I hope."

"Fairly serious," said Celeste. "He was murdered last night at the Blue Pool."

"Good God!" exclaimed Garland. For a moment his mind became quite blank. Stage fright. It was as though he had forgotten his lines. Then he forced himself to make the necessary comments. "The Blue Pool? What on earth was he doing there? I didn't know he went to such places."

Celeste was smiling. "He must have been a dark horse. I always felt he was too upright to be true." She seemed to find pleasure in the thought of Dubois' fatal moral lapse.

"I must say I think your amusement's misplaced," said Garland stiffly.

"Oh, don't be such a prig, Adrian. You know you didn't like him, and I detested the man, so why should we pretend to be sorry?"

Garland had been contemplating some supplementary exclamation of horror, but in view of Celeste's attitude he decided that the moment had passed. "It'll make things very difficult at the office," he said. "Is it in the newspapers?"

"It certainly is." Celeste smoothed a newspaper and handed it to him. "Have you had breakfast?"

"All I want, thanks," he replied. "This news has rather taken my appetite away."

"Oh, you mustn't let it do that," said Celeste, with the amused look again. "Did you catch anything?"

Garland glanced up from the dramatic headlines. "Eh? Oh, nothing to boast about." He returned to the paper. The whole front page was devoted to Dubois. Celeste eyed him lazily as he read it through. As far as he could see, the report added nothing of significance to what had already been announced on the radio.

"Well," he said finally, putting the paper down and frowning into the middle distance, "it's a tragic thing. Most unexpected. It all seems to have been very deliberate. I wonder what the motive could have been."

"Do you think a motive would be necessary with a man like Dubois?" asked Celeste. "I should think an ordinary human reflex would be enough."

"Oh, he wasn't as bad as that," said Garland. "You know, I wouldn't be surprised if there was a woman behind it."

"Wouldn't you, darling? You have such an original mind. Now *I'm* much more interested in the two people at the next table—the white people. I wonder who they were? There'll be a perfectly luscious scandal if their names come out. It's quite probable that we know them. They might even have been to dinner here. I dare say the woman was someone we'd never dream of, like that quiet little Scots wife of David Carew."

"Now, look here, Celeste," Garland protested. "You really mustn't say things like that."

"Why not? It's obvious the Colony's going to be swept by a guessing craze for at least nine days, and I don't see why I should be out of it. It's a pity there aren't more clues."

"Perhaps the police know more than has come out yet." He got up. "Well, I suppose I'd better be getting along to the office. I'll go and change."

"Yes, run along," said Celeste. "The place is bound to be in an uproar. I expect I shall be answering the telephone all day long. Isn't it exciting? You don't think the woman could have been the Governor's wife, do you? Now that *would* be fun. Anyone who wanted Salacity to be called Sally would be just the type. Subterranean urges masked with propriety! Or a nice plump homely body like Mrs. Sylvester, licking her lips over naughty nudity."

"You're incorrigible!" said Garland.

Celeste shrugged. "What else is there to do here but gossip and speculate about other people? Roll on Honolulu, that's what I say. I hope you haven't forgotten. Oh, by the way, Superintendent Jarvis was trying to get hold of you this morning. I forgot to tell you."

Garland started—he couldn't help it. "Jarvis? What did he want?"

"Oh, something about Dubois," said Celeste lightly. "He'll tell you—he's going to call at the office at about eleven. Perhaps he thinks you did it."

"You have a peculiar sense of humour," said Garland in a cold voice.

Chapter Fourteen

Superintendent Jarvis, of Fontego's Criminal Investigation Department, stood in the main office of the Department of Health, waiting for Miss Chang to return and usher him into the Secretary's presence. He was a tall, well-built man in his late fifties, with greying hair and a little grey moustache that contrasted with his otherwise young appearance. The deep golden-brown of his skin could have come from prolonged sunbathing, but was in fact the result of mixed blood, of which he was unduly conscious. The expression on his fleshy face was thoughtful, almost sullen, and his thick lips were thrust out in a pout.

When Miss Chang called him, he advanced upon Garland with the agile tread of a tawny panther. "Good morning," he said in his mellow voice, and shook hands with Garland before taking the seat that was offered him.

At least, thought Garland with relief, it didn't look as though the Superintendent had come to make an arrest. Confidence was beginning to return. The talk with Celeste had passed off smoothly. The feel of the office chair at his back was comforting, and so was the knowledge that there were people around who would unquestionably defer to him. He was back in his own world, the world of men and affairs that he understood.

"Well, Jarvis," he said, taking the initiative, "my wife told me you rang up earlier to-day. I suppose it was about Dubois? A bad business! I hardly know how we're going to manage without him. Have you made any progress with the case?"

Jarvis hesitated. He had been trained in England, and at Scotland Yard had learned that good detectives preferred to ask questions rather than to answer them. However, Fontego wasn't England. Garland was a man of authority, a white man, a man to whom one should show all possible respect. Apart from that, he had a dominating eye.

"It's a little early to expect results," said Jarvis, swinging his cane in front of his massive thighs. "Of course, we shall get our man in time, I'm confident of that, but at the moment we're working very much in the dark."

Garland appeared surprised. "But you seem to have a fairly complete description of the man, if the papers are anything to go by."

"Only of his clothing," said Jarvis. "I'm afraid that won't help us much. The things he was wearing were a disguise that anyone could have concocted. The negro party who saw him just after the murder had all had a good deal to drink, and none of them could give any details that would help in identifying him."

"H'm," said Garland, "you *are* up against it, aren't you? I read something about two white people at a nearby table. What about them?"

Jarvis shrugged. "Even if we could find them, it's not very likely they could add much to what we already know. And, of course, it's doubtful whether we shall find them. We've no idea who they were, or even what they looked like. The only person who can remember anything about them is the waiter, and he's not much use. All he can tell us is that they both wore red masks. So did about ten thousand other people. He thinks the man was wearing a light suit and the woman a long coloured dress! Hopeless!" Jarvis gazed gloomily at the floor. To him, this business of the two white people was one of the more painful aspects of the case. It was bad enough that he should have had to draw public attention to the presence of white people in such a place; their deliberate silence was even more distressing. Not what one had a right to expect from them at all.

Garland made sympathetic noises. "What a lot of trouble Fiesta gives you!"

"Trouble!" exclaimed Jarvis. "Do you know there were seven

homicides last night? This one just happens to be the most sensational. The thing should be stopped."

"I've always rather thought so myself," agreed Garland. "I suppose there's just a chance your two witnesses may respond to your appeal?"

"I doubt it. They were evidently in a great hurry to get away. It's clear they don't want publicity."

"I suppose not," Garland smiled. "But you still think you'll get your man?"

"Oh, we'll get him," said Jarvis stoutly. "There are one or two clues, you know."

The smile faded. "I see. Well, I'm sure you'll make the most of them."

"I shall do my best, of course. There's not very much to go on. The knife that the murderer used was of a common type, and up to a point he was smart. Apparently he held it with a glove or cloth; there were no prints. Then there was the glass he was drinking out of——"

Garland's heart leaped violently. The glass! He'd forgotten the glass! His fingerprints would be all over it.

"Unfortunately," Jarvis went on in a melancholy voice, "the damned fool of a constable who was first on the scene didn't do anything about the glass, and it was taken away and mixed up with all the others."

"Ah!" Garland's tense body relaxed. "That was bad luck for you."

"These black fellows are very difficult to train," said Jarvis, stroking his brown thigh.

Garland nodded. "It's the same in all departments. So actually the clues don't amount to very much?"

"No doubt something will turn up," said Jarvis. "One of the things I wanted to see you about was this piece of paper. We found it under the body. It seems to be something to do with your department, though it's a bit difficult to read because of the bloodstains."

Garland took the paper, inwardly cursing his carelessness. He wondered how many more things he'd overlooked—and he had believed he'd made a good job of the killing! He glanced at the typescript. "Yes," he said, "it's part of a report on the typhoid epidemic." With an ironical expression he added, "One of our million or so documents."

Jarvis held out his hand for the paper. "I'd better keep it for the time being." He looked at it again with a puzzled air and remarked, "It seems odd that Dubois should have been studying a thing like that at the Blue Pool."

"He was unusually conscientious," said Garland.

"I dare say," conceded Jarvis, "but this is just a fragment, and there were no other papers on him. In any case, you'd think he'd have put it away when the other man arrived. You don't suppose he might have been discussing it with the fellow?"

"He might have been," said Garland. "It's not a secret document. But I don't see that it could have had any bearing on the murder. There's nothing controversial in it—nothing to argue or quarrel about."

"That's what I thought," said Jarvis. "In any case, there were no indications of a quarrel. Again, we've only the waiter to rely on, but he seemed to think the two men were quite amicable."

"Perhaps they drank too much," Garland suggested. "You know how quickly these stabbing quarrels flare up at Fiesta after a few *rekis*."

"They both appear to have been quite sober," said Jarvis. "No, from the information we have it looks like a carefully planned murder, for some reason that we don't know about. There seems to have been an appointment—the table was reserved by telephone in the name of Grainger. We've worked on that, but without result. I was wondering, Dr. Garland, if as Dubois' superior you know anything about his affairs that might suggest anyone's having a motive for killing him."

Garland appeared to consider, and then slowly shook his head. "He never talked to me about his private life."

"I'm thinking rather of his public life," said Jarvis. "He doesn't seem to have had a private life in the usual sense. No women that we can trace, at any rate. Most unusual. No, I wondered if you knew of anyone he'd got on bad terms with in connection with his work in the department, or outside it."

Again Garland shook his head. "Dubois had a finger in a lot of pies," he observed, "and I should think he was almost certain to have made enemies. He was ambitious, you know, and he had rivals who might have been glad to get rid of him. Any number. But as far as I know, there was nothing specific. I've never heard of any quarrel or threats or anything like that. In the department, he was always most amenable and co-operative."

Jarvis got up. "Well, I suppose the only thing to do is to go on making inquiries. I'd better talk to some of the relatives; they may know more about his affairs."

"That's possible," Garland agreed. Then he remembered that "relatives" might include Johnson Johnson, and his face became sombre.

"Anyhow," said Jarvis, "I'm very grateful for your help, Dr. Garland. You must have a lot of things on your mind today."

Garland's laugh sounded harsh in his own ears. "Yes," he said, "I have." He added tactfully, "But it'll be a bad lookout when we white people can't give each other a helping hand. Good day, Jarvis—and good luck!"

Chapter Fifteen

Mrs. Sylvester was giving her opinion of Fontego's newspapers to a group of ladies gathered under the Garlands' mango tree. "If you ask me," she said, although no one had, "they are paying far too much attention to this murder. What else do they expect to happen at Fiesta? They should be campaigning against the thing itself."

Celeste was listening with an air of lively satisfaction. She had found the telephone, after all, too arid a medium for full enjoyment of the latest sensation. It would be much more fun, she had decided, to watch people's faces during discussion of the murder. She had therefore invited for tea, besides Mrs. Sylvester, Maisie Andrews—the pretty fluffy wife of the Attorney General—Delia Smythe, a raven-haired divorceé who was at present married to a rich cocoa planter, and Susan Anstruther.

Susan said, "But Dr. Dubois was one of the hopes of the Colony. He had brains. I can understand their making a fuss—it's really quite a tragedy."

Delia Smythe made a sound that was like a snort. "I don't see that it matters to us what these black men do to each other," she said. "They're always cutting one another up on the estate. Only last week a man called Willy something lost his temper over some trifle—I dare say the rice wasn't cooked properly—and he chopped his wife's hand off with a cutlass. Nobody seemed to mind. They patched things up—the relationship, I mean, not the hand—and he visited her in the hospital and held the other hand and she forgave him."

"Yes, but this case of Eke is different," persisted Susan. "*He* wasn't the sort of man to get involved in a violent quarrel, and you can hardly class him with the labourers on your estate. It looks as though this was a civilised murder—you know what I mean—with a proper motive and everything."

"Well, I agree with Delia," said Mrs. Sylvester firmly. "Why should we bother? I don't think we ought to concern ourselves with these people's squabbles."

"They're human," said Susan.

"Oh, darling, don't exaggerate," drawled Celeste.

Susan smiled in spite of herself. It was impossible to talk seriously when Celeste was in a flippant mood.

"Anyway," Celeste proceeded, "it's not the murder that's interesting, but the people who saw it happen and didn't say anything. Isn't it a fascinating thought that there are two white people here among us in the Colony who actually watched a murder committed and perhaps even know who did it and yet daren't open their mouths for fear of scandal?"

"I'm not surprised they daren't," said Mrs. Sylvester. "I've heard that the Blue Pool during Fiesta is the absolute limit. People just don't care *what* they do there."

Celeste looked interested. "Have you been talking to someone who's been there, Marion? Do tell us what goes on."

"Don't be silly," said Mrs. Sylvester. "*You* know what a reputation the place has got as well as I do."

"It looked very dull to me, I must say," remarked Susan.

Four pairs of eyes swivelled toward her. "Susan!" cried Maisie Andrews. "You don't mean to say you were there?"

"I didn't go inside," said Susan. "It was too noisy and everyone seemed drunk."

The group relaxed. "Surely you weren't alone, Susan," said Mrs. Sylvester. "Even you couldn't be so foolish as to wander around town without an escort on Fiesta night."

"I wasn't alone," said Susan calmly. "I was showing Dr. West some of the sights."

"That must have been very nice for you both," said Celeste.

"I wish I had your nerve," sighed Maisie Andrews. "Bob would be livid if I even went near the place."

"It's different for you, Maisie," said Celeste. "The wife of the Attorney General, and all that. If *you'd* wanted to go you'd have had to dress up and pretend it wasn't you at all—the way these people did, in fact." Celeste's eyes were wide and innocent. "Were you in costume, Susan?"

Susan laughed. "I'm sorry to disappoint you, but we weren't even masked. You can't pin anything on me."

"We've only your word for it," said Delia Smythe. "You admit you were near the place."

"That shows she has a clear conscience," Maisie Andrews observed.

"Oh, I'd trust Susan anywhere," said Mrs. Sylvester. "It's just the pioneering spirit with her. She's the very best type of Empire-builder."

"Heaven forbid!" cried Susan.

"When you come to think of it," said Delia Smythe, "we've none of us any proof that we weren't there. At least, I haven't. What were you doing, Celeste?"

"Wishing I had a boy friend to take me out," said Celeste lightly. "Now if Dr. West had offered to take *me* to the Blue Pool I'd have gone like a shot."

"What a chance he missed," smiled Susan.

"Celeste's all talk," said Delia Smythe, who at least had a divorce to her credit.

"You mean I'm discreet," said Celeste.

"You hope you are," returned Delia.

"At least *I* haven't been found out," said Celeste, enjoying herself.

Delia shrugged. "It saves a lot of trouble once you are. Hiding things is a bore."

"I'm sure I could never keep a secret from Bob," said Maisie Andrews.

"He wouldn't be much of an Attorney General if you could," remarked Mrs. Sylvester.

"What I mean," floundered Maisie, "is that if I *had* been at the Blue Pool secretly with a man, and the police were looking for me afterwards, it would be so much on my mind that I should just have to blurt out the truth sooner or later."

The tyres of a car screeched as it turned into the concrete drive. "That will be Adrian," said Celeste. "I wonder if he's heard any news."

A moment later Garland approached. He knew all the women, and his informal greeting was a general acknowledgment.

"Heavens, it's hot," he exclaimed, sinking into an empty chair. "I think the rains will be early this year."

"Never mind the rains, darling," said Celeste, handing him a cup of tea. "Has the case been solved? That's what we want to know. I'm sure you've done nothing but discuss it all day."

"I've seen Jarvis," Garland admitted. "He doesn't seem to have much information. My own guess is that the murderer will get away with it."

"Isn't it a bit early to be so sure?" asked Celeste. "In this Colony someone always talks in the end. That reminds me, Maisie was just going to blurt out something as you came in."

"I wasn't going to do anything of the kind," cried Maisie indignantly. "All I said was that if I knew anything I should blurt it out. But I don't."

Celeste laughed. "We've been having a lovely time, Adrian," she said, "wondering which of us was at the Blue Pool in disguise last night. Any one of us might have been, you know. Or *all* of us. Don't you think it's a delicious thought?"

"You've got a single-track mind," said Garland good-humouredly. "You were saying the same thing when I left you this morning."

His eyes travelled round the circle. Celeste was right—it *was* a fantastic situation. Four women, and any one of them might be the secret witness who didn't want to talk. Mrs. Sylvester was a bit plump, perhaps, but the others filled the bill all right. Any one of them might at this moment be putting on the act of a lifetime, knowing that he was the murderer. It was nonsense to pretend you could tell what people were thinking from their faces—particularly women. And so it would go on, for days and weeks, wherever he moved in white circles. As long as he remained in the Colony he would be wondering. Of course, the time might come when the woman would give herself away by a word or a look. It would be very tempting for her to drop a hint during a quiet tête-à-tête, no doubt. If ever that happened, an entirely new situation would arise. He would have to make up his mind, then, what to do. He wondered if any of these women had a white and purple beach wrap. He couldn't very well ask, and there was no point in speculating—he had quite enough on his hands as it was.

He put down his cup and got up. "I think if you'll excuse me, Celeste, I'll go and freshen up. I'm getting rather tired of talking about this murder. All I know is that it's going to make things very difficult at the office. I shall be worn out before the end of the week."

"Poor darling," said Celeste, "you'll have to go fishing again. It always takes your mind off things."

Chapter Sixteen

Johnson Johnson was perched on the gunwale of *Papeete's* dinghy, trying to get the outboard motor to start. He was stripped down to a pair of khaki shorts, but the sun was fierce and his back glistened with sweat between the shoulder blades. His face wore a look of profound concentration, intended to give the impression that he knew what he was doing. As he tinkered, he hummed a little tune of his own devising.

He was feeling rather cheerful on this Saturday afternoon. On the whole it had been a most satisfactory week. He couldn't remember a Fiesta that he had enjoyed so much. He had spent the whole of the two days in one calypso hut after another, building up his store of experience by listening to the experts. What was more, he had accepted an open challenge to a calypso "duel" by the "Black Jaguar" and had held his own in the ribald personal exchanges for nearly twenty minutes. He had tasted for the first time the honey of public applause. As a result of his success he had been interviewed by a representative of a popular illustrated sheet and had had his picture in the paper. It was true that no financial offer had come his way so far, but he was hopeful. His fellow residents in Paradise Heights had no longer any doubts that they had a talented composer in their midst, and were showing greater respect than ever. Even Delta, the pretty girl who had ignored him when she was washing her hair, had at last begun to smile on him. It was all most satisfactory.

Then, apart from his professional success, there had been the stirring event of Eke's unexpected demise. Who could have hoped for two family funerals so close together? And what a funeral Eke's had been! Johnson had rubbed shoulders with quite a lot of notables and had got gloriously drunk. It had been too bad for Eke, of course, but he rather asked for it. All that self-righteous talk about working hard and making good, and then slipping off himself to watch the strip tease at the Blue Pool when he thought nobody was looking. A bit of a hypocrite, that's what Eke had been.

Johnson gazed thoughtfully at the carburettor jet and prodded it dangerously with a bit of wire. He didn't really know much about engines, but Dr. Garland knew even less, so the outboard motor was always left to him. Perhaps that was why it never seemed to go very well. Actually, he was getting very fed up with working for Dr. Garland. The Doctor was pleasant enough, but there was always something he wanted doing. If it came to that, Johnson didn't particularly want to work for anyone. Now that the interfering Eke was safely out of the way, he could try to find a job which could give him more leisure for composition.

He blew through the jet and replaced it. When he pulled the starting cord the engine miraculously sprang into life. Johnson looked up at the cabin top of *Papeete*, where Garland was peacefully smoking in the shade of a sail, and his satisfied grin invited favourable comment.

Garland watched Johnson slowly collect the tackle for the trip. They were going to try for mackerel a couple of miles off-shore. The surf was beating steadily at the mouth of the lagoon, but there was almost no wind, and from the cabin top the open sea looked calm and inviting.

For him it had been a worrying week. Although things had seemed to be going all right, the possibility of an awkward development had been constantly in his mind. At the moment, he felt much better. For one thing, he had heard that Superintendent Jarvis had made no progress at all and had virtually dropped the case. Dubois' death would soon be forgotten. For another, he now had Johnson under his eye. Happily, Jarvis hadn't considered Johnson an important enough person to be talked to. Now it was too late; he'd missed his chance.

After the carefully planned murder of Dubois, dealing with

Johnson was going to be comparatively simple. There would be a straightforward accident. No one would suspect for a moment that a man like Garland could have the slightest reason for killing a fellow like Johnson. And no one would care. Anyway, Johnson wasn't like Dubois—he was a nobody. By to-morrow Garland's affairs should be tidy and secure. The future seemed promising. Celeste had been noticeably more forthcoming during the past day or two—it must be the result of the promised trip to Honolulu. They ought to have a good time there; it could be perfect if Celeste decided to be nice. And there really wasn't any reason why they shouldn't continue to enjoy themselves. Once all the dangers were out of the way, he could announce his retirement and he and Celeste could make whatever plans they pleased. By to-morrow, the only cloud on the horizon would be the thought of the unknown woman at the Blue Pool—and that would disperse with time.

He felt a sudden impatience to be finished with Johnson. Leaning across the cabin top he said, "Are you going to be long, Johnson? We ought to be starting."

"Jes' ready, sah," cried Johnson. He started the motor again and brought the dinghy alongside. Garland dropped down into it, looking carefully around to make sure that Johnson's preparations had been thorough. It was important, just in case of inquiries, that everything should be precisely as it would have been for an innocent fishing expedition. Tackle, oars, bailing tin, spare petrol—yes, everything seemed to be in order. His eye dwelt on the soft plank amidships. The dinghy was really very old—hardly fit to take out in fact. That, of course, was the reason he had put in an order for a new one that very week!

He settled himself comfortably in the bows. Johnson, seeing that his master was in an equable temper, was all smiles. A good-natured fellow, Johnson, thought Garland. Lazy, but willing. If he hadn't babbled about things that didn't concern him he'd have been all right.

Garland suddenly felt he would like to make quite sure that Johnson *had* babbled. It would be a pity to take life unnecessarily. Besides, if it hadn't been Johnson it must have been someone else, and it was important to get the right man. As soon as the little boat was safely through the line of surf and into open water Garland said, "Have you been sleeping in that mango tree lately, Johnson?"

The black boy grinned. "Ah nah bin neer de tree, sah, nah fo' long times, an' dat's de troof ah's tellin' yo."

"Were you in the tree when Mr. Rawlins talked to me about Tacri?"

Johnson looked a little shamefaced. "Ah bin heer yo tark 'bout dat place long time 'go," he admitted.

Garland nodded grimly. "That's what I thought. Did you hear anything interesting?"

Johnson wriggled uncomfortably. He would have preferred not to talk about it, but at least Dr. Garland didn't seem at all angry so perhaps it was all right. He said, with a gleam of teeth, "Ah bin heer de mans say 'e give yo fifty tousand pound."

"And you told Eke?"

Johnson avoided the direct stare. "Eke say ah nah fo' tark 'bout de Australy mans."

"What made you tell Eke?"

"Eke say ah damn fool nigger an' don't know nuffin."

"I see. I suppose you've told a lot of people?"

"Oh, no, sah." Johnson shook his head vigorously. "No, sah, ah bin keep me mout shet al de times. Ah nah go fo' to tell anyones 'bout dat, nebber."

"No," said Garland thoughtfully, "I don't think you will."

For a few minutes there was silence except for the spluttering engine. Garland was thinking what a simple soul Johnson was. There was no malice in him at all—it was a shame to have to drown him. He obviously had no idea of the significance of what he knew. Still, it simply wouldn't be safe to let him live.

"Have you done any swimming lately, Johnson?" he asked presently.

"No, sah, ah bin workin' al de times in de garden."

"Do you think you could swim to the shore from here?"

Johnson glanced across at the palm-fringed coast line and smiled. "No, sah, ah drown ef ah tries."

"H'm," said Garland. The fellow clearly had no inkling of his danger. "Well, I think we might put a line out now."

He watched Johnson attach the silver spoon as bait and stream the mackerel line overboard. They were alone on the sea, and they must be nearly a mile from land. It wouldn't do to go too far—a mile should be about right. He trailed his hand for a moment in the warm water and glanced up at the cloudless sky. A lovely day for a long swim!

Johnson was busying himself with the second line, and on his face was the absorbed look of a child. He was humming again, quietly. It would be rather *like* drowning a child. Garland forced himself to think of his own danger. He really had no choice—it was his own life or Johnson's. Abruptly he stood up in the boat, seized an oar, and stabbed with all his strength at the soft plank. At the second blow the oar handle went clean through the rotten wood, and as he pulled it back the sea came gushing in.

Johnson turned at the sound, and his mouth fell open. He stared with round frightened eyes at the bubbling fountain, and at Garland with the oar. Then he gave a yell and scrambled forward to try to plug the hole. Garland shoved him back on to the stern seat with his foot. The dinghy was settling. Johnson, gibbering with fear, grabbed the bailer from under this seat and began to scoop the water overboard.

"It's no use, Johnson," said Garland. "You'll have to try to swim."

The boat was filling. Johnson stopped bailing and began to moan and rock himself. "Why you do dis, sah?" he asked pathetically.

Garland didn't answer. The motor coughed and died, the bows of the dinghy dipped, and the two men were in the sea. Garland, peering down into the translucent water, watched the boat's long slow dive until it was finally lost in the depths. That was that. It would never be recovered. All the evidence had gone.

He looked around for Johnson, who had got hold of a floating oar and was swimming fairly well a few yards away, his popping eyes straining for the land. Garland called out, "Keep it up, Johnson, it's not far to the shore." He didn't want Johnson to drown too soon.

Garland was swimming easily, comfortably. In water as warm as this, and as quiet, a mile was nothing of a swim ... A tendril of weed, winding itself round his legs, reminded him that there were other dangers. Spanish men o' war—big stinging jellyfish that left a rash on a man's body like the weals of a cat-o'-nine-tails. And barracudas, too, that could nip off a limb as neatly as a shark and couldn't be frightened away by splashing. It was rumoured that there were some around these coasts. Somehow the thought restored Garland's self-respect. He was running something of a risk himself. At the same time, these natural hazards increased his ultimate safety if he survived them. It would be argued—if the matter ever came up, which it wouldn't—that no man in his senses would scuttle a boat in such waters.

They had covered a hundred yards or so. Johnson was puffing a lot and lashing out with his legs in a way that would soon use up his strength, but the oar was giving him buoyancy. Too much buoyancy. Garland swam up to him and with a sharp jerk snatched the oar away and swam with it out of reach. Johnson looked at him piteously. What had happened was altogether too much for Johnson. He didn't understand. All he could think of, as he beat at the water with quick in-effectual strokes, was that the land seemed very far away and that he didn't want to drown.

Garland began to wonder if he had underrated Johnson. These black fellows had remarkable staying power. Johnson was a little man, puny beside Garland, but he was certainly clinging to life. They must be nearly halfway to the shore— they were getting too close for safety. Johnson might just make it. He was in difficulties, but he might just make it. His difficulties must be increased.

"I'll give you a hand," called Garland and once more swam toward Johnson. The Negro didn't trust him any more and tried desperately to fight him off. Garland put a large heavy hand on the wet mop of hair and pushed the head under water. Johnson kicked violently, there was a stream of bubbles, and the head bobbed up with an agonised gasp. Garland gripped a handful of hair and pushed the head down again. The wildly thrashing body suddenly went limp. Garland turned it on its back, put a hand on either side of the grey face, and began swimming toward the shore again. He swam in a life-saving position, but Johnson's face was under water all the time.

Ten minutes later Garland thankfully felt sandy ground beneath his feet. That last effort had exhausted even his great energy, and he could barely drag Johnson's body out of the surf. At the edge of the water he made sure that the Negro was quite dead. For the sake of appearances, in case anyone should be near enough to see, he made a formal attempt at artificial respiration. Then he staggered up the beach toward the palms, shouting and waving his arms.

Chapter Seventeen

Celeste was lying in the swing seat, watching with a faraway look in her eyes the stately descent of an incoming airliner, when Salacity came bouncing out into the garden and proudly presented the *Fontego Gazette.*

"Al de paper say Massa Garlan' good good man, jes like yo tell me," she announced a little breathlessly.

Celeste took the paper and scanned the headlines. "Coroner Praises Doctor Garland," she read. "Heroic Rescue Attempt."

She skimmed quickly through the opening paragraph: "A verdict of death by misadventure was returned at the inquest on Johnson Johnson, 28, of Paradise Heights . . . ," and turned with an air of concentration to the account of the evidence which she had heard her husband give in court that morning.

Dr. Adrian Garland, in evidence, said that he and Johnson had been out fishing in the dinghy on several occasions prior to the tragedy. On Saturday afternoon they planned to fish for mackerel a mile off-shore.

"Everything went quite smoothly at first," Dr. Garland said. "We had streamed a couple of lines and suddenly we got a bite. I don't know what it was, but it was something much bigger than a mackerel. I saw that Johnson was having trouble with it so I got up from the bows to help him haul in. The dinghy gave a lurch and I lost my balance and fell rather heavily. I wasn't hurt—I thought nothing of it at the time. I scrambled up and went to assist Johnson. Whatever there was on the hook got away after a bit of a struggle. When I looked round I saw to my horror that the dinghy was making water fast."

The Coroner: "You hadn't noticed it leaking before?" "It had been leaking a little, though not seriously. It was an old boat—in fact I had been a bit worried about a bad plank, and I had ordered a new dinghy only last week. I suppose the boat must have been holed when I fell. I shouted to Johnson to steer for the shore while I bailed, and I tried to plug the leak with a handkerchief but the water rose very quickly and in a few minutes the dinghy filled and went down under us. Johnson was clinging to an oar, but after a while he let go of it as he found it was impeding his swimming, and we struck out together for the shore. He wasn't a very strong swimmer and very soon I had to support him. I think we might have reached the beach safely, but unfortunately the poor fellow got into a panic as he felt his strength failing, and struggled so wildly that both of us became exhausted. I did my best, but I'm sorry to say my best wasn't good enough. By the time I reached the shore with him he was dead."

The Coroner: "Did you try to revive him?"

"Naturally. I applied artificial respiration, but he showed no sign of life. I was too tired myself to do much good, so I went up the beach for help and after a little while I found some labourers. I brought them back and under my direction another effort was made to revive him. We worked for nearly an hour before giving up."

After the verdict of misadventure had been returned, the Coroner complimented Dr. Garland on his behaviour. He had evidently done everything in his power to save his weaker companion and had stuck by him and assisted him even when his own strength was exhausted. His loyalty might well have cost him his own life. The whole Colony would rejoice that Dr. Garland had been spared to continue his unremitting efforts to improve conditions in Fontego.

As Dr. Garland left the court he was warmly applauded by the large crowd which had gathered.

After the inquest, Dr. Garland told our reporter, "I am very deeply shocked by the accident. Johnson Johnson was a good companion and a loyal servant and I shall miss him. I cannot help feeling some responsibility."

Celeste put down the paper and lay for a long time very still, thinking.

Chapter Eighteen

The month of May was drawing to a close, and Fontego was parched. For more than twenty weeks no drop of rain had fallen. Under its layer of fine dust the ground was baked. The last of the sugar cane had been reaped and carted, and the stubbly fields were brown. So was the coarse-leaved grass. The leaves on the citrus trees were beginning to wilt as the merciless heat burned down to the roots. Even the fronds of the coco-nut palms seemed to droop. The "bush" had become a crackle underfoot, and fires a constant menace. At the bottom of gullies and riverbeds the dry mud was deeply fissured. In Fontego City the scorched pavements hurled the heat back to the brassy sky and people loitered, gasping, in the shade. The Colony's reservoirs, always inadequate, had fallen so low that many taps and standpipes yielded no more than a trickle of heavily chlorinated water.

That was in the morning of this day, but the climacteric had been reached. The brooding stillness presaged storm. In the thirsty countryside, where the earth looked dead and the animals desiccated, the knowing peasants had their eyes on the eastern sky over beyond Tacri. They were wondering just when the storm would break, and how fierce it would be, and how soon afterwards they would be able to start work in the rice fields.

Just before noon, banks of lurid cloud came sweeping up out of the sea, black and red and green, and shot with lightning. For a while the water took on a leaden hue. Then the wind came roaring over the Colony—less than a hurricane, but not much less. The palms bent on the shore, their fronds streaming out like blown hair. In exposed places, trees and telegraph poles were snapped off short. The air became thick with flying objects—leaves and vegetation and tiles and thatch, and even sheets of galvanised iron torn from the roofs of rickety shacks. Great waves came sweeping into Fontego's inadequate harbour and many small boats were broken up. Over in Darwin Bay the *Papeete* was carried up under the palms by a small tidal wave and left high and dry above the beach.

With the wind came the rain. First there were a few huge premonitory gusts, and then the heavens opened and the water came down in a continuous beating stream, as though a giant bowl had been overturned above the earth. The din was so great that even indoors it was barely possible to converse. Outside, all traffic stood where it had been caught, and every living thing sought shelter. At first the roads and pavements steamed and sizzled, but presently, as the overloaded drains failed to carry off the surface water, floods covered the lower parts of the town to a depth of several feet, and every street became a rushing foaming torrent. Outside the town, down every old dried watercourse, red and yellow floods tore their way, carrying before them half a year's accumulated deposit of vegetation and refuse. Down every inhabited hillside water streamed in cascading sheets, washing away foundations, giving old shacks a new tilt, and applying to others the last destructive touch. Riverbeds filled to the brim and beyond in a matter of minutes, and unleashed torrents hurled themselves upon decrepit bridges and broke them up. One of the first to go was the temporary bridge over the Silver River. High mountain roads were undermined and became impassable as great walls of eroded earth slipped fifty or a hundred feet.

For three hours Fontego cowered and Nature did her worst. Three hours of shattering rain and tempest, of cracking thunder and splitting lightning. Then, as suddenly as they had formed, the clouds broke and passed for the day. Life began again. To-morrow, probably, and on many to-morrows, the rain would return, but in the meantime hot sunshine was breaking through the humid air. The waters abated in the streets and the people emerged from their shelters and went about their business. The pavements steamed again and quickly dried. Cleaners came out to clear away some of the mud and mess and litter. The Office of Works was already gathering damage reports from all over the Colony. The tenants of the hundreds of damaged shacks were beginning to prop and repair, talking without bitterness of this first storm of the season, which had been one of the heaviest in Fontegan memory. Out in the country, peasants strolled barefooted between the reeking verges of the roads, stopping to chatter happily beside the placid pools where green rice would soon be springing.

Everywhere men sweated and sweated in the close moist air.

Chapter Nineteen

Little Miss Chang was sorting Dr. Garland's mail when the door of the outer office was flung open with a vigour that set the flimsy partitions rattling, and Martin West strode in.

"Good morning, Dr. West," she said. Her impassive face rarely registered surprise, but she looked mildly interested when she saw that his clothes were damp and stained and his hair tousled. "We weren't expecting you this morning. Is anything wrong?"

Martin said curtly, "Is Dr. Garland alone?"

"Yes," said Miss Chang, "but——"

Martin pushed open Garland's door unceremoniously and plunged in. Directly Garland saw who it was he sensed trouble. The leprosarium—always the leprosarium! Why couldn't he be allowed to forget it?

"Hello, West," he said in a voice that held no shade of welcome. "What on earth are you doing here so early?"

"I'm paying a personal visit because there's no telephone on that damned island," said Martin grimly. "I've some bad news for you."

"Oh!" Garland braced himself. "You'd better sit down. Well, what's happened?"

"Tacri was almost washed away yesterday afternoon."

"I dare say," said Garland. "So was Fontego." Relief made him sound almost amiable.

"Two patients were drowned," went on Martin in the same grim tone. "Bed patients. They were swept into the sea."

"Good God!" exclaimed Garland. "That certainly is bad news. How did it happen? Wasn't there anyone in charge?"

Martin made an obvious effort to speak calmly. "*I* was in charge.

I don't think you quite realise what conditions were like. It rained so hard for two hours that water poured down that rock face like a small Niagara. What with the rain and the wind it was almost impossible to move. You've no conception."

"Was there much damage?" asked Garland in a serious tone.

"The male infirmary was washed off its foundations—that's where the two drowned men were—and it's now lying on the slope of the hill at an angle of forty-five degrees, smashed up. It's a miracle more people weren't killed. Two of the residential huts were undermined and we've had to evacuate them. Several of the latrines have been blown to blazes, and one of the kitchens is unusable. They're the major items, but the fact is that the whole place is in chaos. I'd have come yesterday, but I couldn't leave Mortimer until we'd cleared up a bit. We need help badly."

"Of course, my dear fellow," agreed Garland. Now that he realised the extent of the disaster his attitude had changed. "You must have had a dreadful time. What would you like me to do? What do you need? Shall I come out there?"

Martin thought of the tired attendants, the tangles of wreckage, the neglected patients. It was difficult to know where to begin. "We need a working party of labourers," he said, "to start repairs and clean things up as far as possible—and at least three additional attendants to lend a hand until we get straight. If we ever do."

"Of course you will," said Garland. "Heavens, man, you mustn't get dispirited over a storm. It's bad luck, but it was an act of God and couldn't be helped."

Martin's smouldering anger flamed. "It wasn't an act of God and it could have been helped," he said savagely. "You know that as well as I do. The place isn't fit for the job, as I told you before. If you'd seen crippled bed cases trying to crawl out of an overturned hut on their stumps, shouting and yelling and sliding about in the mud with all hell loose, you'd agree with me. It's a disgrace that they should be there, a damned disgrace!"

Garland watched him with an anxiety he tried to hide. "We can hardly reopen the debate on policy at a moment like this. How big a working party do you think you'll need?"

126

"Ten men at least," said Martin. "Chaps who can turn their hands to pretty well anything. And we'll need a big launch right away. I'll have to evacuate twenty-five cases to the mainland this afternoon."

Garland, his hand already on the telephone to call the Office of Works, dropped the receiver as though it were hot. "Why?" he asked sharply.

"I told you—we've no male infirmary now. There are twelve bed cases in very bad shape, and we may have some more deaths if they don't get proper attention. There are another dozen that we can't possibly accommodate with two huts out of commission. As a matter of fact, the whole place should be evacuated. That's my recommendation, and I'll put it in writing. There may be another storm. If there is, I'll do my best, but I want to make it quite clear that in my view we're not justified in taking the risk."

"I will take full responsibility," said Garland. Great dangers had suddenly leapt into view. It was bad enough that the story of the disaster would probably leak out and receive unwelcome publicity. If, in addition, large numbers of patients were evacuated, the whole Tacri scheme would be jeopardised. It would be an official admission of the unsuitability of Tacri. People would ask what was the use of developing a place that might continue to be dangerous. Of course, the contract was signed; the contractors couldn't lose, and his money was safe. But the very last thing he wanted was to have the whole Tacri project re-examined.

Martin was pressing his demand. "Whatever you do about a general evacuation," he said, "I'll have to have those twenty-five patients out. That's the minimum."

"I think we must try to keep our heads," said Garland. "In my view it would be much better to make temporary arrangements on the spot. We'll send out some beds and equipment and you can put the displaced people in the administrative offices for the time being."

"We can't handle them," repeated Martin firmly. "You've no idea of the disruption."

"I'm afraid you'll have to try," said Garland. "I'm sorry, but we can't have them here. As for the bed cases——"

"Well?" asked Martin, with a dangerous glint in his eye.

Garland gave a little shrug. "You've got Mortimer to help you now. You ought to be able to manage. I would suggest clearing one of the residential huts for a temporary infirmary and doubling up somewhere else."

Martin stared at Garland incredulously. "You can't mean that," he said. "As the medical officer in charge, I'm telling you it's beyond the present capacity of the leprosarium to give those twelve patients the attention they need. Surely that's a matter on which you must accept my judgment."

"You're a little shaken," said Garland, "quite understandably, of course. For the moment I think a cooler judgment is required."

"But——" Martin began. He was almost speechless with indignation. "Why, your attitude's unbelievable. I tell you again, these patients need help that we can't give them. They *must* come here. You don't want to murder them, do you?"

Garland's eyes had a frosty gleam. "Your choice of words is extreme. Once and for all, I am not going to have a panic evacuation from Tacri. Do you understand, that's final! Perhaps these twelve can be brought over in a few days, when the excitement has died down. Anyhow, that's my decision. Now perhaps we can get on with the arrangements."

Martin's chin went up. "I can't accept your decision. It astounds me. I don't understand your motives—that's your affair—but I feel obliged to tell you that I regard your attitude as unprofessional and damnably inhuman."

A dark flush rose in Garland's face. "I won't have you talk like that, West, do you hear? Who do you think you're speaking to? If you can't observe a little discipline, I shall know what steps to take."

"You can take what steps you damn well like," cried Martin. "I'm not intimidated. You leave me no alternative but to take the matter to the Colonial Secretary, and that's what I propose to do—right now."

"I forbid you to do anything of the sort."

Martin got up. "I'm afraid you're not the judge of men that I thought you were."

Garland strode across the room and faced him, massive and formidable, his cold eyes full of menace. "You'll do as you're told, West, or live to regret it. Nobody has ever defied me in this department."

"Then it's time someone began," said Martin. He gave his chief a searching look. "Frankly, I think you must be ill," he added, and turned to go.

Garland fought with self-control. Surging anger struggled with common sense. He realised that he'd been a fool to behave in such a high-handed manner. He'd dealt too long with black men. He was bludgeoning where he ought to be subtle. He must be losing his grip. He couldn't possibly let this fellow go to Anstruther.

"Wait a moment, West," he called. "Perhaps I was a little hasty. Come and sit down."

Martin, puzzled, returned slowly to his chair.

"As a matter of fact, you're quite right," said Garland, dabbing at his face and neck with a handkerchief. "I *am* feeling the strain of this job a bit. I apologise."

"Oh, that's all right," murmured Martin uncomfortably. "I'm afraid I lost my temper too."

"We'll send a launch out this afternoon," said Garland, "and bring your patients back right away. They can go in one of the old army huts behind the workhouse."

Martin listened silently, wondering at Garland's sudden change of attitude.

"I'll tell Anstruther what's happened," Garland went on, "and what we're doing about it. You get back to Tacri and hold the fort, and I'll have the working party there by tea-time. We'll have a bit of trouble getting attendants at short notice, but I'll scrape them up from somewhere. You can leave the whole thing in my hands. I'll come out myself tomorrow, and we'll go over the place together. Of course, you realise that an incident of this kind couldn't happen once Tacri is rebuilt?"

"If it ever is," said Martin. "Most of the timber which was delivered is now floating in the Bay. The cement was dumped in the open and is probably useless. And the machinery for the new laundry is beginning to rust."

"That's bad," said Garland. "Still, it's the contractor's concern." He accompanied Martin to the door, quite affable now. "I hope," he said, "we shall manage to avoid any sensational publicity about this affair. The press will leap on the incident if it gets the chance, and that won't do the department or the leprosarium any good. *Or* the patients, for that matter. I'll see that a brief statement goes out through the Information Office, and beyond that the less we say the better."

Martin smiled wryly. "I don't suppose anyone will come out to interview me on Tacri. I'll see you to-morrow, then."

Garland nodded, and closed the door after him. Alone, his affable expression faded. West had had his own way. He was a tough customer, in spite of his youth. And persistent. Always bringing up this question of Tacri. Never really accepting the situation. Still, this misfortune on the island would soon be forgotten; they'd get the mess cleared up quickly, and the bed patients could be sent back there as soon as a new hut had been put up. All the same, it was disturbing. And just when it seemed that everything was going smoothly at last. West's remarks had been innocent enough—they must have been, but all the same there had been one or two that Garland hadn't liked at all. "I don't understand your motives——" —that had jarred. It would be a pretty dangerous thing if West started delving. Dangerous for West.

Chapter Twenty

Three weeks had passed since the great storm. Martin, feeling the need for relaxation after many arduous days, was sitting beside Susan in her speeding Lagonda. It was to be a busman's holiday for him, for they were on their way to join the field party on the Spencers' estate: Garland's rural health drive had begun. Martin had been glad to accept the Health Secretary's invitation to take part, for he wanted to see how such a campaign was organised in local conditions so that later on he might use similar machinery for a leprosy survey. Susan, always eager to learn something new, had offered her services as housekeeper to the party, and Garland had readily agreed. He would have preferred to have his wife along, but Celeste couldn't bear the moist heat of the cocoa plantations and had shown no disposition to accompany him.

It was still early morning, and the clouds had not yet begun to mass for the customary midday downpour. The air was as hot and humid as the inside of a greenhouse, but it blew exhilaratingly enough past the open sports car. In spite of a considerable load of cares, Martin felt extremely cheerful. He enjoyed being with Susan. He hadn't seen much of her—not nearly as much as he would have liked—but since his stay at the Anstruther home over Fiesta he had taken to dropping in whenever he was on an official visit to the mainland, and he and Susan had fallen into an easy comradeship. Martin admired the competent way she ran her father's house, becoming neither submerged in domesticity nor confined by the narrow social life of the town. She had an independent character and a lively ranging mind. Her interests were far broader and more varied than those of most of the women he had met—and yet no one, he reflected, could look more feminine and attractive than Susan. No matter how much she rushed about, she was always well-groomed and cool. He wondered if his desire for her good opinion meant that he was falling in love with her.

Conversation was intermittent. Occasionally Susan would draw his attention to something she particularly wanted him to see, but the rush of air and the beat of the powerful engine made talking difficult. Martin was well content to sit beside her, soothed by a pleasant sense of companionship, and gaze out on the sights of a new country. This was the first time he had been outside Fontego City, and everything he saw was fascinating.

Susan negotiated one of the road's infrequent bends and slowed as a road block came into view. "That must be for the broken bridge," she said, turning off to the left along a minor road in obedience to the "Diversion" sign. "It's really too bad the way nobody does anything here until it's too late. Sylvester might have known it would fall down when the rains came. He was warned often enough." She swung the car on to a level patch of grass beside a creaking bamboo. "What about a nice long drink?"

"Good idea," said Martin. "I never say no to that." He leaned over and handed Susan the picnic basket from the back. "I think you've been maligned," he remarked. "You're not nearly as reckless a driver as I'd been led to expect. How is your hand, by the way?"

Susan looked at the unsightly cross of sticking plaster. "It's been giving a bit of trouble, actually, but I think it will be all right soon. Cuts don't heal very well in this heat, I don't know why."

From the hamper she produced sandwiches and a large vacuum flask of iced lime-squash. Martin drank deep and gave a sigh of enjoyment. "Marvellous!" he said. "Wonderful stuff!" He put the glass down and took a sandwich. "You know, I was afraid I was going to miss this trip."

"It didn't look very promising for you after the storm, did it? How are things at Tacri now? How's Mortimer shaping?"

"Oh, he's all right as long as the place is running smoothly. It's a great relief to have him."

"Have you repaired all the damage?"

"More or less. I must hand it to Garland—he can certainly get things done when he wants to. He managed to lay hands on a really good foreman for the working party, and he came out himself three times to make sure that they weren't slacking. I've never known such zeal. They ran up a new infirmary in eight days; an inadequate place, of course, but it holds the beds."

"What happened about the evacuees?"

"One of them died, but I think he would have done so anyway. The rest have gone back."

Susan regarded him thoughtfully. "You're not very happy in your new job, are you?"

Martin sighed. "No," he admitted. "It's no use pretending I am. To tell you the truth, Susan, I don't know what to do about it. It may sound feeble to you, I'm afraid, but I've a very good mind to resign."

"As bad as that? Did the storm make all that difference?"

"Good Lord, no, not the storm. I'm prepared to believe that that was a freak. It's simply that I can't see the faintest hope of ever being able to do any decent work there. I don't mind difficulties provided there's a chance to grapple with them, but on Tacri there's no chance. I wasn't exaggerating when I said it was a hopeless place. Imagine how you'd feel if, you were asked to make a comfortable home at the bottom of a coal-mine. Well, that's roughly how I feel about Tacri. There are some things that just don't make sense and Tacri's one of them. I chafe the whole time. I have a picture in my mind of the job I might be doing on the mainland, and I can't persuade myself that it's a dream. God, how I loathe that rock!"

"It *is* a shame," said Susan.

"I suppose I ought to have made a greater fuss to start with," said Martin, lighting a cigarette, "but when you're new to a job you don't like starting off with a thundering row. All the same, I believe now that it was a mistake even to give the place a trial."

"Was it Daddy who persuaded you?"

"No, I wouldn't say that. There didn't seem to be any real alternative at the time. That's probably still true. Think what it would mean if I really kicked over the traces. Virtually, I should have to present an ultimatum: 'Close down Tacri or I go.' Well, what happens then? Look at it from the Colony's point of view. To cancel the contract would mean paying out a tremendous sum of money to the contractors in compensation, for absolutely no return. Garland would fight tooth and nail to save the scheme, and nobody else seems to care. I think he'd win."

"Nobody else knows much," said Susan. "You'd have to tell them all about it."

Martin gave a little, smile. "I told your father, and, with all respect, he was for the path of least resistance."

"Oh, I know he's easy-going," said Susan. "He's a moderate, a conciliator. He doesn't like rows, and anyway it's his job to smooth them out. But he isn't a bit happy about Tacri. If a row started in a really big way, if it was unavoidable, I'm sure he'd be on your side."

"It would have to be in a big way to be worth while. But, Susan, it's not my line of country. I'm a doctor, not an agitator. And that's not all. I'm a civil servant, and etiquette is strict. I can't move except through the usual channels, and you know what that means. A memorandum to Garland, passed on very reluctantly to your father, possibly passed on by your father to H.E., possibly referred by H.E. to the Colonial Office, and there almost certainly stuck in a pigeonhole. My resignation would be accepted with regret, a stooge would be appointed instead, and Tacri would go on. Don't think I'm scared about resigning; I think it'll come to that anyway. I'm just not convinced that it'll do any good to make a fuss. And yet—I don't know."

"I think you'll have to," said Susan. "If what you've been saying all along about Tacri is right, then someone will have to, one day. It might just as well be you; you've got the urge. Why not draft a memorandum, anyway—you'll feel better when you've written it all down, even if it doesn't get you very far."

"Will you read it?"

"Of course, if you'd like me to. Do you feel you need support?"

Martin nodded. "I do, as a matter of fact. I'm rather isolated on Tacri, you know. There's not much opportunity to make friends and influence people! You're right, Susan—it *will* be a relief to write it down. Garland will be furious, of course. He's got the devil of a temper."

"So I've heard," said Susan. "He's always very polite to me."

Martin laughed. "That's no great strain."

"Ah, but with him it's a politeness of indifference. He's so blinded by Celeste that all other women look like coconut palms to him. I don't blame him—she *is* rather dazzling. Anyway, how are you getting on with him?"

Martin hesitated. "Ought I to talk to you about him?"

"Oh, don't be so official. I promise not to chatter to Daddy."

Martin regarded her dubiously. "You're sure? It wouldn't do, you know. Well—I think he's pretty odd."

"Is that so?" said Susan dryly. "Now I have a complete picture." They both laughed. "What exactly do you mean by odd?"

"He strikes me as a bit of a Jekyll and Hyde."

"Isn't that rather melodramatic?"

"No, that's my considered view. One side of him is admirable. He's the quietly efficient administrator, doing a socially useful job with great zeal and not sparing himself. But there's another side to him that you probably wouldn't know about. When Tacri was hit by that storm, he flatly refused to evacuate the battered bed cases until I threatened to appeal to your father. He was afraid it would undermine public faith in the reconstruction scheme. He seems to have a positive bee in his bonnet about that scheme."

Susan looked puzzled. "But I thought those patients were hurt and couldn't be treated on the island."

"So they were—that's just the point. I've never been more staggered in my life. I was making a proposal that was so obviously necessary it just couldn't be argued about, and he flew into a fearful rage about it. Honestly, he was quite prepared to let them stay on Tacri whether they could be treated or not. I can still hardly believe I didn't dream it."

"He has a reputation for toughness, of course," said Susan, "but I've always put it down to his desire to get on with the good works. This sounds like sabotage. I'm very surprised."

"It was outrageous," said Martin. "I can still get angry about it. I told him I thought his conduct was unprofessional, and he looked as though he was going to assault me. He was as near losing all control as I want to see him. I suppose the fact is he's backed this Tacri scheme a hundred per cent and thinks that if anything happens to it now his prestige will suffer. That's natural enough, but you'd think that where lives were at stake he'd put his pride in his pocket. I was very shocked. Then, just as I was going to walk over to your father's office, he suddenly gave in completely. He became Dr. Jekyll again and was as amiable as could be. If that isn't odd, I don't know what is."

Susan was still dubious. "I can't help thinking," she said, "that perhaps he didn't realise just how ill those people were. He may have thought you were trying to make decisions that were really his to make. He hates anyone to oppose or disagree with him. Daddy's often found that. If he feels he's being pushed he digs his toes in and won't budge."

"He budged this time, anyhow," said Martin grimly. "Complete surrender—and that was almost as odd as the rest of his behaviour. He said he was tired and overworked."

Susan raised her eyebrows at that. "Garland admitted being tired? Well!"

"That's what he said. We had a rather embarrassing reconciliation after that; I felt he'd put me at a disadvantage by more or less appealing to my sympathy. I'd arrived at the department more than half inclined to make the storm the ground for a real showdown, but when he gave way on the evacuation I let the opportunity go by. He's quite disarming when he's friendly."

"Oh, well," said Susan in a lighter vein, "it's just as well you made it up. Otherwise he wouldn't have asked you to come on this trip."

"Would you have minded?" asked Martin recklessly.

Susan stubbed out her cigarette and pressed the starter. "I'm sure it will be an invaluable experience for you professionally," she said, "and there's a splendid beach for swimming." She gave him a mischievous look. "Or perhaps you fish?"

Chapter Twenty-one

The district chosen by Garland for the special health drive was a remote rural area known as Fontenoy, with a total population of about eight hundred people scattered around the single village of Faux. The only access to the district was along twelve miles of tertiary road which snaked its way through dense "bush" and was studded with deep potholes along its whole length. No one ever traversed that road for pleasure. The people of Fontenoy almost all got their living—such as it was—from agriculture. In narrow valleys between the low hills they worked on plantations of citrus and cocoa and tapped the rubber trees when the price was sufficiently high. A few of them fished, but without enthusiasm, for the market was a long way off and the sea was treacherous. They lived in huts of the most primitive pattern but were not conscious of lacking modern amenities, except perhaps a reliable water supply in the dry season. Possibly because they had so little contact with the outside world, they dwelt together in complete amity. There were two very modest churches, but the main external influence in their lives was the school—a tiny broken-down building in charge of a Negro headmaster who rose above all his material difficulties and enjoyed the trust and affection of the whole community.

Partly, but not entirely, because of its remoteness, Fontenoy had been barely touched by public health measures. Very occasionally a divisional medical officer or a district nurse would bicycle laboriously to Faux, but the visits were too infrequent to have much effect. The village midwife, kindly but unskilled, attended all the births; one or other of the parsons attended all the deaths. Between birth and death, Nature took her course. Disease flourished because no one did anything about it. It was something that had to be borne with fortitude, like the storms that blew in from the sea. The health record of Fontenoy was blotted by malaria, hookworm, yaws, syphilis and gonorrhoea, tuberculosis and tropical ulcers, scabies and head lice, malnutrition and anaemia and bad teeth. In other respects, as a Colonial Report might say, it was satisfactory.

Garland had singled the place out, not because there was any reason to suppose that its health was very much worse than that of many other rural areas, but because of its isolation. It was the perfect spot for a test-tube experiment. Here, in a week or two of intensive effort, it should be possible to examine everyone, to let no one at all slip through the net. Here, a survey could be complete and treatment thorough. At one time Garland would have hoped that dramatic results achieved in this one district would pave the way for more generous expenditure and an extension of effort to other parts of the Colony. Now, his interest was narrower. He had the single-minded curiosity of the research worker; he simply wanted to know what would happen if the knowledge and drugs available to modern science were suddenly applied to a closed, disease-ridden community. Or rather, he wanted to *see* what would happen; he wanted to observe the miracle. Though his mind had been increasingly occupied with personal anxieties in recent weeks, there was still a compartment of thought and concentration set aside for this campaign. It might well be his last major activity in Fontego, his final achievement; its lessons might be wasted by his successors; but he would still carry it through with conscientious efficiency because he was technically interested and could work in no other way.

The task of organisation was already far advanced. By the time Susan and Martin arrived on the scene the field crew were well established in the Spencers' house. In addition to Garland himself there were two medical officers, a ward sister and a couple of nurses, a medical orderly, a follow-up worker, and a driver. Garland believed in concentrating his forces, and the personnel was hand-picked and spoiling for the engagement. The old house made an excellent headquarters. It was a large square wooden building, lavishly equipped by a wealthy planter in the heyday of cocoa, but now showing signs of age and depleted family fortunes. At its centre was a vast sitting-and-dining room, opening at one end on to a veranda. Around the other three sides numerous bedroom were arranged, opening in their turn upon another veranda. The place was somewhat gloomy, especially when the daily storm clouds gathered; and the "bush" seemed to be brooding over it and pressing in on it, as it had invaded and crushed and overgrown so many other famous houses in the past century. Still, the building had survived and was hospitable—a monument to an almost forgotten age when a shilling was a good day's pay for a labourer and planters carried whips.

It took Susan only a short time to get the domestic side of the enterprise running smoothly, for the Spencer's had left plenty of servants for the house and an odd-job man named Obadiah to attend to the water pump and the electricity plant. There was a little trouble at first about laundry, for in this soaking heat great demands were made on it and the Negro maids declared that if they washed and ironed on the same day they'd get a "fresh cold." They also believed that if they crossed water after laundering, misfortune would befall them—a conviction which was all the more awkward because several of them lived in huts which could not be reached without crossing water. However, a little tact and persuasion on Susan's part soon put these matters right. She was used to the local superstitions and accepted them with tolerant amusement. In a day or two the staff couldn't do enough for her, and Obadiah in particular had become her devoted slave. He made a point of giving her car a more brilliant polish than any of the others, and in the heat of the morning he would often come in out of the plantation with his cutlass under his arm and the delicious water of a decapitated coconut as a token of his esteem for Susan. He was always seeking for some new way of pleasing her, and told her of a place he knew where there were some baby alligators he would like to show her when she could spare the time. The Spencers' coloured steward called once to make sure that everything was in order, but for the most part he was busy running the plantation from his own house and no one saw much of him.

From the start, Martin found Garland very friendly. Whatever the man's real feelings, he was certainly behaving as though he'd forgotten the sharp quarrel they had had in Fontego City. Martin couldn't help mentally contrasting the Secretary's unexceptionable attitude to the Fontenoy health drive with his incomprehensible prejudices about Tacri, but he was tactful enough not to voice his thoughts. Garland proved enthusiastic, interesting, and informative about the work in hand, and was evidently anxious to carry Martin along with him and win his approval. As the only two white men in the party, their relationship had a special quality. The only trouble about all this, Martin felt, was that it would make it more difficult for him to return to the attack over Tacri when they got back to Fontego City. Perhaps Garland realised that, and was being consciously disarming. Anyhow, Martin had accepted the invitation and had an obligation to be civil. As long as he didn't think about Tacri it was easy, for Garland at the moment was very much the Jekyll, and Martin was finding the whole enterprise immensely stimulating.

The first problem was to win the co-operation of the villagers. Their interest had already been aroused. The descent of the field crew was quite the most exciting thing that had ever happened to Fontenoy, and on the first evening, when work in the fields was over, all of the eight hundred inhabitants except the babes and the bedridden congregated in the open space beside the school to hear what was going to happen to them. Susan had slipped down to join the party and stood beside Martin watching the faces of the wide-eyed, open-mouthed multitude, squatting on the ground. Garland, far from appearing tired, seemed very much on top of the situation. Whatever his private views about the black people, he could certainly handle them when he liked. He stood in the middle of them, a strong, almost handsome figure, one foot raised on a fallen log, his hands thrust into the pockets of his shorts, his manner casual and chatty. He couldn't talk the coloured man's patter, but he spoke with a simple directness which they understood.

In case there should be any doubt about that, he was followed by the headmaster, who with much gesture and an incredible vernacular seemed to be promising a new Heaven and a new Earth. When the talking was over, a film unit was brought on to the scene, and the impact of the propaganda films was unmistakable. No one in Fontenoy had ever seen a moving picture before.

"You've certainly got them on your side," said Susan to Garland after dinner that evening. "They think you're some sort of witch doctor. Don't you agree, Martin? They expect magic." The field crew had dispersed throughout the house, and the three of them were sitting alone on the veranda.

"As a matter of fact," said Garland, "that's just what they're going to get. I've complete confidence in the results. What you ought to do, Susan, is to come down here in a few weeks' time and see the difference. Phillips, the head teacher, complains that the people here are listless and apathetic. Of course they are, but when we've finished with them he won't know them. They'll be doing twice the work in the fields."

"That should please Mr. Spencer," said Susan. "I remember Dubois used to argue that all our efforts at health improvement were really designed to get more work out of the labourers."

"H'm," Garland grunted. "That's the sort of thing he would have said."

Susan remembered that Garland hadn't been particularly fond of Dubois. He *had* been a bit of a worm, of course, but he'd certainly taken a good deal of work off Garland's shoulders and according to his lights he'd worked hard for the Colony. She found herself resenting Garland's offhand contempt.

"You must miss him, all the same," she said. "Unless, of course, you prefer being without him. I suppose he might easily have been a thorn in the flesh of some people."

Garland's eyes flickered with annoyance. How the devil had they managed to get on to the subject of Dubois, he wondered. He got up, pushing his chair back sharply. "I think I'll turn in," he said abruptly. "We start work at six. I'll see you at the clinic, West, if not before. Good night."

Martin grinned as Garland walked away, "You seem to have put your foot in it, Susan. Dr. Jekyll caught off balance!"

"Oh, he's just prejudiced," said Susan. "Eke had a lot of faults but he *was* keen, and I suppose Garland thought he might take some of the credit for the department. Odd, though, that he should rush off like that. He *is* getting a bit short-tempered these days."

"My dear Susan, you should see him when he's roused."

"Oh, well, you're a bit prejudiced too. He's probably worried. It must have been a frightful ordeal for him when that servant of his was drowned."

"I hope he was more concerned about the servant than he was about my patients."

Susan was still inclined to find excuses for Garland. "You must admit he's doing a fine job here. I think he's rather terrific; I admire him."

"I think it's time I went to bed too," said Martin. "I'm not in the mood to listen to a panegyric on Garland." He said good night rather sulkily.

Left alone, Susan sat watching the fireflies dancing against the mosquito wire. She felt slightly guilty, and couldn't understand why. Everyone seemed to be very touchy all of a sudden. Her thoughts dwelt on Martin, and presently she found herself wondering what it would be like to live with him on a leper island. When drowsiness forced her to her own bed she had still reached no definite conclusion on the subject.

During the next few days, work from dawn till dusk left no time or energy for social exchanges. A couple of bell tents had been erected in a clearing to serve as an improvised clinic. The one hundred and fifty families had been organised into groups and attended the clinic in orderly rotation, shepherded and exhorted by the tireless head teacher who had set his heart on a full muster. Garland was anxious to get the examinations over quickly, for the slides and specimens had to be sent into Fontego City for report and the staff there were standing by.

The general health picture was already clear enough. Nutrition was extremely poor; at least a third of the people were anaemic;

many were suffering from yaws and syphilis; one in eight had scabies and a quarter were troubled with head lice. Martin was immersed in the work, which had temporarily driven all other thoughts out of his head. For him, this campaign was a unique and memorable experience. Sometimes in the evenings he and Susan would take their chairs on to the veranda and discuss the work of the day, or simply sit peacefully listening to the night sounds and watching the gorgeous moon. But not for long; early to bed was the rule.

Once the examinations were completed there was a brief respite. Treatment had begun for the complaints that had been already diagnosed, but the tempo was quieter. The people with scabies were painted; those with head lice were dusted with D.D.T.; the obvious yaws and V.D. cases were given a rapid course of penicillin injections. The villagers were still cooperative, for the first results of the treatment had impressed them. They were free from body parasites for the first time in their lives.

As soon as the laboratory reports came in, the pressure of work rose quickly. More than a third of the villagers needed treatment for malaria, and such a high proportion had hookworm that Garland decided the simplest course would be to dose the whole population over two years of age without exception. Difficulties were encountered for the first time. The patients seemed to have no objection to the rather painful shots of penicillin, but they didn't like their medicine at all. Rumours began to circulate that some people, having drunk their draughts of tetrachlorethylene, had turned giddy and felt tipsy, and attendances at the clinic became ragged. Garland got hold of the head teacher and together they toured the area with a loudspeaker mounted in a station wagon, urging the people to take their medicine. As there was still some reluctance, the hookworm unit was established in one of the cars, and from morning till night huts were visited individually and the draughts administered at the roadside by the nurses.

The moment came when even Garland was satisfied. The back of the work was broken, and there was little more to be done except to clear up and await results. The field crew gathered at the house before dinner on that first free evening, tired but triumphant, and Susan suggested that they should celebrate the end of the campaign by taking the cars down to the beach and having a swim and a cocktail before dinner. The idea was received enthusiastically, and a few minutes later the convoy of cars and wagons was rolling along the sandy track beneath the coconut palms which lined the long open beach. Night had fallen, but the moon was brilliant and the water at blood heat. For fifteen minutes the whole party made merry in the surf, and then Susan went off to her car to get the cocktail flask and Martin went with her.

He was unusually quiet, and after a sidelong glance at him Susan said, "Is anything on your mind, Martin?"

To her surprise he looked confused. "Lots of things, some more than others."

"It's been worthwhile, hasn't it?"

"The trip? Good Lord, yes. I wouldn't have missed it for anything. There's only been one thing wrong with it." He looked at the line of surf, the yellow moon, the gracefully waving palm fronds above their heads. "It seems a pity to have wasted all this."

Susan laughed. "Must you have a romantic back-cloth?" she asked, and dimples Martin hadn't seen before lurked near her mouth. Her smiling eyes met his, and with a swift movement he gathered her into his arms. "Darling Susan," he murmured, "I think I'm in love with you."

She pressed close to him for a moment, her head against his shoulder, her mouth upturned to his. Then she released herself and resumed her usual bantering tone. "Well, take the cocktails," she said, "and make up your mind on the way back. I'm going to remove this wet costume."

Martin made his way along the beach like a man in a dream, not noticing that he was ecstatically hugging the vacuum flask. At least she'd let him kiss her! Had seemed to like it! Surely he could get up the courage to ask her to marry him.

"Susan's just coming," he announced as he joined the party on the sand. He began to take the glasses from the picnic basket, self-consciously aware of interested glances. In a few moments

Susan came serenely toward them, looking very smart in a well-cut beach wrap.

"Come on, Susan," called Garland, "our tongues are hanging out." He looked at the flask with a smile, but the smile froze on his lips. Susan's beach wrap was white, with an intricate design of purple arabesques.

Chapter Twenty-two

Everyone had gone to bed, and the house was silent. Garland sat sweating in his darkened room. Though the doors leading to the veranda were wide open, the mosquito wire seemed to keep out all the air. The steamy heat was stifling. He wondered if other people were sleeping—if Susan were sleeping. He felt that he would never sleep again until he had made up his mind what to do about her.

Even now, hours after the shock on the beach, he had not accustomed his mind to the discovery that Susan had been the woman at the Blue Pool. She was venturesome enough, he knew—the type to try most things at least once. But would she have behaved as that woman had behaved at the Pool? Would she have deliberately flaunted her nudity?

Garland stared blankly into the darkness. When it came to deciding what a woman might or might not do, he knew that he was out of his depth. He could have sworn that Susan, of all people, wouldn't have behaved like that, but what did he really know about her? Nothing, in point of fact, that wasn't on the surface. All he knew was that she behaved decorously in public and that he'd never heard any unpleasant gossip about her, but that didn't mean much. As the Colonial Secretary's daughter, she'd naturally watch her step. And wasn't a woman who had to be so careful in public just the sort of person to have a wild fling when a safe opportunity occurred?

Anyhow, it *must* have been she. Everything pointed the same way. Nothing could be more distinctive man that beach wrap. She was about the right height, and her figure was about right too. Put a kerchief over her hair and a red mask over her face, and she'd completely fill the bill. She'd been at the Pool that night—she'd said so herself. Garland remembered Celeste telling him. She'd been there with young West. She'd pretended she hadn't gone inside, of course, but why should anyone believe that?

Naturally, she'd kept her own counsel all this time. Probably she hadn't even told West that she'd recognised the murderer. She couldn't have done; Garland felt sure he would have known if West had had anything like that on his mind. She had kept the secret to herself.

That made sense, but why had she worn the wrap again? She must have known that Garland would recognise it. She must have wanted him to do so. And wearing the wrap wasn't all. Garland recalled the conversation which had annoyed him so much the other day. Her reference to Dubois must have been calculated. What was it she'd said? "Perhaps you prefer being without him." And something about Dubois having been a thorn in the flesh. At the time, Garland hadn't attached any deep significance to the remark, but he could see now that it must have been carefully premeditated. It was Susan who was being a thorn in his flesh. Why? What was she up to?

She must want something pretty badly to come out into the open like this. The whole thing smelled of blackmail—the quiet start of the campaign, the innocent-sounding remarks directed at him, the wearing of the wrap as a warning of what might follow. Garland frowned into the darkness. Susan Anstruther and blackmail! It didn't sound right. Could she need money so badly? One could never tell, of course. In any case, how could she blackmail him when, if he wished, he could tell so much about her? Hadn't he decided long ago that the certainty of scandal was his safeguard? And yet was he so safe? If it came to a battle of bluff, and the calling of bluff, where did he stand? Her reputation against his life. How could he afford to take the risk? And there was only his word as evidence of her actual behaviour. She might insist that she'd gone to the Blue Pool solely because Dr. West, an interested newcomer, had been anxious to see the sights—a sort of sociological visit. There'd be a few more raised eyebrows, but probably she'd get away with it. With such a story in mind she might well think that her position was strong enough to make blackmail safe.

Or perhaps it wasn't money she wanted. Perhaps it was something else that had made her show her hand. Could it be anything to do with West? She and West were obviously interested in each other. Perhaps West had told her of the quarrel over Tacri, and this was her contribution to the battle. Blackmail of a different sort.

Anyway, her motives were of only secondary importance. Whatever they were, they could spell no good for Garland. Now that she had revealed herself, his peace of mind was shattered. He had been hurled out of his fool's paradise, right back to where he had started. His danger was now greater than ever, for he had to deal, not with black men, but with a clever, subtle, and determined white woman.

His mouth sagged into bitter lines. He had killed two men to win safety, so why stop short of safety? He hadn't wanted to kill them, particularly Johnson. He'd been forced to; he'd had no choice. Had he a choice now? Could he carry on from day to day, knowing that Susan Anstruther had him in the hollow of her hand and could crush him whenever she felt like it? He knew it was impossible. Much better to get her out of the way before she could carry her plans any farther.

Killing Susan, he reflected, would be much more unpleasant even than killing Johnson. He hadn't the least desire to kill her. He had always rather admired her, in a detached impersonal way; she was certainly one of the nicest women in the Colony. At least, he'd believed so. Now that he knew what kind of a woman she was, of course, the position was altered. A whited sepulcher!

He gave an unpleasant laugh in the darkness. What nonsense he was telling himself. He'd always tried to face facts, and he'd face them now. It was her neck or his—that was the root of the matter. There were no other considerations whatever. He'd just have to be callous.

He got up and went quietly out on to the veranda. From the beach came the low roar of the surf. Away in the "bush" a monkey was raising its ugly voice. The moon was just sinking. Sweat rolled down Garland's bare chest. A man couldn't think in this heat.

Suddenly he had a desperate desire to get the job done and finished with. If only by morning he could feel free again! He listened. Everything was still around him. Two rooms away, Susan slept, and her doors to the veranda stood open. A dozen steps! With his strong hands he could choke her as she lay, quickly, noiselessly—in the dark, where he couldn't see her face. He rubbed his moist palms together. To get it over, and let morning do its worst! One of the medical officers had the room between them, and appeared to be sleeping like a log. On the other side was West. That wasn't so good. West was as likely to be awake as not—probably thinking about his damned leprosarium. Or about Susan.

Garland drew back. No, it would be madness. He'd been lucky twice, but his luck would fail if he killed Susan here in this house. The choice of suspects would be too limited. Himself or West, that was what it would amount to. There was always a possibility that a coloured man might assault a white woman, but to make that seem likely here, the stage would have to be set. It would need more thought. He must wait for his opportunity—or make it.

Garland crept back to his room. He would think of a way. If necessary, it shouldn't be difficult to contrive a chance meeting with Susan in some quiet spot. She was always moving about the Colony on her own, and he had his car. If he could come upon her in a lonely place he could kill her and hide her body in the sugar cane. No one ever went into the grown cane except for the reaping, and by the time the next "crop" came round there'd be nothing left of her but unidentifiable bones. The ants would see to that. She'd simply have disappeared, and that would be all. The only thing was that it might take a little time to arrange. In the meantime he must be on the watch for any opportunity.

He lay on the bed, sweating. Not much chance of sleep! He could see that woman now, so plainly, across the gap between the two tables at the Pool—her wrap falling apart, the white gleam of her body. The thought excited him. God, how he wanted to be back with Celeste!

Chapter Twenty-three

Sounds in the big dining-room soon after dawn roused Garland from a fitful doze. He had expected that the field crew would sleep late, now that the pressure of work was relaxed, but someone was evidently stirring. He rose, his head heavy and his eyelids pricking, and took a shower. As he dressed, his thoughts turned again to Susan. The decision he had come to in the heat of the night seemed just as valid now. His course was set. He went into the kitchen to get some orange juice from the icebox, and found one of the maids, Evelyn, at work there.

"Is someone up already?" he asked her. "Or was it you in the dining-room?"

"Dat wah Miss Susan, sah," said Evelyn. "She bin go wid Obadiah fo' to see de gaters."

"Oh?" Garland looked interested. "And where are the alligators?"

"Dey down close by de bridge, sah, thru dey trees." She pointed across the cocoa plantation. "Mis Susan say she nebber see gaters an' Obadiah 'e know wey de lil baby gaters is an' 'e say 'e show ah."

"H'm," said Garland. "I'll follow them down. I've never seen any baby alligators either."

He walked thoughtfully out of the house. It was hardly likely, he realised, that an opportunity would present itself so soon, but now that Susan knew his secret he felt he wanted to be where she was. He wanted to keep an eye on her.

Though it was not yet seven o'clock, the sun was already too hot for comfort, and Garland plunged with relief into the gloom of the cocoa plantation. Narrow overgrown paths ran between the thickly massed immortelles and banana trees which gave shade to the cocoa bushes. The ground was wet after the rains, the paths sticky, the drainage gullies full of water. Walking was difficult. Sometimes the paths were obstructed by coffee branches, heavy with their load of green berries. The undergrowth stirred with life, the air hummed with myriads of winged creatures, the plantation gave off a rich and heavy perfume. Garland began to feel the sweat gathering again under his white shirt, and walked more slowly. There was no hurry, he told himself. He mustn't be carried away. Impetuosity could ruin him, as it might so easily have ruined him during the night. He must wait for the right moment.

The stream seemed a good deal further away than Evelyn had led him to believe. Not just at the bottom of the first hill, but up another rise and down another hill. A good mile from the house. The paths were becoming less clearly defined. Garland wasn't sure of the way, and began to wish he had stayed at the house and kept cool. He stopped and shouted a "Hello, there!" but no one answered. Presently, deep among the trees, he spotted a gang of workers clearing the undergrowth ready for new planting, and he got directions from them. A few minutes later, as the ground fell away, he saw an open space ahead of him and the little wooden bridge that he had been seeking. Susan was there, leaning over the railing. Obadiah, standing beside her, was pointing with his cutlass.

Susan looked up as Garland approached. She waved, showing no great surprise at seeing him, but as he walked up she gave a warning "Sh!" Garland made his way quietly to the bridge, and for a moment or two watched a large alligator and a small one sunning themselves on a patch of grassy bank beside the water. They looked unpleasant and sinister with their gleaming teeth and staring eyes, but they were easily scared and presently waddled one after the other into the water.

"Sorry," said Garland. "I'm afraid I did that."

"We'd been watching them for quite a while," said Susan. "Ugh! Now I can believe in the evil eye!" She gave Garland a friendly smile. "You're up early."

"I heard you moving about," said Garland. "And in any case, I always think the first two hours of the day are the least unbearable." He wiped his forehead and neck with a damp handkerchief.

"I think some coconut water would be a good idea," said Susan. "What about it, Obadiah? Do you feel like a climb?"

"Ah try, missee," said Obadiah, proud to have shown off his alligators and by now more devoted than ever. He took his cutlass and set off up the hill toward a cluster of tall palms.

Susan spread a dry banana leaf on a fallen log and sat down carefully, as though she suspected alligators of lurking in its shadow. Garland was wondering what she was thinking, and wishing that she would put all her cards on the table. Again, he had difficulty in believing that she was really the woman who was hiding so much. It just showed how mistaken one could be. There must be a devil in her, concealed behind that frank and friendly expression. He stared at her, seeing her again in the beach wrap and the mask, wantonly displaying herself. His eyes dropped to her bosom, exploring its contours. Incredible, and yet it must have been she. He kept coming back to that. It *must* have been. She was just playing with him.

Susan had begun to stir uneasily under Garland's uninhibited gaze. She had always felt comfortable in his company until now, but this morning he certainly had a disturbing look in his eye. She hoped he wasn't going to start anything. He wasn't her type at all.

Her suspicions appeared to be confirmed when he sat down beside her on the log and said with a nervous huskiness quite unusual in him, "I thought that was a very attractive robe you wore last night, Susan."

"I had it sent from New York," Susan answered in a tone of studied indifference. "I think it's rather special myself." Her eyes travelled up the hill to the palms. Obadiah was already at the top of one of the trees, hacking at a bunch of green coconuts. She hoped he wouldn't be long. It would be a beastly bore if Garland made a pass at her.

Garland was looking sideways at her, trying to read her thoughts. It wasn't easy; eyes didn't really tell much. The sudden sharp glance she had given him when he'd mentioned the wrap might have meant anything—interest, fear, expectation, surprise. It hadn't been an ordinary glance, he was sure of that. It had meant something. "Rather special," she had said. The wrap had certainly been that Susan probably knew very well that it was the only one of its sort in the Colony. And she had just got it from New York—perhaps nobody had seen it. That, no doubt, was why she had dared to wear it at a place like the Blue Pool. He turned his face to her, and his eyes probed.

Susan avoided his gaze. "Martin and I are going back to town to-day," she said. "I suppose you are too. Celeste will be getting lonely without you."

"I'm not expected until to-morrow," said Garland, still staring. She had a slim neck, he thought; he could strangle her very easily. But not now. Strangling would leave marks, and the marks might be traced to his fingers. Besides, there was Obadiah. . . . He *mustn't* let his impatience get the better of him.

"West is a pleasant young fellow," he said, fighting his urge.

"*I* like him," said Susan simply.

"So I imagine. I suppose you saw a lot of interesting things at Carnival?"

Susan's eyebrows went up. Garland was certainly in a very strange mood to-day. She felt now that she didn't want to talk to him at all, particularly about personal things. "Quite interesting," she said shortly.

Still secretive, Garland told himself. Still playing him on a hook. He said, "Particularly at the Blue Pool, eh?"

For the first time, Susan looked at him with distaste. "Everywhere," she answered.

"It's a great relief to be able to conceal one's identity for a time. To see without being seen. One learns a great deal."

"Perhaps," said Susan. She saw with satisfaction that Obadiah was on his way back.

Garland leaned toward her. "What exactly is this game you're playing, Susan?" he asked in a thick voice.

Her eyes opened wide. "I haven't the slightest idea what you're talking about," she said.

Obadiah came plunging down the hill and poured an armful of green coconuts at Susan's feet. She thanked him with, a smile, and watched while he skilfully sliced off the top of a nut with the razor-sharp cutlass. When he had trimmed the cup to his satisfaction she took it gratefully and quenched her thirst. Garland took a nut in silence. He was no longer trying to understand Susan or get any sense out of her. He was looking at the cutlass, and he thought he could see a way.

He would have to kill Obadiah as well, of course. He would say that he had walked down to the stream and found Susan struggling in the arms of the black man. As she broke away he had seen Obadiah strike her with the cutlass. He had rushed up, thrown himself at Obadiah, snatched the cutlass away, and beaten the Negro down with it. Two corpses, and a convincing story. Nobody would be left to tell the truth. Attempted rape of a white woman, sudden violence by her attacker after a struggle, and summary punishment. Who would ever dream that Garland himself had killed her? It would be a bloody business, but it would soon be over. In five minutes he would be free of Susan, free of the vague menace that was worse than a spoken threat, and the last danger would have gone. After that, no more worry at all.

He looked round the clearing. There was no one in sight, nor were there any sounds of people nearby. He would have to take the slight risk that someone might be watching, but it was very slight and he was desperate. The sooner it was done the better. The cutlass gleamed at his feet. All that was necessary was to get Obadiah out of his way for a couple of minutes . . .

Garland said in a peremptory voice, "Obadiah, go and see if the alligators are back. I'd like to have another look at them."

"Dey no come back, sah," said the Negro, but he got up from the ground, conscious of Garland's fierce eye upon him. "Ah go an' see, sah." Garland was watching him, willing him to leave the cutlass behind. If he took the cutlass with him . . . Obadiah seemed to hesitate, then strolled away, leaving the cutlass where it lay.

"I don't suppose they will come back," said Susan, thankful that

Garland's interest had switched away from her. "Anyway, I'm ready for breakfast." She was just going to move when she caught his expression, and something in it froze her. She was used to his hard cold stare, which she had come to regard as no more than a mannerism, but this was something different. It was a look almost of madness. She said, "Dr. Garland, are you ill?"

He didn't answer. Alarm seized her and she looked around for Obadiah. It was absurd, she told herself, to think that Garland could intend to harm her, but now there was no mistaking the menace in his face. His eyes were narrow slits, and his features were contorted with the intensity of his purpose, like those of a man making a supreme physical effort. His body seemed braced to lunge at her. She met his gaze, knowing rather than seeing that his hand was on the cutlass. Still she couldn't believe it. What had she ever done to him? She saw him raise the cutlass. God in Heaven, he was going to kill her! She shouted, "Obadiah!" at the top of her voice and thrust herself back, away from him. It was too late to run for it—he was going to strike! She covered her face with her hands.

An age of seconds passed, but nothing happened. Then she heard Garland's voice saying, "I'm sorry, I'm afraid I frightened you. I was only trying the cutlass. Dangerous weapons, aren't they?"

She looked up and saw that his face was pouring with sweat and quite grey. For a moment neither of them moved. Then Garland slumped down beside the cutlass and the tension was broken. Susan found that the power of movement had not after all deserted her. She turned for the house and ran as though all the demons of hell were after her.

Garland himself still sat beside the cutlass, mopping his face. Another second, and it would have fallen on her neck as he had intended it to do. He had braced himself, clothing her in his imagination with the beach wrap and the mask and the white kerchief. But the picture had gone wrong. The hand with which Susan covered her eyes had a white cross of sticking plaster on it—quite a big cross. And in that moment of faltering, Garland remembered Susan's accident. At the time of Fiesta her hand would still have been heavily bandaged. But the other hand hadn't been bandaged. It had been smooth and golden, like the arms that had rested on the table. The enemy was still at large. And it wasn't Susan.

Chapter Twenty-four

Martin had finished shaving and was carefully knotting his tie when there was a sound of rapid footsteps at the door, and a distraught Susan almost fell into the room.

"Martin!" she gasped, and the next moment she was in his arms. She was fighting for breath and could hardly speak. Her hair felt damp against his face. He held her close to him, fiercely protective, his own heart hammering at the thought of some unnamed calamity. "There, there," he said soothingly, as though she were a child. "Whatever it is, you're all right now."

"Oh, Martin," she said again, and clung to him. "Thank goodness you were here!"

"What is it, darling? Tell me."

She released herself, still trembling, and sank into a chair with a long sigh. She looked exhausted.

"Can I get you anything?" asked Martin anxiously.

She shook her head.

"Are you sure you're all right?"

"Just give me a cigarette. I'm sorry to be such a weak fool. Martin, Garland's mad! Absolutely insane! He's just nearly killed me."

Martin stared at her incredulously. "*Susan!* Darling!"

"I know it sounds fantastic but I swear to you that he's just made a very nearly murderous attack on me. What stopped him I don't know, but thank God something did. Another second, and I'd have been a nasty sticky mess, quite defunct." She laughed shakily.

"Better tell me from the beginning," said Martin gently. "And take your time."

"Well," Susan began, "I got up early and went off with Obadiah to see the alligators . . ."

With a tense, grave face, Martin listened while she told her story, watching her closely.

When she had finished he said, "Darling, I hate to sound unbelieving, but are you *sure* you're feeling quite well? You know I'm not very keen on Garland, and God knows I've no reason to take his side in anything, but it *is* an extraordinary story and a frightfully serious matter. You couldn't have made a mistake, could you? You're sure you didn't *imagine* that he was going to attack you?"

"Quite sure," said Susan. "If you think I'm suffering from a touch of the sun, you're wrong. I tell you Garland sent Obadiah away on purpose, and when he picked up the cutlass he meant to use it. If you had seen the expression on his face, Martin, you wouldn't have been in any doubt either. I was petrified. So completely frozen that I just stayed there like a little rabbit, waiting for the blow to fall. Only it didn't. And when I *could* move—well, I didn't know I could ran so fast. The dignified Miss Anstruther! Oh, Lord, you must think I'm a frightful coward!"

"That's absurd. An experience like that would shake anyone. It's shaken me just hearing about it." Martin was still looking at her as though he'd like to give her a thorough overhaul, but she seemed quite composed now and he had to believe her.

"Well," he said finally, "if everything you've told me is true, it's obvious that Garland has become a dangerous lunatic. There can't be any other explanation."

"I'm sure he has," said Susan. "I wonder what's happened to Obadiah. I hope Garland isn't going to run amuck. Not that he looked capable of it when I left him. He seemed just about all in."

"I'd better go and find him," said Martin. "He may need help. I'll take one of the other fellows along with me in case he isn't co-operative. You'd better have some coffee—and don't worry any more. I won't be longer than I can help." He got up. "There have been signs of this coming on, I suppose," he said, as though trying to convince himself. "His behaviour to me after the storm, for one thing."

"And he did tell you himself that he felt tired and overworked," said Susan. "I dare say we ought to feel sorry for him, though I must say it's rather difficult just at the moment."

"Very difficult," said Martin grimly. He paused at the door, seemed about to depart, and then half turned as though something was still on his mind, "Susan, I suppose he *is* mad?"

She looked startled. "You just said yourself that there couldn't be any other explanation."

Martin walked slowly back from the door. "I know—but there's something about his behaviour that doesn't strike me that way. His conversation with you, for instance; it had a sort of pattern. Not a very clear pattern, I admit, but he seemed to be driving at something."

"That's what I feel," said Susan. "When he made that remark about my beach wrap, out of the blue, I thought he was just being come-hitherish, but he's never been the least bit that way with me before, and now I can't believe it was that at all. He gave the remark such significance."

"I can't think why," said Martin.

"Nor I, but he did. And the other things he said too—they sounded as though he wanted some information. Something is nagging at him. I'm sure. All those innuendoes about what you and I were doing at Fiesta! I could understand Celeste taking a morbid interest, but why should Garland? And that last remark of his: 'What exactly is this game you're playing?' Why, I hardly know him. I've met him at parties and in public quite a few times, but that's all. What game *could* I be playing? It didn't make any sense to me at all, but it must have done to him."

"Of course," said Martin, "if he's a homicidal maniac with delusions there's no point in trying to find a rational explanation. But is he? I'm blessed if I know what homicidal lunatics talk about before they kill their victims, but I should have expected some stronger indication of an unbalanced mind. Something more than systematic curiosity, anyway." He frowned. "Susan, I don't like it. I don't like it a bit. I suppose he couldn't have had a reason for *wanting* to kill you, could he? Deliberately, I mean."

"But that would be murder," said Susan, staring.

"That would be murder," said Martin.

Susan shook her head. "I'm sure he couldn't. As I told you, we've had hardly anything to do with each other. It would be different if I'd had an affair with him or anything like that, but I haven't."

"I should think not," said Martin indignantly.

A smile flickered over Susan's face. "Honestly," she said, "I can't think of the faintest reason why he should have a grudge against me."

Martin shrugged. "If he did what he did without a reason, then he *is* mad. I dare say that is the answer. After all, he showed the same carelessness about human life over those chaps on Tacri. There couldn't have been any intention to murder there."

"I think he ought to be shut up at once," said Susan. "He seems to be a danger to everybody." She followed a train of thought. "You know," she said, "a thing like this makes one wonder about other things."

"Could you be less cryptic?"

"I was thinking of that servant of his who was drowned—Johnson Johnson. I suppose it *was* an accident?" She tried to recall details of the case. "Yes, it must have been—I remember now, he tried to rescue Johnson. He was a hero."

"H'm." Martin had a reflective look in his eye. "There was only Garland's word for what happened. The only actual fact was that he brought the man ashore, dead."

"It *was* a bit odd," Susan mused, "that a boat should sink so suddenly in a calm sea. You'd think that the two of them together could have plugged the leak. And Garland's a magnificent swimmer. Still, why on earth should he want to kill that inoffensive little man?"

"Why should he want to kill you? We're back where we were. I suppose homicidal maniacs have a catholic taste. I certainly can't imagine any link between you and Johnson that would give Garland a sane reason for wanting to kill you both."

Susan agreed. "I only saw Johnson once in my life, and then he was asleep. There couldn't possibly be any connection. I think we'd better forget Johnson; we've nothing to go on at all."

Martin tried another tack. "Why do you suppose Garland changed his mind at the last moment about using the cutlass?"

"I just can't imagine," said Susan. "It was certainly nothing that I did or said."

"There must have been something. Some check to the homicidal impulse, perhaps—or some sane reason? If we only knew what it was that was worrying him!"

"Well, we know roughly. The main thing on his mind was that you and I had been together at the Blue Pool, seeing lots of interesting things without anyone knowing who we were. That was the theme."

Martin chewed that over. "It doesn't make any sense. Why should Garland be interested in our Fiesta activities, particularly after all this time? Did the subject come up naturally?"

"Good gracious, no," said Susan. "Garland plunged straight into it as soon as we were alone, and he went on asking questions even when I made it as plain as I could that I didn't like them."

"It's very strange," said Martin. "The Blue Pool—why should he bother about the Blue Pool? Did anything happen at the Blue Pool during Fiesta time that could concern Garland in any way?"

"I shouldn't think so," said Susan. "It was hardly the sort of place he'd have any associations with." A startled look leapt into her eyes. "Eke was killed there, of course. Dubois."

"Dubois! Good Lord!" Martin's voice had an edge of excitement "That's an association, anyway. His right-hand man. There's a peculiar element of coincidence creeping into this affair. There've been two unnatural deaths and a——"

"A near miss," shivered Susan.

"Exactly. And Garland is connected with them all. What's more, Dubois' death at least wasn't the result of any crazy impulse. He was deliberately murdered."

"Garland wasn't in town over Fiesta," said Susan. "He was on his boat, fishing. Don't you remember Celeste told us when we dropped in on her that day?"

"How do we know he was fishing?"

"Well, he was certainty out of town. He wasn't around any of the usual haunts. We'd have heard."

"He might have been disguised," said Martin. "Almost everybody was. Didn't the chap who killed Dubois wear a turban and a robe?"

"And a mask, yes."

"There you are then. What could be easier than for Garland to rig himself up in a costume of that kind? On his boat he could have done it at leisure. And there was certainly nothing to prevent him coming secretly into town on Fiesta night if he wanted to. By Jove, Susan, if he did do that, and he killed Dubois, it's not surprising he should show an interest in what we were doing at the Pool."

"He's taken his time," said Susan. "And if he was in disguise I don't see why he should be worried."

"Perhaps he wasn't too happy about his disguise. Still, this is all speculation. If only we could find out whether he was in town over Fiesta—that would be a start."

"I think we might do that," said Susan.

"How?"

"Well, Garland keeps his boat at Darwin Bay and the only way to reach it is to drive through the Base. They take the numbers of all cars—they've taken mine often enough—and I expect they keep their records for a little while. We can probably discover how many times he made the journey."

"Would the Base people tell us?"

"I'm sure I could find out," said Susan. "I know some of them. Of course, even supposing there is anything fishy about his journeys, he's bound to have an explanation."

"He'll need to have," said Martin. "We'll face that when the time comes."

"We haven't got very far, have we?" said Susan. "I'm just bursting with questions we can't answer. Why should he want to kill Eke? What connection could there possibly be between Eke and Johnson and me? And you were at the Pool too—why should he concentrate on me? Oh, and lots more."

"I know," said Martin. "Perhaps we'll get to them in time."

"Meanwhile, what do we do?"

"I think I'm going to talk to Garland."

"Oh, Martin, is that wise?"

"I'll be careful. It's just possible he might make a false move if he thinks we're on his trail. He's obviously pretty rattled already."

"That's what I'm afraid of. He must be quite desperate. I'm almost sorry I came to you."

"Now you're being absurd again. Who else should you have gone to? Susan, darling——"

"Yes?"

"Oh, Lord, what a morning this is!" Martin sighed, and ran his fingers wildly through his hair. "It isn't at all what I planned. You know, Susan, I lay awake last night imagining myself making a pretty speech to you. I was all set to do it, and then we got plunged into this wretched business."

"Does that mean I'm to be deprived of the speech?"

"I'm afraid it does. It wasn't a very good one. Susan, will you marry me? I'm terribly in love with you."

"I expect I will," said Susan. "Even if it does mean living on Tacri!"

"It won't," said Martin. "I've made up my mind. Either Tacri goes or we go. We'll fight it out together once we've settled this thing with Garland. Susan—darling!"

He kissed her and she clung to him. The tie between them seemed all the stronger because it had nearly been cut. For a while they forgot Garland and Tacri and everything but each other.

Suddenly there was a knock at the door. The little black maid peered in and then precipitately withdrew.

"Good Heavens," cried Susan, "what on earth am I thinking about? It'll be all round town that we spent the night together."

Chapter Twenty-five

Martin, striding purposefully toward the outside of the house, came upon Garland by the station wagon, having his luggage put in.

"I thought you weren't leaving till to-morrow," he said.

"I've changed my mind," said Garland shortly. "I'm off right away."

"Without saying good-bye?"

Garland scowled. He was evidently in the worst of tempers. "What the devil do you expect me to do? Go round and kiss the maids?"

"Nothing that you did would surprise me, said Martin.

Garland glared. "What exactly do you mean by that?"

"I'm thinking of your strange behaviour this morning. Susan tells me you threatened her."

"Threatened her? What nonsense! She must be out of her mind."

"On the contrary, she gave me a most lucid and circumstantial account of what happened. I want an explanation."

"You won't get one. I don't like your tone. Clear off, West, I'm not in the mood to talk to you."

"Perhaps you'd prefer to talk to Superintendent Jarvis?" said Martin.

Garland came up menacingly. "You damned young puppy! What are you insinuating? I've a good mind to knock your head off."

"Haven't you been violent enough for one morning? Susan says you brandished a cutlass at her. Why did you do it?"

"She's imagining things," said Garland. "The heat must have affected her. I happened to pick up the cutlass to have a look at it, that was all. Why should I threaten Susan? Don't be a damned fool."

"I suppose you 'just happened' to send Obadiah out of the way before you examined the cutlass?"

"I won't discuss the matter with you. Susan's making herself ridiculous over a trivial incident. The whole thing's quite absurd. I warn you, West, if you try to make trouble about this imaginary occurrence, you'll regret it."

"I *am* going to make trouble about it—as much trouble as I can. I've come to the conclusion, Dr. Garland, that you're a very dangerous man. I'm sorry to have to say it, but I think you intended to kill Susan this morning. I don't know what's going on in your mind. If you're ill, of course—if you're conscious of being ill—we'll all help as far as we can. It's up to you."

"Are you suggesting that I'm insane?"

"That's the kindest explanation I can think of."

"The kindest explanation of what?"

"Of your behaviour this morning—and other things."

"What other things?"

"Why were you so interested in what Susan and I were doing on Fiesta night?"

"I'm not in the least interested."

"Susan says you talked about it."

"I tell you she can't be well," said Garland. "We never mentioned the subject."

"I see," said Martin. "And I suppose you didn't ask her what game she was playing with you?"

"Why should I? What game could she be playing? You're talking gibberish."

"Perhaps. Dr. Garland, what were you doing yourself on Fiesta night?"

"I was at Darwin Bay, sleeping quietly, though what it's got to do with you I'm damned if I know."

"Yet you tell me all the same! You weren't by any chance in Fontego City?"

"Oh, go to hell! I'll not answer your questions. You're all crazy."

"You'll have to answer a lot more questions before long. Superintendent Jarvis will ask them. I don't know what you've been up to, Garland, but whatever it is you went too far this morning. You've started something you can't stop."

Garland's face had turned purple with anger and his hands were clenched. "You chattering fool!" he shouted. "By God, I'll shut your mouth if it's the last thing I do."

"It *will* be the last thing you do. There happen to be people in the house."

Garland suddenly turned, climbed into the car, and drove off without another word.

Martin walked slowly back to the house. A most illuminating conversation! It ought to lead to action of some sort. He went in to tell Susan.

Chapter Twenty-six

Garland was driving bard toward Fontego City. He knew that a crisis was imminent. In the course of a single morning the situation had got completely out of hand. He had given himself away to Susan utterly. Having gone so far, he ought to have silenced her while he could. Now the position was irretrievable.

No doubt plenty of people would believe his account of what had happened, if it came to rebutting charges, but West would never believe him. West was in love with Susan, and he was angry. He accepted her story, and all sorts of suspicions had been aroused in his mind. No wonder! The clues in that fatal talk with Susan had been plain as a signpost to anyone interested in them. If West now started to delve, as he would, there was no telling what might turn up.

The only course, Garland decided, was to get out of Fontego at once. The more he struggled, the deeper he seemed to sink into the bog. There was nothing more he could do here. It was no good trying to eliminate any more people—there were too many involved. Susan would tell her father, and West would tell Jarvis. Questions would be flung at him, dangerous questions that could tie him in knots. He'd had a hint of what could happen in that brief talk with West.

No, the thing to do was to leave. He could pack up now and clear out before the storm broke. The job on the Spencer estate was finished; it would seem quite natural that he should go on leave. He had already told people that he and Celeste were going to Honolulu. Well, they could go to Singapore instead and pick up the money. To-night if possible. Directly he got back he would contact the air terminal and reserve two places on the night plane. Celeste would be delighted, and once abroad they needn't come back. He could plead a sudden breakdown, and send his resignation by post. Perhaps, after all, things weren't as bad as he feared. He would have money and Celeste, and provided he wasn't available to be questioned, they wouldn't get far with the case.

After all, he reflected, suspicion was one thing but proof was quite another. They couldn't arrest him on suspicion. It wasn't as though, he was an obscure person, a nonentity. Adrian Garland, the Secretary of Health, was well known as one of the Colony's mainstays—the *only* man with guts and drive in the whole place. They'd need cast-iron proof before they dared to touch him—something much more convincing than the tale of a hysterical girl. If he continued to deny everything charged against him that morning, he'd be safe enough. They'd have to assume that Susan had been mistaken. They'd *have* to.

But what about other evidence? What could West dig up? Garland thought back over the past, trying to reassure himself. Everything had become so complex. The Johnson Johnson incident, at least, was closed for ever. The dinghy was sunk in twenty fathoms and could never be recovered. There couldn't possibly be a shred of evidence. The verdict of the coroner's jury would stand. There was nothing to worry about there.

What about Dubois? That was a different matter. The situation had changed for the worse. Previously, when Jarvis had been searching for clues, there had been nothing to connect Garland with the case. Now there might be, if West went on using his imagination. "I don't know what you've been up to," he'd said. But he obviously had a shrewd idea.

West was a disaster. He knew more than he thought he knew. That episode after the storm had shaken his faith in Garland. Sooner or later he might fit Tacri into the rest of the jigsaw. Garland couldn't see how, but he might. No good worrying about that, though. The thing to concentrate on now was making sure that no material clues had been left behind anywhere.

Garland thought back to his interview with Jarvis. There had been one or two bits of evidence, harmless enough as long as Garland was under no suspicion, but possibly significant now. That piece of paper from the department's files, for instance. The police had assumed at the time that Dubois had taken it to the Pool with him, but now they could equally assume that Garland might have brought it. Still, there really wasn't much in that. It was a pointer, perhaps, but no more.

They would check his movements over Fiesta, of course. They would ask where he had been, and unlike West they would be in a position to insist on an answer. All the more reason for getting away quickly, out of their reach. In any case he had his story. If he declared that he had spent all the time on his boat, what could they do? No one had seen him except in disguise.

Suddenly, with a pang of fear, he remembered the Base. He'd overlooked the Base! The number of his car would have been taken on the double journey. What a crass fool he'd been! They would know now that he had been in town. He felt his wet shirt clinging to the back of the seat.

Well, what of it? They still couldn't prove anything. He could invent some reason why he'd driven back; he could even say that he'd had an itch to take a look at the Fiesta crowds. There was time to think of something. He could do it at his leisure in Singapore, just in case they ever caught up with him. Any explanation would do. They needed proof.

The shock of his oversight had passed, but he was more anxious now about other things. What else could they do? They might search the boat. It was a pity that it hadn't been sunk in the storm, instead of being driven ashore. Garland wished now that he'd been more thorough in destroying all traces. The blanket and towel might look harmless enough, but it would have been better if they hadn't been there at all. A smart policeman—supposing there was one!—with the Moslem disguise in mind might take a second look at such likely raw material. There wasn't anything else, though. The absence of the knife would cause no comment. Now that Johnson was dead, no one knew that he had had one.

Garland thought of the mask. Had he been careful enough about that? He had rather taken it for granted that no one would ever look for clues on the boat. He remembered giving a few cuts to the canvas from which the mask had been made. They were lying there now in the locker, those few shapeless pieces of canvas. But were they shapeless? Suppose some busybody, with the mask in mind, began to try to fit the pieces together. The shape of the mask might suddenly emerge. That would be proof, by God. Conclusive proof. He *had* been careless. He cursed aloud, shouting above the noise of the engine.

Time was precious, but he would have to go to the boat and destroy that evidence, at least. He would go there after he had completed his jobs in Fontego City. It was going to be a tight schedule. First he must make sure of the plane reservations. And he must call in at the office and leave everything tidy there. He would see Celeste, and get her started with the packing, and then later in the day he would drive to the boat and clean up. There'd still be time to get the plane.

He brought the car up sharply outside his house and strode quickly across the garden. It was good to be back. He felt an urgent need to hold Celeste's smooth body, to get his sense of proportion back. She didn't seem to be about; probably she was lunching at the Club. He called "Salacity!" and the maid appeared, smiling a welcome.

"Yo sho back early, sah," she said. "Missus say yo no comna home befo' to-morrer."

"Where is your mistress, Salacity? Out?"

Salacity nodded. "She bin go out in de auto de mornin' early. She no say wey she go."

"Did she say when she'd be back?"

"She say in de evenin', sah."

"For dinner?"

"Ah nah know, sah."

"Blast!" exclaimed Garland. "All right, I'll be having lunch here." He went to the telephone with a scowl, and dialled the air terminal.

Chapter Twenty-seven

There was an air of satisfaction about Susan as she hung up the receiver and joined her father and Martin in the garden. "Well, we were right—he *was* in town," she announced. "Station wagon X-707 passed through the Base four times during Fiesta, twice each way. What do you think of that?"

"It's certainly a point," conceded her father.

The Colonial Secretary was hunched in his chair and his face showed lines of strain. Susan's story had been a tremendous shock to him. Though she was safe now, he still felt shaken by the narrowness of her escape.

It had hardly occurred to him to question the accuracy of her recollections. Her vivid and detailed account had been only too convincing. Against all his inclinations, almost against his reason, he had to accept the fact that the Secretary of Health had intended that morning to make a murderous attack upon his daughter, and had almost done so.

And as though that wasn't bad enough, there was just the possibility that Garland was already a murderer, that the episode had been the result not of madness but of criminal intent. Horrifying!

Anstruther passed a hand across his forehead in a dazed manner. "It still seems incredible to me," he said. "I'd have trusted Garland implicitly."

"So would I," said Susan, "until this morning." She leaned over the back of his chair and for a moment laid her face against his. "Poor Daddy! It *is* all rather a shock, isn't it?"

"It's appalling," he said. "I'm not quite sure what we ought to do. If it were a clear case of mental collapse, there would be no great problem, but the mere possibility of deliberate murder makes things very difficult We'll have to be most careful. I think before we do anything at all I'd better have a quiet word with H.E."

"Isn't it a bit late for discretion?" said Susan. "I think he ought to be arrested at once."

"It's never too late for discretion, my dear. The greater the crisis, the more need for caution."

"You wouldn't say so if you'd had the sharp edge of a cutlass brandished at *you*," persisted Susan.

He smiled at her. "I don't expect you to look at the matter quite as I do, Susan, but I can't break the habits of a lifetime. The immediate danger has passed, and now we must consider the matter coolly."

"There *is* the possibility that he may get away," put in Martin.

"And I'm not so sure that the danger *has* passed," said Susan. "He knows now that we're suspicious. He may have another try. After this morning, I should think that Martin's a potential victim, as well as me. If the man has one or two murders on his conscience already, what is there to hold him back? I think we should tell Jarvis everything, and leave it to him."

Anstruther shook his head. "It's no good being impetuous, Susan. Whatever we may think or suspect, we can't go levelling capital charges at a man like Garland, or anyone else, without at least a good prima facie case. What actually *is* the case against Garland? What are we going to tell the police if we go to them?"

"We can start by telling them that Garland threatened me with a cutlass."

"And he"ll deny it. He's already denied it to Martin. He's made it quite clear what line he proposes to take. You were feeling the heat, and you imagined things. *You'll* say that you saw a dangerous look in his eye, and that he raised the cutlass. *He'll* reply that you were mistaken about the look and that he was merely examining the cutlass."

"But——" began Susan indignantly.

"I'm merely trying to look at the thing from the police point of view," said Anstruther. "It'll be your word against Garland's. You have some status here, and your word will command respect, but they'll never arrest Garland on the strength of your word alone. We couldn't expect them to. After all, nothing actually happened. It would be different if Garland had struck you."

"It certainly would!" Susan exclaimed. "In the interests of justice it does seem a pity that I wasn't slightly mangled."

Her father put his arm around her. "That's the position, anyway. What do you think, Martin?"

"I agree," said Martin, "if we take that incident by itself. It isn't even as though Garland shows any obvious signs of insanity. He's sane enough, and clever enough, to make us all look pretty foolish."

Anstruther nodded. "And we'd get nowhere. Well, what else have we got against Garland? You two have persuaded yourselves that he killed Dubois. What's the evidence for that?"

"At the very least, suspicious behaviour," said Martin. "The police might be interested, I should think. He lied about what he was doing over Fiesta—there's obviously some thing on his conscience."

"It might not be murder," said Anstruther dryly. "There could be a dozen explanations for that."

"He was in town, anyhow," said Susan. "He *could* have killed Dubois."

"I dare say," said Anstruther. "Let's agree that he had the opportunity. That's not going to get us very far. So did about fifty thousand other people."

"Yes," persisted Susan, "but look at the way he's behaved since. It's as plain as can be that he's worried about something he thinks Martin and I saw at the Blue Pool. Why should he worry if he wasn't there?"

"He could have been there without killing Dubois," said Anstruther.

"Well, he'd hardly try to murder me simply because he thought I'd seen him having a quiet drink. I believe he killed Dubois, and for some reason or other imagined that I knew and wanted to shut me up."

Anstruther stared thoughtfully at the ground. "It's pure surmise, you know. I agree that that conversation this morning was most curious, but I suppose it could bear some other interpretation. Parts of it, certainly. Men like teasing pretty women, and Garland may have been doing only that."

"Teasing! with a cutlass at the end of it! Oh, Daddy!"

Her father stirred restlessly. "I know, Susan, but everything else is so unsubstantial. You may be right about the significance of his remarks—you may easily be right—but they're far from constituting a *case*. They're puzzling, intriguing, suggestive, but by themselves entirely insufficient. In the hands of a good lawyer I'm sure they could be given several innocent interpretations. Besides, as I said before, Garland denies the whole thing. As evidence, that conversation is almost useless. In any case, why would Garland kill Dubois? So far there isn't a hint of motive. We've nothing solid to go on at all."

Susan looked despondent. "I suppose you *are* right," she admitted. "And yet I'm so sure that man's a murderer. To me, there couldn't be any stronger evidence than what I saw in his eyes. Couldn't the police show a bit of your discretion, Daddy, and make inquiries privately?"

"You know Fontego," said Anstruther with a little smile. "How long do you think it would be before Garland found out that we'd made allegations against him? I can see him suing us all for slander in no time."

"Not if he's guilty," said Susan.

"More than ever if he's guilty. He couldn't afford not to. And he'd win his case, you know. At the moment, there isn't a shred of evidence to put before a jury."

"So what do we do?" demanded Susan. "Just sit around and wait for him to carve up someone else?" She caught her father's pained expression. "I'm sorry, Daddy, but you can't expect me to feel very amiable about Dr. Garland. We *must* do something."

"The only thing I can think of at the moment," said Anstruther, "is that I should offer him protracted leave of absence on health grounds, and hope that he'll leave the Colony. Considering everything that's happened, he might jump at it."

"He rather gave me the impression that he could use some sick leave," said Martin, "after we'd had our row over Tacri."

174

Anstruther looked up sharply. "I didn't know you'd had a row."

"Oh, we patched it up. It was after the storm. Garland refused to move some desperate cases to the mainland for fear it should undermine public faith in Tacri. I threatened to appeal to you, and he gave way."

"Extraordinary!" said Anstruther. "I must say he has been behaving in a most peculiar manner, one way and another. His attitude over Tacri has often puzzled me."

"It absolutely defeats me," said Martin. "I'm completely at sea."

"I'm at sea about everything," said Susan. "It's all most unsatisfactory. I feel certain there's a tremendous amount to find out, but I just don't know where we can begin. I hate the idea that Garland is going to get away with things, and that's what it looks like."

"I wouldn't be too certain about that," said her father. "I can imagine that the fruits of murder aren't always what they're expected to be. Things often go wrong."

"They do in books," said Susan. "I wonder what fruits Garland expected from killing Dubois? Do you suppose he kept a coloured mistress on his boat, or something, and Dubois found out?"

"I can think of nothing less likely," said Anstruther dryly. "Anyhow, we're just beating the air. We can't possibly form any useful conclusions without data. I'd better get back to the office."

He uncoiled his legs and got up. "What are you going to do, young fellow? You don't seem to be spending much time on Tacri these days."

"No," said Martin, meeting Anstruther's quizzical glance with a frank smile.

"H'm. Susan, I'm beginning to think you're a bad influence on Martin."

"Oh, darling, that's awful," said Susan. "Because I'm going to marry him."

Chapter Twenty-eight

A great round moon was rising above the motionless palm fronds that fringed Darwin Bay, lighting the yellow sand and throwing a silver bridge across the still water of the lagoon. The evening air was scented and caressing. Above the water's edge the yacht *Papeete* lay almost upright, firmly embedded in the soft sand where the storm had driven it. Its hull glimmered white in the moonlight, and its masts stood out sharply against the velvet sky. Its main hatch was open, and so were its portholes. On the shoreward side of it there were footmarks in the sand—a man's and a woman's.

Below decks, on one of the softly furnished settees in the cabin, some clothes were carelessly thrown. A woman's clothes, gossamer thin, hardly a handful all told. A man's clothes— the tropical uniform of an airline pilot. On the floor stood a picnic basket, open. On a little extending table stood two glasses, each with its amber content of whisky and ice. On the rim of one glass there was a smudge of lipstick.

On the other settee, beneath an open porthole through which the moonlight streamed, Celeste lay naked, her beautiful body gleaming, her fair hair scattered round her satiny golden shoulders. Beside her lay a young, good-looking man whose skin was tanned a rich brown from much sunbathing.

Celeste, surveying her companion's nude body, thought again what a handsome pair they made, and how well he matched her physically. Not, she reflected, that there was anything wrong with Adrian's body. He might be a much older man, but he kept himself fit. He was as muscular as this Dave Lawrence, and just as passionate. But he was her husband. He was around all the time. And then he was so serious. Whereas Dave, although a wonderful lover, was no more serious than she was. Also, being a pilot, he wasn't in the vicinity too often. Their meetings were infrequent, lighthearted, and completely carnal. It was an arrangement which suited Celeste perfectly.

Dave, raising himself on one elbow, passed her glass across and clinked his own against it. "To us," he said. "Gee, you look beautiful to-night, honey."

"Don't I always?" said Celeste provocatively.

"I'll say you do, but there's something extra special about you right now. Maybe it's the moonlight, or maybe it's because I haven't seen you for so long. What went wrong last month?"

"Adrian didn't go fishing after all. He had a conference or something."

"Too bad. I sure felt deprived. I got really steamed up over the ocean, and when I flew in over your garden and saw the white cloth wasn't there I felt like turning the ship round and flying straight back."

"You'd have consoled yourself, I don't doubt," said Celeste.

"Why, sure." His dark eyes smiled into hers. "You wouldn't have me waste all my youth and beauty, would you? But it would have been anticlimax. *You* know that. You've spoilt me for the ordinary models." His hands slid over her, softly following the curve of hip and thigh.

Celeste shivered under, his touch. "Don't do that; you'll make me spill my drink." She sipped the iced whisky. "How do you like this rendezvous? I think it was very nice of Adrian to let the boat run aground in such a heavenly spot, don't you?"

"He'd be pretty mad if he knew how convenient you find it, I'll bet." Dave looked out of the porthole. "It's certainly a humdinger of a spot for necking. Not a leaf stirring, and all that moonshine. It wouldn't be quite so marvellous if that husband of yours took it into his head to come and have a look at his boat to-night, all the same."

"You're not scared, are you?"

"I might be, at that. From what you tell me, he sounds quite a hunk of a man. What's he doing this trip, anyway?"

"He's away on a cocoa plantation, darling, trying to improve the health of the natives, don't ask me why. You needn't worry. He doesn't come here now—not since a servant of his was drowned when they were out on a fishing trip. Besides——"

"Besides, what?"

"Oh, I can handle him. He's a bit afraid of me."

Dave looked amused. "Now why would a woman like you go on living with a sap like that?"

Celeste smiled. "We're not so casual about marriage as you are, my boy. And, anyway, no one better has cropped up so far."

"You mean nobody with more dough?"

"That's rather the idea. I might even run away with you if you'd got a million dollars."

"Wait till you're asked, you shameless little gold-digger!"

"But you like me, don't you?"

"I think you're adorable." Dave pressed close to her and they kissed with sensuous passion.

Celeste drew her head back. "Do you love me?" she asked.

"Do you want me to?"

"Not particularly."

Dave laughed. "At least I bring you nylons."

"Darling, you're sweet. I've never had a more satisfying lover."

"And you never will, honey. Unless you can find a guy who'll shower mink coats on you every time he arrives in port. Say, these bunks are narrow."

"They're not meant for two side by side." Celeste shifted her position slightly, and Dave rolled over. The settee springs creaked.

Presently Dave sat up and reached for a cigarette. "Honey, I know when I'm beaten. Don't forget I've got to fly tomorrow."

"That's just as well," said Celeste, admiring the sheen of her hair as it cascaded down her arm. "Adrian gets home tomorrow."

"Panting for his loving spouse, no doubt."

"Don't be coarse."

Dave grinned. "Okay, honey, I know how you feel. 'It'll be hateful, but you'll have to do your duty'."

Celeste looked at the smiling face, so confident of its charm.

Dark wavy hair, brown skin, white teeth. Dave was certainly good to look at. Fun to be with too, for short periods. He was gay and debonair. Young as he was, he knew most of the answers. She couldn't pull the wool over *his* eyes, and it was somehow a relief. All the same, once appetite was satisfied he hadn't really got much. She wondered how she would feel about him when they returned from Honolulu—always supposing she hadn't found herself a millionaire there.

She stretched like a cat, almost purring with physical contentment. "Pour out another drink," she said, "there's a good boy, and throw me my clothes. We'll have to be going."

"It's a shame to cover all that up," said Dave, but he wasn't really interested any more. He fixed the drinks. "Well, here's to the next time." He raised his glass.

"Happy landings," said Celeste. She took a long drink, then lifted her head and listened. "Isn't that a car?" she said.

Dave peered out of the porthole again. The sound of the engine became unmistakable. A moment later headlights flashed among the palm trees not fifty yards away.

"Christ!" said Dave, and made a dive for his clothes. He began to dress, his fingers clumsy with nervousness. "What do we do now, kid?"

Celeste's eyes were wide with excitement. "What on earth can have brought Adrian here to-night? My God, he'll kill you, Dave!"

"That's a nice thing to say," said Dave, buttoning his tunic. His face was pale and his apprehension was growing but at least he felt better with his clothes on. "It's too late to skip, anyway," he muttered, looking out across the sand. "I suppose it *is* your husband?"

"No one but Adrian would come here in a car," Celeste answered. "Give me a cigarette, will you?" She too was pale, but she showed no sign of panic. Dave held the lighter for her, and the flame was unsteady. Heavy shoes crunched outside among the shells. Then Garland's voice called harshly, "Who the devil's in there? Come out, do you hear?"

Dave stood up, bracing himself against a bulkhead. Celeste sat where she was, on the bunk, her cigarette glowing between still fingers. Feet appeared on the companion ladder, lit by a shaft of moonlight, and Garland's head followed as he glared down into the cabin.

For a moment he remained quite motionless, scarcely believing what he saw in the half-light. Then he came slowly down the companionway. "Celeste!" he exclaimed in a hoarse voice. "Celeste, what does this mean?"

"Isn't it rather obvious?" said Celeste.

Garland looked across at Dave. He could have broken the boy's neck, but it hardly seemed worth it. It was Celeste who mattered. He suddenly saw quite clearly how utterly he had deluded himself. Nothing that had happened since that first day with Dubois had given him such a jolt as this.

Dave, pressed against the bulkhead and watching Garland, said with feigned calm, "If you're going to slap me I guess we'd better go where there's more room."

Garland, not looking at him, said, "Get out!" When Dave didn't move he shouted again, "Get out, do you hear, you little swine?"

Celeste, from the bunk, motioned to Dave to go. "Wait outside," she said. The young man squeezed past Garland and climbed the ladder.

Celeste gave a long sigh as the tension eased. "That was very sensible of you, Adrian. Thank you."

"How long has this been going on?" asked Garland in a low voice.

Celeste gathered her belongings. "Adrian, I refuse to talk here. And before anything else, I must take Dave back—he hasn't a car. I'll see you when I get home."

"You expect me to go home?"

"Why not? You needn't stay if you don't want to, but we must have a talk."

"I can say all that I want to say in a couple of minutes," said Garland harshly.

Celeste stood up. "No doubt," she said coolly, "but I may have a few things to say too—things that will surprise you."

Leaving Garland open-mouthed, she climbed the ladder and joined Dave on the beach.

Chapter Twenty-nine

Celeste stood on the terrace of her home in the luminous chirruping darkness, listening for the approach of the station wagon. She had disposed of her pilot, quietly and without fuss, and for all that he mattered to her now he might never have existed. If it would help repair the situation she was quite ready to appear remorseful, but she didn't think it would. On the other hand, if it should be necessary, she was equally prepared to be defiant. She hadn't wanted a showdown with Adrian, but if he forced one she would fight for what she had with all the weapons in her considerable armoury. She was, in fact, awaiting has return with more curiosity than alarm.

She had had a shower and changed into a severely becoming gown, and now felt braced for what could hardly fail to be something of an ordeal. In the mirror she had seen a picture of sophisticated propriety, of elegant composure. Yes, she thought, she could handle Adrian, as long as he didn't become violent. She had never doubted his capacity in that direction. He had been hurt so much himself to-night that he might want to hurt her. She shrank from the thought of his muscular hands and was glad that Salacity was within call.

Lights suddenly flashed at the end of the road, and the station wagon screeched to a standstill at the gate. The angry slam of the car door was like an explosion. Celeste went indoors to meet her husband. The sooner it was over the better.

Garland came in with heavy aloof dignity. He flashed her one brief inimical glance and stalked over to the sideboard to pour himself a drink. At least, Celeste saw with relief, he wasn't going to start throwing things. His determined self-control was patent. She began to wish that he would speak— the smouldering look in his eyes was unnerving. She could cope with a noisily angry man, but this charged silence was infinitely more difficult to deal with.

Garland drank his whisky at a gulp and stood by the window mopping his forehead. Celeste realised that he had had a great shock and that it would be necessary for her to use the utmost tact. She must be careful not to provoke him further.

From the arm of the settee, where she had taken up a graceful position, she said in a subdued, almost penitent voice:

"I'm sorry this has happened, Adrian. You must believe that I feel horribly humiliated."

He turned angrily. "Humiliated? You? You're beyond humiliation!"

"Adrian!" she said in a wounded tone.

"You belong in a farmyard," he sneered.

Celeste's lips tightened a little. It looked as though penitence wasn't going to work. "Abuse isn't going to get us very far, Adrian, do you think? And, anyway, I'm not particularly interested in your opinion."

Garland's eyes flashed. "So it seems. You're no better than a bitch in heat."

"If you're going to talk like that I shall leave. Understand once and for all that the way I behave is my own affair. I'm not asking for approval. And I'm not in the least sorry for what I did. All I regret is that you found out."

"We've got to the truth at last," said Garland, his face working.

"I might as well be frank. You shouldn't have spied on me. I suppose that's what you were doing?"

"I was doing nothing of the kind," he answered furiously. "I had business on the boat. I had no idea that you were there. I can still hardly believe that you were. It's like a nightmare."

"I really don't see why it should strain your credulity," said Celeste. "These things do happen, you know—quite often. It's unfortunate that you should have found us like that, and although you mayn't believe it, I do feel humiliated. But I've hardly made history."

"You've made history for me," he said.

Celeste assumed a softer expression. "I can understand your being hurt and angry—"

"Hurt and angry! You just can't imagine how I felt! How should you? You've never cared about me as I did about you. You were the one person in the world I relied on. I thought I could trust you. I don't know why I should have done—but I did. You meant everything to me. You were the one stable thing in life, the one thing that mattered. And I find you behaving like a filthy little slut. My God, it's unbearable!"

"Having an affair with a presentable young man doesn't make me a slut," said Celeste, "and you know it. I'm afraid you're very old-fashioned."

"If I were," said Garland, "I'd thrash you. Are you in love with that fellow?"

"Don't be absurd. He doesn't mean a thing to me"

"Does anyone?"

Celeste shrugged. "I have a certain respect for you, darling, though you may find that difficult to believe. The weak woman and the strong man, you know." A smile flickered over her face. "I've always admired your strength. Poor old Dave showed up in a very poor light by comparison when you came into the cabin. It almost made me despise him. It was nothing more than a passing affair, you know, although I don't suppose that will make any difference to you."

"It robs your intrigue of any shred of decency, that's all. If you'd been in love with him it wouldn't have been so bad."

"Well, I'm sorry to disappoint you, but I'm not. I went to bed with him because I felt in the mood, and that's all there is to it. Personally, I can think of no better reason."

"It's not the first time, I'll be bound."

"No, it isn't," said Celeste, "and I dare say it won't be the last. Considering everything, I must say I think you're being ridiculously conventional."

"I'm quite sure I am, by your standards, and I shall continue to be. Don't think you're going to get away with this, Celeste. I've been made a fool of long enough. When you've been dragged through the divorce court and stripped of what little self-respect you've got, you may regret your attitude. I'm going to ruin you. When I've finished with you you'll be on the streets, where you belong."

Celeste gave a long sigh. "My poor Adrian! For a man of the world you're surprisingly stupid. Was I on the streets when you married me?"

"Not quite."

"Now thats very horrid of you, and not a bit true. I may have married partly for position, but lots of women do that. I could easily do it again, you know. All the same, I don't think I fancy being divorced—not at the moment, anyway. It wouldn't be very pleasant for you, either, to have our affairs paraded before all the people we know. Can't you imagine how they'd lick their lips? 'Poor old Garland,' they'd say, 'he must have been blind.' They'd be sorry for you; would you like that? Surely you can see how much better it would be to behave in a civilised fashion. You know what I mean—keep up appearances the way people do. You don't have to sleep with me if you don't want to."

"I don't want anything more to do with you. I hate the sight of you, can't you understand?" Garland turned away, conscious that his words were final, but that his mood swung miserably between hatred and longing.

Celeste sat still, and thought hard. Divorce might have its advantages. What, after all, could Garland give her now? She might be well out of things. She'd exhausted all his possibilities. He'd never be able to give her all the things she wanted, she realised that at last. All the same, if they were to part, it should be in her own time, not his. And with dignity. She wasn't going to be flung out by Garland or anyone else. For one thing, she had no money to speak of. It might take a little time before she could find the right sort of husband. Her requirements were greater now than they had been when she married Garland. No, it wouldn't do to have a financially embarrassed interregnum. She could remember only too vividly the time, not so very long ago, when she had lived the precarious life of a woman without man or means. It hadn't been at all satisfactory. She mustn't make the mistake of throwing away dirty water before she had some clean.

She got up from the settee. "You know, Adrian," she said silkily, "I strongly advise you to change your mind about a divorce. For your own sake."

Something in her tone jarred very unpleasantly on Garland's ears. "Don't talk nonsense," he said sharply. "What do you mean, for my own sake?"

"I've been very patient with you," said Celeste slowly, wondering how long it would take Salacity to reach the sitting-room. "I've put up with this high moral attitude you've adopted because I didn't want to quarrel, but if you insist on being insufferable, you force my hand. You've asked for it, and now you're going to get it. Tell me, in your opinion is adultery so very much worse than murder?"

Garland stared at her as though he hadn't heard clearly "*What did you say?*"

"Believe me, I didn't want to bring it up," she assured him. "I knew it could only make life very uncomfortable. But you see, I happen to know that you killed Dubois."

The blood drained from Garland's face. "You're out of your mind," he muttered under his breath. He walked quickly to the door and made sure that it was shut. "What on earth makes you say a thing like that?"

Celeste gave him a benevolent smile. "It's no good, Adrian dear; you're a dreadfully poor actor, and it wouldn't make any difference if you weren't, because I happened to see you do it. If you must know, I was the woman at the Blue Pool." She made a wry little face. "I'm afraid I wasn't behaving very well, but after all, it *was* Fiesta and I was rather drunk."

"You're lying," said Garland thickly. "The whole thing's a pack of lies. You're making it all up for some reason of your own. I suppose you think this cock-and-bull story will frighten me out of divorcing you. Well, you'll see." His eyes bored into hers. "It *couldn't* have been you——"

"Why not?" asked Celeste, amused. "Do you think I'm too pure or something? Or perhaps you think I wouldn't have been wearing the clothes you saw? Of course, that's it. So you *were* there?" She gave a little satisfied laugh at her own cleverness. "But why should I bother to trap you? I saw you, my dear, with my own eyes. I recognised you when your turban fell off. I was wearing a beach wrap, a white one with a wavy purple design. Remember? Now are you satisfied?"

"You haven't got a wrap like that," he said hoarsely.

"No," said Celeste, "I haven't. It belongs to Susan. She left it here by mistake one day when we'd been swimming, and I thought it would be a sort of disguise if I wore it. I knew Susan wouldn't be at the Blue Pool anyway. There now, darling, isn't it nice to know you won't have to worry any more about who that woman was?" She sat back and beamed at him. "You might just as well admit it. It would be a frightful bore otherwise. If you want me to, I can give you lots of corroborative detail. Do you remember how I stared at you after you'd struck Dubois? I had a glass in my hand. Remember that horrible nigger who bumped into you? Remember the piece of paper you showed Dubois?"

Garland collapsed into a chair, a long trickle of perspiration rolling down from his temples. "*You!*" he gasped.

"Yes, me!" Celeste nodded brightly. "So at last you believe me?"

"Yes," he said slowly, "I believe you. I wouldn't have done a couple of hours ago, but now I do. I can just imagine how you enjoyed exhibiting yourself to the world that night. And the man you were with—I suppose it was the same fellow I saw to-night?"

"The same one. I'm not nearly so promiscuous as you think. But don't start lecturing me again, darling. I couldn't bear it."

Garland gazed at her in bewilderment. For the moment, at least, her sexual adventures had taken second place. All he could grasp was that the situation seemed to have passed from his control. "What are you going to do about it?" he asked. "About Dubois, I mean?"

"Do?" echoed Celeste in a tone of surprise, "why, nothing. Unless you make me. I told you I didn't want to start anything. It isn't as though any harm's been done. I never liked Dubois anyway, and as for Johnson . . . I suppose you did kill him too? I couldn't ever quite believe that story you told the Coroner. You're such a splendid swimmer, and it wasn't really very far, was it?"

Garland sat fascinated. "I don't understand you, Celeste. I don't begin to understand you. You knew all this, and yet you didn't say anything? It's inhuman."

"Oh, I don't think so, darling. Feminine, if you like. Women often know things they don't think it wise to talk about."

"But weren't you going to say anything at all?"

"I suppose I might have done sometime. I don't suppose I could have kept it in for ever. We'd have been bound to have a quarrel sooner or later, and then I expect it would all have come pouring out. But only to you. I'd never have given you away, and I wouldn't have said anything even to you if I could have helped it, because it was obvious it would make things awkward. And, besides, it was rather fun knowing a really guilty secret and not telling."

"But now that you've told me—aren't you afraid?"

"Of you?"

"You've good reason to be. How do I know you won't tell? I killed Dubois, and Johnson Johnson, and I nearly killed Susan Anstruther because of the wrap——"

Celeste looked shocked. "Oh, Adrian, that would have been a pity. She'll make such a charming wife for that nice Dr. West. I know you don't like him, but he is rather sweet." She smiled amiably at him. "No, I'm not afraid, not when we're sitting and talking like this. I know you can be rather ruthless. It's one of the things about you that's always attracted me. But you seem quite controlled now, and anyway I'm sure Salacity wouldn't approve if you started being brutal to me."

"You're a devil," said Garland. "My God, I thought I had strong nerves, but you're incredible. Aren't you—aren't you going to do *anything*? Aren't you appalled? Can you take murder in your stride so easily?"

Celeste laughed. "Look, Adrian, I know this has all been a bit of a shock to you, but try to relax. You're all strung up." She caught his eye. "I'm sorry, darling, perhaps that wasn't a very happy phrase, but you know what I mean. The whole trouble about you and me is that we took so long to get to know each other. You were all romantic about me and put me on a bit of a pedestal, when in fact I'm really an adventuress. I don't want to go into sordid details, but I was brought up in a very hard school, if you can call the gutter a school, and that's why I'm not easily shocked. You simply expected the wrong things from me. And I was just as stupid about you. I had no idea what sort of a man you were until I saw you kill Dubois. After that, I felt I could get quite interested. By the way, why *did* you kill Dubois? It's puzzled me a good deal."

"He knew too much," said Garland. "He'd have ruined me. The fact is, Celeste, I allowed myself to be bribed by that contractor fellow, Rawlins, the man whose firm got the contract for rebuilding the leprosarium. Johnson Johnson heard us arranging it, and he told Dubois. I had to kill them. I had no choice."

It was Celeste who looked fascinated now. "Well, you *have* been keeping things to yourself," she said. "Dr. Adrian Garland, the upright administrator, taking a bribe! Amazing!"

"If you can swallow murder," said Garland, "I should think you can swallow that."

"Oh, easily, but I *am* a little astonished, I must say. Did you need money so badly?"

"You did," said Garland briefly.

"Darling! You mean you did it for me? But how sweet of you! Of course, I see now—that accounts for Honolulu. And we have spent rather a lot lately, I know. I'm afraid I'm dreadfully extravagant. Oh, darling, now we shall get along perfectly. Don't you see, we're birds of a feather! We've different vices, of course, but we're both fairly vicious. If only I'd known, I'd have been so much nicer to you. I think virtue is so tiresome. Everywhere I went people told me how wonderful you were, and you always seemed to be doing good among those dreadful natives. Even when you wanted to make love to me I felt I was going to bed with a well-run department—it was terribly off-putting. Darling, how much was the bribe?"

"Fifty thousand pounds," said Garland, not without complacency.

"Fifty thousand pounds! But that's a fortune. Has the man actually paid it?"

"He paid me ten thousand in cash, and the rest is safely tucked away in Singapore."

Vistas of endless luxury floated before Celeste's eyes. She said wistfully, "It would have been rather nice to share it with you. We could have had fun."

"I had everything arranged," said Garland, his bitterness returning. "When I went to the boat this evening, it was to clear up some bits of evidence that I'd overlooked. After that, I intended that we should go off to Singapore together at once—for good. I've made all arrangements. I've actually got the plane tickets in my pocket."

"Couldn't we still go? What time does the plane leave?"

"Midnight. But I don't want to take you any more. I'll never get that cabin out of my mind as long as I live."

Celeste gave him her tenderest smile. "You will, you know. It was only because you were away so much, darling—I got bored here all by myself. You shouldn't have left me, it wasn't fair. You were such a stuffy old thing, too, at least I thought you were. It'll be quite different when we're together all the time, and you haven't got your work to worry about. Think of it, my sweet, one long honeymoon! Doesn't that appeal to you?"

"You're shameless," said Garland. "And transparent. Don't think I can't see through you. I've learned my lesson."

"I know, darling. We can both see through each other and nothing need be hidden any more. Isn't that the perfect basis for a perfect marriage?"

"You don't mean a word of it," said Garland. He was consumed with jealousy and self-pity, and oppressed by the weight of his anxieties. "You're simply trying to sell yourself to me all over again."

Celeste pouted. "You do put things so crudely. At least you'd have a much better bargain this time."

"How do I know that? I wonder how long it would be before

you found some other good-looking young fellow half my age and started your tricks all over again."

"I keep telling you, angel, I don't really like young men. They bore me."

"You'd say anything to get your way. I can see now that you always have. How can I possibly trust you after what's happened?"

Celeste showed the tips of her claws. "If it comes to that, darling, after what's happened have you any alternative?"

"Yes. I can kill you, or myself, or both of us."

"Oh, let's not be melodramatic. It would be such a dreadful waste. Things may seem a bit difficult just now, but they won't when we get away. We *must* try it, Adrian. We're in this together, and we'll pull through together. Life can start all over again. In a few days you'll have forgotten all about Fontego. Well put it right out of our minds and begin again. I'm sure everything's going to be marvellous."

"I wish I could believe it."

"You will when you get away. Look at me, Adrian. Aren't I lovely? Don't you want me more than anything else on earth? Isn't that why you've done everything you have done? Darling, I'll be all yours from now on. I promise. I'll be terribly well behaved. Isn't that a better prospect than—well, than some of the other things that might happen?"

"Is it? I shall always be in your power."

Celeste laughed lightly, knowing the tide had turned. "Of course you will, you solemn old thing. Always, for one reason or another. Haven't you always been? What does it matter what the reason is? Naughty passions or murder—the result's the same. You can't do without me, and you know you can't. Adrian, we were made for each other. We suit each other. I've been very foolish; I can see that now. Do let's have another try."

She got up and stood where the soft light of the single shaded lamp fell on her. It was a kindly light, and made her look pure as a Madonna. "It shouldn't be a difficult choice for you," she said. "Me—all of me for yourself, or——" Delicately, she left the sentence uncompleted. "Well?" she said, smiling.

"You're a devil," cried Garland hoarsely. "You know you drive me crazy. I'm a fool, a damned weak fool, but, by God, Celeste, I need you. I'll have to take you—I can't help myself."

"Darling!" murmured Celeste. "I promise you'll never regret it." Suddenly she became business-like, aware that she was about to become an open accessory after murder. "Adrian, I suppose no one suspects you?"

"Of course they suspect me," said Garland. "That's why I'm so anxious to be off. Susan knows I was going to kill her, and young West is treading on my heels. But they can't *prove* anything."

"Are you sure of that?"

"Certain. I've tidied up all traces. They haven't an inkling about Tacri, and there's no way they can find out. The only thing I'm afraid of is a lot of probing questions by the police. If only we can get away quickly, I'm positive everything will be all right."

"You're so clever, darling," said Celeste. "Let's go and pack."

Chapter Thirty

"Celeste, we must leave," Garland called urgently, as the clock struck eleven. "I'm sure we've got everything that matters."

The Garland home had been thrown into chaos by ruthless rummaging and packing. Celeste, unwilling to sacrifice treasures she couldn't replace, was having a last look round. Garland had gathered his own things together and was satisfied that he had overlooked nothing vital. He felt on edge. Salacity had at first tried to be of assistance, but she had been ordered away and was now hovering resentfully in the kitchen. She had always helped Celeste on previous occasions, but this time both master and mistress seemed to have gone crazy. A fine way to pack for a holiday!

Garland hurried Celeste into the car. "It's going to be a close thing," he muttered, ramming in the gear. "That detour round the broken bridge will take us an extra ten minutes at least. Hold on—I'm going to drive fast."

"Good, it'll be exhilarating," said Celeste, settling herself comfortably and nestling up close to Garland. "Well, I'm glad thats over. What a whirlwind! I do hope I haven't forgotten anything."

"We may be able to have the rest of the stuff sent," said Garland, "if all goes well."

"Yes, of course," agreed Celeste. What did it matter, she thought. They could buy new things now.

Her eyes sparkled as for the last time she looked out upon the noisy streets of the eastern suburbs. "It's wonderful to think that we shall never see Fontego City again," she gloated. "What a shoddy place it is! All galvanised iron and shops."

Garland grunted. It would be time enough to start feeling cheerful when they were out of their difficulites. He still couldn't think very straight about Celeste. It was wonderful to have her there, that was all he knew. It was what he had always dreamed of, to have Celeste warm and friendly and clinging, and wholly with him. Nothing else mattered—except catching that plane.

Once out on the Main Trunk Road he gave the lively little car all she had. The road lay ahead invitingly wide and open, a swathe of macadam between the sugar canes. The close air became a refreshing breeze with the speed of their passage.

"After we've collected the money," said Celeste, her lips parted in an ecstatic smile, "let's fly to Honolulu as we planned. Everybody raves about it."

"It'll certainly gladden my eyes," said Garland.

"I'll have to do a lot of shopping, I'm afraid. I haven't a rag to wear. There'll be dancing and shows—I believe they have some first-rate cabarets. Oh, what a gorgeous change it's going to be! And what shall we do after that? Perhaps we ought to go to some *really* cool place. Do you remember fresh air? I'd like to be made to shiver."

"That may be easier than you think," said Garland grimly.

"Darling, how morbid! Seriously, though, I've had enough of the tropics for the time being. I'd like to get thoroughly cool and eat a nice crisp apple."

Garland permitted himself a slight smile at Celeste's chatter.

"I'm sure it's a very modest wish," she went on.

"That's a change for you."

"Oh, Adrian, don't be an elephant. We've started our new life."

A brilliant beam of overtaking headlights suddenly flashed on the windscreen, and in a moment or two there was an imperative honk behind them. Garland, fearing pursuit without expecting it, felt his heart leap. He slowed, and a huge streamlined limousine swept past, dangerously close, and roared ahead on an erratic course. It seemed to be full of Negroes. They were shouting and singing in raucous disharmony, and one of them was waving a bottle.

"How I hate *reki*," said Celeste.

"Damned fools," growled Garland. "Look at them—all over the road. That driver must be drunk as an owl." Unconsciously he drove faster himself, pressing the accelerator to the boards and roaring after the wildly swaying car in front. But it had more power than he had, and its rear light slowly faded.

"What's the time?" he asked anxiously.

"Twenty-five past eleven, darling. I'm sure there's no need to worry—you know how casual they are at the airport. We'll make it all right."

"God, I hope so," muttered Garland.

They took an easy bend at seventy. The red light had disappeared. At this speed the road seemed unfamiliar. The brilliant headlights made the verges dark. Garland peered anxiously ahead. "The detour ought to start somewhere here," he said, slowing to sixty.

Suddenly he caught sight of a dark shapeless object close to the near-side verge. He swerved to avoid it. Something hit the side of the rushing car with a horrible thud, and was flung away.

"What on earth was that?" cried Celeste, frightened. She peered out, trying to penetrate the receding darkness. Surely that was a red light, among the canes. "I say," she called, "I believe that car's had a smash. Did you hear someone shout?"

"No," said Garland. "Serves them right anyway, the drunken idiots. Where's that turning? Damn it, we ought to have reached it by now." He slowed to fifty.

"Perhaps a miracle's happened and they've repaired the bridge," said Celeste. "So much the better; now we'll do it easily."

"They *haven't*," yelled Garland, hideous panic in his voice. Tyres shrieked, the car rocked, the ramp of a bridge rushed toward them and a dark chasm gaped. Celeste grabbed Garland's arm and gave one long piercing scream. The car leaped and plunged—down, down, in shattering noise and an agony of fear. Swirling muddy water poured through the open windows, stifling the scream, choking life. The car sank, and slowly settled in the brown ooze twenty feet below.

Chapter Thirty-one

News of the accident on the Main Trunk Road came through in driblets. The first reports spoke only of a wrecked limousine and several dead Negroes—an event so common that it barely warranted headlines. Further investigations suggested that there might be a car in the river. Not till the late afternoon did the newspapers of Fontego produce their largest type, and then they really went to town. To judge by the zest with which they threw themselves into the reconstruction of the tragedy, there had been no more satisfactory calamity in the history of the Colony. Hardly any dramatic element was lacking. Not merely were there plenty of bodies in every state of mutilation, but there was quality as well as quantity. The famous Adrian Garland and his lovely young wife, plunged to muddy death on the eve of their holiday!

From the press reports it was plain enough what had happened. The road block guarding the broken bridge had, it appeared, consisted of no more than a light pole balanced on two wooden trestles. There should have been a red hurricane lamp in front of it at night, but according to the story of a survivor, no such lamp had been burning. The limousine, recklessly tearing through the night, had scattered the frail road block and precipitated its load of nine drunken passengers into the cane. The Garlands' car, following close behind, had driven straight on—"to its dooms," as the report put it. Thus the Colony had suffered the loss of one of its most notable figures. Many columns of obituary notice followed.

Martin and Susan were working together in the garden on the Tacri memorandum when Anstruther, informed by Superintendent Jarvis, arrived home with the news. After the initial shock, the feeling uppermost in the minds of all of them was relief. At least Garland could do no more harm. And relief was followed by a return of curiosity.

"He must have been driving terrifically fast," said the experienced Susan, "not to see the turning or the wreckage of the road block. My guess is that he was running away. I suppose he was so determined to catch the plane, his mind wasn't on the road. Did you know he was going, Daddy?"

Anstruther shook his head. "I was told this morning that he'd gone. Most irregular, I'm afraid. He must have made up his mind very quickly. It's suggestive, to say the least of it, but we'll never know for sure."

"It's most annoying," said Susan. "I hate being left with a tangle of loose ends and surmises."

"*I'm* quite content," said her father. "We've all been saved a great deal of anxiety and trouble. A merciful intervention, I'd call it."

"H'm," murmured Susan. "Perhaps so. A pretty rotten finish for Celeste!"

"Yes," said Anstruther gravely. "I'm afraid for the moment I wasn't thinking of her."

"Anyhow," said Susan more cheerfully, "there's one thing to be thankful for. This should help to bring the Tacri scheme to an end. Martin and I have prepared a terrific indictment."

Anstruther frowned. "I shouldn't bank on anything, Susan. I know that Garland was the biggest obstacle to any revision— the biggest personal obstacle—but there are plenty of others."

"But it's a clear case," said Susan. "It's absolutely overwhelming."

"I don't doubt it, my dear, but there's still the little problem of money to get over."

Susan looked so crestfallen that Martin couldn't help laughing. "It's no good, darling. I told you we'd got to be realistic. Your father's quite right."

"But it means so much to you," said Susan. "And to me," she added ruefully. "Oh, Lord, I'd really begun to think we should get somewhere with that man out of the way."

"We still may," said Martin. "We've got to try, anyhow, while everything's fluid. If we can't get the scheme revised now, I doubt if we ever will. And we'll have to hurry. Material is beginning to pour into Tacri."

"Yes, that's the trouble," said Anstruther sympathetically. "The work is well under way at last. Frankly, Susan, I don't think there's the least hope that the Finance Committee will back out of its contract at this stage. The cost in compensation alone would be enormous. It isn't as though the Colony can afford to fling away hundreds of thousands of pounds."

"They should have thought of that before," said Susan indignantly. "Stupid idiots!"

"I'm not defending them," remarked Anstruther. "I'm just telling you what's likely to happen so that you won't be too disappointed. Finish the memorandum, by all means, but don't expect miracles."

Susan got up. "So Garland wins after all. It's too bad—he didn't deserve to."

"I shouldn't make a personal thing of it," said Anstruther with quiet irony. "He can hardly be enjoying his victory—if it turns out to be a victory."

She frowned. "I still wish we could have got to the bottom of everything. Do you know, I think I'll pop over and see if I can get any sense out of Salacity."

Anstruther raised his eyebrows. "Do you really think that's wise at this stage? Wouldn't it be better to let things rest?"

"In peace?" said Susan. "Not if I can help it."

Chapter Thirty-two

It was nearly two hours before Susan reappeared, a little breathless and with an excited gleam in her eye. Martin mixed her a drink and she sat down with the portentous air of a person about to impart tidings.

"I've been thinking," she announced.

Both men smiled. "That's gratifying news," said Anstruther. "To some purpose, I hope."

"You wait, and perhaps you won't be so snooty. Garland *was* running away, there's no doubt about that. Headlong flight, I'd call it. His place is a shambles."

"H'm," said Anstruther. "Interesting—but I don't know that it carries us much farther, does it? He hasn't left a confession, by any chance?"

"The way he and Celeste packed is as good as a confession. After all, they were supposed to be going away for a holiday, but it's obvious that they weren't. Celeste took hardly any clothes—imagine that!—but she cleaned up every scrap of jewellery, and all her old letters and photographs. And Garland practically emptied his desk of papers. Oh, they were going for good, there's no question about it. And they were in such a hurry to get off, they didn't even make any arrangements about having the car collected from the airport. I suppose they were just going to leave it there. They couldn't even stop to get a taxi, and they went off virtually with what they stood up in. I think it's all most significant."

"It certainly looks as though Garland lost his nerve at the end," said Anstruther. "Well, whatever there was on his conscience he's taken the proof of it with him."

"I'm not so sure," said Susan. "After I'd talked to Salacity and had a good look round, I sat down among the litter and imagined that scene last night when they were packing, and suddenly I got on to something. Do you realise that all the time we've been concentrating on *Garland*—on Garland's actions and motives? I believe that was a mistake. *I* began to put myself in Celeste's place, and the results were quite fascinating." She leaned forward eagerly. "Don't you think it's peculiar, to say the least, that Celeste should pack up and go off with Garland at a couple of hours' notice, for good?"

"Is it?" asked Anstruther mildly.

"Why, of course it is. Celeste hated doing anything quickly. She was a leisurely, deliberate sort of person—almost lazy, in fact. Did *you* ever hear of her rushing off anywhere? And that's not all. You know how proud she was of her home— well, she's just abandoned it without even leaving instructions. And all those lovely clothes of hers—my dear stupid men, she's left them all behind! Practically all! I can't imagine what she'd wear. Don't you see? It's not like her. She'd never have cleared off like that unless she'd had a terrifically powerful reason."

"I thought wives accompanied their husbands more or less automatically," said Martin with a grin. "Or am I about to make the mistake of my life?"

Susan ignored the red herring. "Celeste wasn't that sort of wife. It was she who ran that households—*you* know that's true, Daddy. It was quite incredible how she used to wind Garland round her finger. She didn't do what *he* wanted; she pleased herself. Why, she wouldn't have walked to the end of the road simply because he thought it was a good idea. If Celeste decided to leave Fontego for good at two hours' notice, it was because Celeste wanted to, and for no other reason. I'd stake my life on that."

Anstruther looked as though he were inclined to agree with her.

"I've been trying to think what might have happened at their house when they met last night," Susan went on eagerly. "According to Salacity, Celeste came in first, a little before nine, and Garland soon afterwards. She says she heard them talking very excitedly part of the time. Until then, neither of them had said a word to her about leaving that night. But by eleven o'clock they had packed and gone. Something pretty dramatic must have happened. I know, I simply *know* that it wouldn't have been any use Garland just saying that he had a sudden hankering to live somewhere else for a change, or that he'd got urgent private reasons for leaving and that Celeste must come along with him. She'd just have laughed in his face. She'd have wanted to know what all the hurry was about. She'd have wanted to know everything."

"That seems reasonable," said Martin. "Well, perhaps Garland took her into his confidence and told her of the danger he was in. That would have been dramatic enough."

"I don't think he told her," said Susan, bringing out her ace. "I believe she knew all the time."

"You mean she was an accomplice?" said Anstruther, startled.

"Perhaps not quite that, but I'm sure she knew. I've been shockingly dim-witted, but once I started thinking about Celeste it all came to me."

"Well, it hasn't all come to me," said Anstruther with a glance at Martin. "Perhaps you'd enlighten us, my dear?"

"It's quite straightforward, really," said Susan. "You see, I couldn't forget that conversation I had with Garland by the bridge. You know how it is when a bit of a puzzle's missing— you can't help thinking about it. From what Garland had said, I felt sure he suspected me of having seen him at the Blue Pool, and I just couldn't imagine what had suddenly put the idea into his head after all that while. He'd seen me several times since Fiesta and had behaved in a perfectly normal way. What was suddenly different about me? I naturally thought of clothes—and then I remembered his peculiar remark about my beach wrap." She paused, with a mischievous glance at the two men. "Have I your attention, gentlemen?"

"What about the wrap?" asked Martin.

"Only that when I began thinking about the wrap I remembered that I didn't have it at Fiesta. I'd left it at Celeste's by mistake. *Now* do you begin to see?"

"Good Lord!" said Martin.

"*I* think she must have been at the Blue Pool herself, and that it was she who was one of the missing witnesses. It was silly not to think of it before. After all, she was quite a likely person, only she talked so much about it she threw dust in our eyes. I wonder who the man was."

"So you think that she and Garland had a showdown last night?" said Martin, frowning.

"Yes, I think it all came out, and that's what the excitement was about."

"Just a minute!" Anstruther interposed. "Are you suggesting that Celeste would have gone off with him last night, knowing he was a murderer? I didn't know Celeste very well myself, but it seems to me most unlikely. Think of the risk she'd be running. She'd have had to be quite infatuated with him to do a thing like that, and I must say she never showed the least sign of infatuation. What possible inducement could there have been?"

"That's what I was coming to," said Susan. "She must have had a very good reason. Something that really appealed to her—something that made up for all the things she was sacrificing, and even made the risk of going off with a murderer seem worth while. There's only one thing I can think of—money. Lots and lots of money."

"Oh, come!" said Anstruther. "Garland hadn't any money. At least, he never seemed to have. I always fancied he was living up to the hilt, like most of us."

"I'm sure he was," Susan agreed. "Celeste saw to that. She was a terrific spender. The times I've envied her clothes! She adored luxury and beautiful things, and I honestly believe she'd have done anything to get them. She'd *never* have cleared off with Garland if all he'd been able to offer her was what he'd saved from his salary and the prospect of a paltry pension. She could no more have done that than she could have joined the sleepers-out on the pavement. She'd want something glittering."

Anstruther, who had been following Susan's rather intuitive reconstruction with a slightly teasing expression on his face, suddenly became grave. "What exactly are you suggesting, Susan?"

"I'm suggesting that Garland had something to offer her that we don't know about—a lot of money, that he couldn't have come by honestly. It might even explain Dubois' murder. Daddy, you're the man of affairs—how could he have got hold of a lot of money?"

Anstruther sipped his drink thoughtfully. In a long lifetime of colonial service, he had learned that civil servants rarely became rich men, unless by crooked paths. What crooked paths had been open to Garland? He had certainly been in a position of great authority, a little dictator in his department. Some sort of graft? That *could* have happened. It happened in many departments—only too frequently—but so far there had been no case to his knowledge of a white administrator going off the rails. Anstruther was proud of the service he controlled—he hated to think that anyone in Garland's position could have betrayed his trust. But it couldn't be ruled out—not now. If the man had been a murderer, he had doubtless been capable of the lesser sins as well. But if Garland had done anything like that it wouldn't have been on any petty scale. He wouldn't have been content to rifle the cash box, or raid the stores, or monkey about with receipts. The Colonial Secretary silently reviewed Garland's major activities.

Finally he said, with slow emphasis, "The only really big thing that Garland handled was—Tacri."

There was a moment when all sat thinking, mentally poised between darkness and light. Then knowledge came like the break of day.

"Tacri!" Martin repeated. "*Of course!* We haven't been very bright, have we?"

"You always said there was something phoney about Tacri," said Susan jubilantly.

"Well, he was so preposterously wrong," said Martin. "So stubbornly and violently wrong. It always seemed quite incredible to me, but if he was making money out of it, that would explain his attitude. Yes, by Jove, it would explain all that fantastically swollen expenditure, and all those idiotic frills. It would account for everything, including the row after the storm—and nothing else would."

Anstruther made a sound that was almost a groan. "Garland, of all people! Good Heavens!"

Susan said, "He *has* rather let the side down, hasn't he?" But she didn't look as though she shared her father's despondency. "Now all we've got to do is prove it," she said.

"I wonder what sort of arrangement he could have made," mused Anstruther.

"Daddy," Susan broke in, "what would happen about the Tacri contract if we could prove bribery?"

The Colonial Secretary gave a thin smile. "*If* we could prove it, I doubt if the firm would feel like arguing. It's possible that they don't know about it themselves—this could have been a private deal between Garland and that fellow Rawlins. But they'd almost certainly be prepared to cut their losses and let the matter drop, for the sake of their reputation."

"So the Tacri scheme would be at an end, or at least it might be brought to an end, and we could start all over again," cried Susan. "Oh, Martin!" She turned and gave him a hug.

"Now don't go too fast, my dear," Anstruther warned her, "That is still all speculation. How do we begin to prove it? Garland's dead—he can't talk. Rawlins obviously won't. Where do we start?"

"There must be an opening somewhere," said Susan. "Surely it would be a big help if we could prove that Garland had a lot of money that couldn't be explained in any honest way. He must have made some secret plans—he'd have to live when he got abroad. He was probably going to pick the money up somewhere. Why was he flying to Singapore all of a sudden? When Celeste talked to me about their holiday, it was Honolulu they were going to. Mightn't he have some documents on him—a passbook or something?"

"Do you suppose anyone has looked in his bags?" asked Martin.

Anstruther shook his head. "Most unlikely, I should think. Jarvis wouldn't have had any reason to do so—it was a straightforward accident, and he had no grounds for suspecting Garland of anything. I imagine the bags are still unopened."

"There *might* be something," said Martin.

Anstruther seemed undecided. "It would be rather dangerous, you know, for Garland to have had money deposited for him in Singapore. I'm not quite sure how it could have been done—not in any safe way."

"You're hardly an expert, darling," said Susan. "Couldn't the contractor man have paid in money for Garland under a different name?"

"I suppose so," said Anstruther dubiously, "but there'd still be a risk of discovery, I should think."

"Surely only if suspicions were aroused," said Martin. "And Garland never expected any inquiries to be made. Don't you think, sir, the time has come to put all this on an official basis with Jarvis? We're obviously at the end of our resources. I think we ought to tell him everything we know and leave it to him to make a thorough investigation."

"You're probably right," agreed Anstruther, though with obvious reluctance. He got up. "I must go and talk to H.E. about it first, and if he agrees I'll see Jarvis." He turned to Susan, with an odd quizzical look. "You realise, young woman, that this immense superstructure we've built up rests almost entirely on your reading of Celeste's character?"

"That doesn't frighten me," said Susan. "I'm sure what I said about Celeste was right. I could never feel she was a very *nice* person, though I always shall think she was amusing."

"H'm," said Anstruther. "I seem to have more in common with Queen Victoria than I supposed."

Chapter Thirty-three

A long week passed. Martin, back on Tacri, watched with growing exasperation the progress of the futile improvements, and began to wonder as the days went by whether the police would ever produce results. Susan crossed over twice in the launch, and the memorandum was completed. They were going to be married in a month—that, at least, was satisfactory.

There was still no news when Martin went to the mainland to spend the week-end with the Anstruthers; but on the first evening, just as the cocktails were being taken out into the garden, Superintendent Jarvis rang up. If it were convenient, he would like to come round. Half an hour later he was striding up the path. His step was as elastic as ever, but his expression was funereal.

Susan, hardly able to contain her impatience, found him a chair and a drink, and the Superintendent made himself as comfortable as his obvious uneasiness permitted. To him, the whole episode was in the highest degree distasteful. However often he reminded himself that a criminal was a criminal whatever his colour, it was still repugnant to him to have to ferret out the crimes of a man like Garland, a man whom he had always respected, a white man like himself. He felt resentful. One had a right to expect certain standards from the Colony's white administrators. A part of Jarvis' limited world had crumbled. He swung his cane restlessly between his thighs and tried to avoid Anstruther's eye.

"Well, Jarvis," said the Colonial Secretary, "you might as well get it off your chest. Were we right about the money?"

"Not exactly," said Jarvis.

"Oh," cried Susan, with deep disappointment. "You mean you couldn't trace it?"

"There doesn't seem to have been any money," said Jarvis.

"But there *must* have been—"

"Come on, Jarvis," broke in Anstruther, a little impatiently. "There's no need to be so mysterious. Just give us the facts."

"Well," began Jarvis, in the tone of a man forced by fate into unpleasant paths, "we opened Dr. Garland's bags, as you suggested. We went through everything. There were a lot of private papers, but nothing that hinted at any bank account in Singapore. In fact, there was nothing suspicious there at all. We emptied his pockets, but there was nothing at all on paper—not an address or a name or anything that would help us. There was, however, a bunch of keys."

"Aha," said Anstruther encouragingly.

"We accounted for most of the keys," Jarvis went on in a depressed monotone, "by trying them on various locks in the Garland house and in the department. In the end, there were two that we couldn't explain. They were rather well made, unusual keys—they both had the same number on them, and the name of the manufacturer. I got in touch with the manufacturer, and I found out that the keys had been speciality made for a strongroom and safe deposit company—at Singapore."

Susan glanced at Martin and her hand stole into his.

"The police in Singapore were very co-operative. So were the safe deposit people. I had duplicates of the keys flown over, and the safe was opened. Inside—"

Three people waited tensely.

"Inside," said Jarvis, "there was nothing. Nothing at all."

"But that's incredible," said Anstruther.

Jarvis sighed over the duplicity of human nature. "It rather looks," he said, "as though Dr. Garland was taken in by someone more experienced in crime than he was. We don't know, of course, what the agreement was, but evidently only a part of it was carried out. The safe was rented in the name of Arthur J. Whiting, with a specimen signature which will no doubt prove to be in Dr. Garland's handwriting. The keys were dispatched according to promise, but no money was deposited."

"What a horrible man!" exclaimed Susan.

Martin grinned. "Can you imagine Celeste's face if she'd arrived in Singapore and found the cupboard bare after all?"

"Can you imagine Garland's?" said Anstruther grimly.

"The fellow was taking an enormous risk. I suppose he was banking on the fact that Garland wouldn't dare to make a fuss, but I doubt if a man who'd done at least one murder would have taken such a thing lying down."

"Rawlins wouldn't have known that he was dealing with a potential murderer," said Jarvis. "Anyhow, he took the risk."

"So where does that leave us?" Martin asked. "Without a nice convincing wad of money, isn't it going to be difficult to clinch the case?"

"That isn't quite the end of the story," said Jarvis, with a gleam of professional satisfaction. "I naturally insisted on some further inquiries. My training at Scotland Yard stood me in good stead. We found out that Rawlins had stayed in Singapore for a couple of days shortly after the Tacri contract was signed. He appears to have visited the safe deposit, and rented the safe. One of the staff there, a woman, thinks she recognises him from the description given."

"Good," said Anstruther. "Is there any other evidence?"

"Yes," said Jarvis. "We've had the auditors go through Garland's private accounts. It's been done as discreetly as possible, though I'm afraid it won't be possible to hush everything up."

"There's no question of hushing anything up," said Anstruther sharply.

"I suppose not," said Jarvis, in a tone of regret. "Well, Dr. Garland's expenditure in the past few months doesn't tally with his withdrawals from his bank in Fontego. Evidently he has made very considerable cash payments in addition. We estimate that they amount in all to nearly two thousand pounds. It looks as though he received some money from Rawlins in advance."

Anstruther nodded. "It seems to be a clear case," he said.

"I'm afraid so," said Jarvis. "Dr. Garland appears to have been a quite unscrupulous man. The only question now is whether what has taken place can be brought home to the contractors."

"You'll have to leave that to us," said Anstruther. "On that evidence, incomplete though it is, I very much doubt if they'll feel like trying to hold us to the contract. Well, thank you, Jarvis. I must say I think you've done an excellent job. Scotland Yard would be proud of you."

"Thank you, sir," said Jarvis solemnly.

Anstruther's eyes twinkled. "And I say, Jarvis—cheer up! This has been a bit of a blow to all of us, but it hasn't any great significance, you know. There are bound to be white sheep in every community."

"Of course, sir," said Jarvis uncertainly. He walked slowly back to his car, trying to puzzle it out.

Anstruther relaxed in his chair when the policeman had gone. "Let's have another drink, Susan," he said. "*What* a business! Still, I suppose you two are feeling very happy."

"Very," said Susan, "and full of plans."

"Oh—what plans?"

Susan laughed. "What plans would you expect a prospective bride to have? Plans for a new leprosarium, of course!"